HARDCASTLE'S QUANDARY

HARDCASTLE'S QUANDARY

Graham Ison

This first world edition published 2018
in Great Britain and 2019 in the USA by
SEVERN HOUSE PUBLISHERS LTD of
Eardley House, 4 Uxbridge Street, London W8 7SY.
Trade paperback edition first published
in Great Britain and the USA 2019 by
SEVERN HOUSE PUBLISHERS LTD.

British Library Cataloguing in Publication Data
A CIP catalogue record for this title is available from the British Library.

ISBN-13: 978-0-7278-8855-6 (cased)
ISBN-13: 978-1-84751-979-5 (trade paper)
ISBN-13: 978-1-4483-0192-8 (e-book)

All Severn House titles are printed on acid-free paper.

Severn House Publishers support the Forest Stewardship Council™ [FSC™],
the leading international forest certification organisation.
All our titles that are printed on FSC certified paper carry the FSC logo.

FSC
www.fsc.org
MIX
Paper from
responsible sources
FSC® C013056

Typeset by Palimpsest Book Production Ltd.,
Falkirk, Stirlingshire, Scotland.
Printed and bound in Great Britain by
TJ International, Padstow, Cornwall.

ONE

On the whole, the month of March 1927 had been a miserable one, the weather changeable, the temperature fluctuating between a bare forty degrees Fahrenheit and the mid-sixties. And it rained and rained.

On this Wednesday morning – it was the thirtieth of March – heavy rain bounced off the windowsill of Divisional Detective Inspector Ernest Hardcastle's office on the first floor of Cannon Row police station in Westminster. In a fit of ill temper, Hardcastle slammed the window shut and, crossing to the fireplace, put another knob of coal on, making a mental note to speak to the station officer about the duty constable's failings in this regard. But it was not the rain or that the station constable had omitted to make up Hardcastle's fire that was irritating him.

This morning, he was wearing a pair of new shoes, and they were pinching. And if that was not bad enough, the shoes, his spats, his socks and the lower part of his trousers had been soaked through while he waited for the tram to bring him from Kennington to Westminster. This particularly irritated him as he took pride in his appearance, and his wife always ensured that there was a clean shirt ready for him every day. Although a man of ample build and only an inch above the five feet eight inches demanded by the police, he was extremely agile. His Kitchener-style moustache was always neatly trimmed, as was his greying hair.

But his mood was about to be made even worse.

'Excuse me, sir.' Detective Sergeant Charles Marriott, the first-class sergeant in charge of the junior detectives, appeared in Hardcastle's office doorway. Smartly dressed, his chiselled features and handsome bearing always made women afford him a second glance, but he was happily married to Lorna, a strikingly beautiful, tall and slender blonde, the mother of the couple's two children, although they could hardly be called children any more. James was eighteen and had already decided to become a barrister, and his sister, Doreen, was a sixteen-year-old young woman who showed all the signs of being as much of a beauty as her mother.

'If you're going to ask me if your promotion's come through yet, Marriott, the answer's no, it hasn't,' said Hardcastle, reaching for his pipe and beginning to fill it with his favourite St Bruno tobacco. Marriott had been selected for advancement to the rank of detective inspector some months previously, but promotion in the Metropolitan Police was painfully slow, and vacancies depended upon officers either retiring or dying in service. However, those above Marriott seemed intent upon staying for ever and, despite the ravages of police duty, seemed a remarkably healthy lot with but one or two exceptions. And it was one of those exceptions that was about to saddle Hardcastle with another murder investigation.

'No, of course not, sir.' On almost every occasion that Marriott appeared in the DDI's office, Hardcastle would make the same comment, but Marriott knew that the DDI would tell him the moment the memorandum arrived from Commissioner's Office, if for no better reason than he would expect Marriott to buy a celebratory drink for him and the other two detective inspectors on A Division. 'Mr Wensley's clerk just telephoned, sir. Mr Wensley sends his compliments and would like to see you at your earliest convenience.'

'I wonder what he wants,' mumbled Hardcastle, as he took his bowler hat and umbrella from the stand in the corner of his office. When the Chief Constable CID asked to see you 'at your earliest convenience', it meant immediately. And being the divisional detective inspector in charge of the CID for the A or Whitehall Division, Hardcastle's office was only across the road from New Scotland Yard where Frederick Wensley had his office, but it was one of Hardcastle's eccentricities that he would never be seen outside his police station without his bowler hat and umbrella.

One of the drawbacks of this close proximity to the Yard was that Hardcastle was far too handy for any odd job that happened to be going. Apart from that, Wensley, in common with many detectives who had served in the East End of

London, believed that the Central London divisions were soft postings.

'By the way, sir, have you seen the paper this morning?'

Hardcastle stared at his sergeant over his recently acquired half-moon spectacles. His wife, Alice, had long been a critic of the wire-framed glasses he wore for reading, and he had, at last, relented. 'What are you talking about now, Marriott?' he asked patiently. It was noticeable that since Marriott's selection for promotion, the DDI's attitude towards him had softened, albeit slightly.

'Segrave's done it, sir.'

'Who the hell is Segrave, and what's he done that's so important he gets himself in the newspaper?' demanded Hardcastle. 'He's not a CID officer, is he?' The DDI prided himself on knowing the names of all the senior CID officers in the Metropolitan Police, and he had not heard of one named Segrave.

'Major Henry Segrave, sir,' continued Marriott. 'He broke the land speed record yesterday at Daytona Beach in Florida. The report says that he achieved over two hundred miles an hour, the first man to do so.'

'Oh, that Segrave,' said Hardcastle, who hated being caught out, especially by a junior rank. 'I wonder why he bothered. He'll finish up killing himself like that Parry Thomas did at Pendine Sands a few weeks ago.' (Three years later, Hardcastle's prediction came true when Segrave died in an accident on Lake Windermere just after creating a new water speed record.) 'It seems that we go too fast as it is, Marriott. Why do we need to go any faster? I really do think that the world's passing me by. What's more, I don't know half the detectives we've got next door now that Keeler, Lipton and Wilmot have been posted or have retired. The new men all joined the Job after the war. And now Mr Wensley's clerk telephones when he used to walk across here and deliver messages in person. It's impolite, that's what it is. Perhaps it's time I thought about retirement. And before you get too excited that there might be a vacancy in the offing, I'm not thinking of going just yet.'

'Of course not, sir.' Marriott restricted himself to that mild and minimal response. He recognized the onset of one of

Hardcastle's diatribes and knew better than to encourage further outpourings.

'You wanted to see me, sir?'

'Yes, Ernie.' Wensley turned from the window and, with a wave of his hand, invited Hardcastle to take a seat. Immaculately dressed, the chief constable wore a winged collar, even though fashion nowadays favoured the double collar, and a pearl pin adorned his silk necktie. Known to the newspaper industry as 'Ace' on account of his detective prowess, he was referred to irreverently as 'Elephant' by the officers under his command because of the size of his nose. 'I want you to read this letter,' he said, handing Hardcastle several sheets of paper. 'As you'll see, the writer is the Reverend Percy Stoner, the vicar of Southfork, which is somewhere in Norfolk.'

Donning his new half-moon spectacles, Hardcastle quickly scanned the letter, and then glanced up. 'What does this have to do with me, sir?' he asked, although he was certain he was about to find out.

'Arthur Fitnam has gone sick again, Ernie,' said Wensley, 'and his deputy is up to his eyes in a fraud case. As this job is centred on Ditton on V Division, I'm going to ask you to take it on. Frankly, given the state of his health, I don't think that Arthur will last in the Job too much longer. He's bound to get cast if he doesn't die first.' It was well known in the Force that Arthur Fitnam, V Division's DDI, had been unwell for some time and the consensus among the unqualified was that he was suffering from cancer.

'Very good, sir.' Hardcastle was unhappy at being given a task that was so far from Westminster, but a request from the Chief Constable CID was in fact an order. 'May I keep this letter, sir?'

'Of course, Ernie, and attach it to your report to the Director of Public Prosecutions.' It was a typical Wensley comment and implied not only that there been a murder but that Hardcastle would solve it.

'Marriott, come in my office,' shouted Hardcastle, as he passed the open door of the detectives' room.

Hurriedly donning his jacket, Marriott followed his DDI.

'You needn't look so expectant, Marriott. Mr Wensley didn't send for me to announce that you were about to become an officer and a gentleman.' Hardcastle handed Marriott the Reverend Percy Stoner's letter. 'In short, Marriott,' he continued, 'the reverend gentleman thinks his nephew's been murdered.'

'Where do we start, sir?'

'In Norfolk, Marriott, obviously. It's where the clergyman lives. Find out how we get there.'

Marriott returned within minutes. 'Train from Liverpool Street station, sir. According to *Bradshaw's Guide*, it will take about two hours to get to Norwich, and I'm told there's a good bus service from Norwich to Southfork.'

'A bus!' exclaimed Hardcastle, his face expressing horror. 'I've told you before, Marriott, that a DDI does not travel by bus to investigate a murder. I can see that you're not thinking like an inspector yet.' He shook his head. 'We'll take a cab from Norwich to this clergyman's place, Marriott. Good grief, man, you've worked with me long enough to know my habits.'

'Yes, sir. I'll make a telephone call to arrange an appointment. Provided, of course, that the vicar's connected.'

'D'you mean you can actually telephone to Norfolk, Marriott?' Hardcastle stared at his sergeant in wonderment.

'Oh, yes, sir. In fact, it's even possible to telephone New York now, but it costs fifteen pounds for three minutes.'

'Fifteen pounds?' Hardcastle laughed. 'Who the hell would want to telephone New York anyway, Marriott?' he asked, before turning to more important matters. 'See you at Liverpool Street station at half past eight sharp tomorrow morning, and when you're buying your newspaper, get me a *Daily Mail*. I don't suppose my copy will have been delivered by the time I leave home.'

Within minutes of his arrival at Norwich Thorpe railway station, Hardcastle had condemned Norfolk as a flat, uninteresting and inhospitable place.

'See if you can find a cabbie who knows where this

Southfork place is, Marriott.' Hardcastle was clearly not in the best of moods.

To exacerbate the DDI's increasingly bad temper, the taxi was a Vauxhall saloon car that doubtless had many miles on the clock, and clearly needed some work doing on its springing. The cab driver appeared to be at least seventy years of age, and was wrapped up in a heavy overcoat, a woollen scarf wound around his neck, and a cloth cap pulled down so firmly that he could only just see beneath the ragged peak. As the journey progressed, it became evident that he had serious adenoidal problems and sniffed for most of the half an hour it took to arrive at the vicarage where the Reverend Percy Stoner lived.

Although the village of Southfork was quite a distance from the coast, the angle of the trees testified to the strength of the winds that frequently blew in from the North Sea. The vicarage was a symmetrically built large stone dwelling with bay windows on either side of a porched front door, and three sizeable dormer windows on the first floor.

'These here clerks in holy orders do all right for themselves, Marriott,' said Hardcastle, as he alighted from the taxi and stretched his aching limbs.

Marriott knocked at the door, but it was several minutes before a woman appeared. Some sixty or so years of age, she wore a white apron over a black bombazine dress which, contrary to the current fashion, almost reached the floor. Her iron-grey hair was gathered up at the back of her head and held in place by an unattractive metal claw.

'Yes?' The woman's greeting was far from welcoming.

'I've come to see the vicar,' said Hardcastle.

'Oh, have you indeed? Well, I doubt he'll be able to fit you in on account of him having some important visitors from London.' The woman glared suspiciously at the two 'foreigners' on the doorstep.

Hardcastle was about to point out that he and Marriott *were* the important visitors from London when the vicar appeared. 'It's all right, Mrs Rudge, I'll deal with these gentlemen.'

With a toss of the head, Mrs Rudge disappeared, presumably to the kitchen.

'Mr Hardcastle, is it? And Mr Marriott? I'm Percy Stoner,' said the clergyman, extending a hand. He was probably in his late fifties, but his wispy, greying hair and stooped posture made him appear much older. His green cardigan and brown corduroy trousers – strangely at odds with his clerical collar – had clearly seen better days, and Hardcastle wondered if he was unmarried. His own wife would make her disapproval strongly known if he ever walked about dressed like that.

'Good morning, Vicar.' Hardcastle shook hands with Stoner, as did Marriott.

'Come along in, Mr Hardcastle, and you too, Mr Marriott. It's too miserable a day to be hanging about on the doorstep. Mind you, it's a lovely place to live in the summertime,' he added, as though justifying having accepted the living of Southfork.

Stoner led the way into a cosy sitting room. There were several comfortable armchairs and a blazing log fire. A large tabby cat was asleep on a silk Persian rug in front of the fireplace but woke up to inspect the newcomers. Apparently satisfied that they posed no threat to its well-being, the animal stretched, yawned and promptly went to sleep again.

Stoner invited the two detectives to take a seat. 'If you're anything like the local policemen—' he began, but was obliged to break off by the onset of a hacking cough.

Hardcastle was about to protest at being likened to what he imagined was a police force comprising, for the most part, ex-farmhands and yokels, when the vicar, now recovered from his coughing fit, continued.

'I'm sorry about that,' said Stoner. 'It's the climate here in Norfolk, you know.' He paused to blow his nose with a colourful handkerchief before going on. 'I was about to say that if you're anything like the local policemen, you'll not be averse to a drop of Scotch whisky, particularly on a day like today. It's a chill wind that comes off the fens, you know.'

'Most kind, Vicar,' murmured Hardcastle, mentally revising his opinion of the clergyman.

Stoner poured malt whisky into three crystal tumblers.

'I take it you'll not be wanting water or soda,' he said, in a manner intended to brook no argument.

Hardcastle took a sip of whisky and nodded his appreciation. 'I understand from the letter you wrote to Scotland Yard that you're concerned about your nephew, Vicar,' he said, determined to get on with the reason for his visit.

'Indeed, I am,' said Stoner, his face assuming a grave expression. 'It was bad enough worrying about him during the war, but I didn't expect to be doing so once it was over.'

'It would be useful if you'd outline what gives you such grave concern, sir,' said Marriott.

'My nephew Guy was a captain in the Royal Field Artillery during the war. In fact, I think the RFA and the Royal Garrison Artillery have now been joined together into one regiment that's called the Royal Artillery.'

'Yes, that's correct,' said Marriott, glancing up from his note-taking. 'In 1924.'

Hardcastle said nothing but was secretly pleased that the clergyman was so pedantic. A man with such an eye for detail and accuracy was likely to give a reliable account of the events troubling him.

'After the war was over, Guy and another officer set up in business in Ditton in Surrey.'

'Doing what, sir?' asked Marriott.

'It was a chicken farm, but unfortunately they couldn't make a go of it.'

'It happened to quite a few of them,' said Hardcastle, not unsympathetically. Too many ex-officers had spent their gratuities and savings on a chicken farm without having explored the difficulties or the market, and all too many of them foundered, often within weeks.

'But then, according to Guy, they decided to turn it into a conventional arable farm, but he didn't say how he was going to go about it. As far as I recall, he had no experience of farming, but maybe his partner did.'

'Was it a success?' asked Hardcastle.

'I've no idea,' said Stoner, placing his hands together in an attitude of supplication. But then he paused. 'Mind you, Inspector, that was his intention, according to the last letter he wrote. However, I don't know whether this farm business actually came to fruition. As I implied just now, Guy never struck me as having the qualities needed for farming.'

'You went on to suggest in your letter that you thought some danger may have befallen your nephew.'

'I didn't suggest it, Mr Hardcastle,' said Stoner sharply. 'I wrote that I was convinced he'd been murdered.'

'But what possible grounds can you have for coming to that conclusion? Did you ever visit your nephew in Ditton?'

'No, I must admit that I'm getting a little too old to make such a tortuous journey.' Stoner drank a good measure of his whisky and leaned back in his chair. 'Guy always wrote to me once a week without fail, Inspector, even when he was in the army and stationed in Flanders. But when I'd heard nothing for a month, I began to worry. It was so unlike him. We liked to keep in touch since his parents are both dead.'

'When did they die?' asked Hardcastle.

'In December 1914,' said Stoner, 'when the Germans shelled Hartlepool. It was where they were living,' he added unnecessarily. 'Rather ironic when you think about it, that it should have happened when Guy was at the Front. In the Ypres Salient, as a matter of fact. Now the family comprises just him and me.'

Hardcastle remembered the audacious attack by German battleships that began, without warning, at just after eight o'clock one morning in mid-December. Eighty-six people were killed, and more than four hundred wounded.

'You say he went into partnership, sir,' said Marriott. 'Do you know the name of that partner?'

'Yes, I do, but I'll make absolutely sure I've got it right. At my age, it's always dangerous to rely too much on one's memory.' Stoner crossed the room to a bureau, and after ferreting among a collection of loose papers, he produced a small notebook. 'Ah, here we are. It was a Captain Holroyd, Rupert Holroyd, who was also in the Royal Field Artillery.'

'Did you ever meet the man Holroyd, sir?' asked Marriott.

'No, never.'

'To get back to the question I asked just now, Vicar,' said

Hardcastle, 'what caused you to believe your nephew may
have been murdered?'

'I'm not a rich man, Inspector – few clergymen are – but
my brother left a decent sum to me when he was killed in the
raid on Hartlepool that I mentioned just now, and rightly left
his son, Guy, the bulk of his estate. He'd been a successful
industrialist in the north-east, and there was a large memorial
service for him when he was killed. He was an alderman as
well, so all the town council were there. However, none of
that's important. The point is that a week ago I received a
letter purporting to come from Guy, but it was not in his
handwriting. The excuse was that he had injured his hand
attempting to put out a fire at this farm in Ditton, and he'd
asked Rupert Holroyd to write the letter at his dictation. In
the letter, he said that the insurance company had declined to
pay their claim and they were on their beam ends. He asked
if I could help him out on this occasion. Frankly, I found it
difficult to believe. Guy had always had a head for figures,
and I don't think he'd have allowed himself to get into such
a parlous state.'

'What did you do, Vicar?' asked Hardcastle.

'I wrote to Scotland Yard, Inspector,' said Stoner, in a tone
implying that to have done so was the obvious course of action.

'Do you still have the letter you received, apparently from
your nephew, sir?' asked Marriott.

'Yes, I do.'

'D'you think we might take it, together with another letter
you know to have been written by him? Oh, and a photograph
of your nephew would be helpful.'

'Of course.' Stoner returned to his bureau and after a brief
search handed over the letters that Marriott had asked for,
and a photograph of Captain Guy Stoner in army uniform.

'Your nephew didn't have a moustache, sir,' commented
Marriott. 'A bit unusual for an army officer.'

'He shaved it off in 1916, Mr Marriott, when the army said
that to have one was no longer obligatory. Rather a silly rule
in the first place, I thought.'

'Very well, Vicar.' Hardcastle stood up. 'I shall return to
London and look into the matter.'

'Thank you, Inspector.' Stoner rose to his feet also. 'I trust you'll keep me apprised of the outcome.'

'I most certainly will.' Hardcastle believed that this country clergyman was seeing a mystery where none existed, and that he would find Captain Guy Stoner alive and well, even if, as the letter had claimed, he was a bit short of funds.

TWO

On Friday morning, the two detectives took a train from Waterloo to Thames Ditton which, Marriott had assured Hardcastle, was the nearest railway station to Ditton. Hardcastle had proposed taking a taxi for the entire journey from London, but Marriott pointed out that it was close to twenty miles from Cannon Row and convinced him that it would be much quicker to go by train.

When Hardcastle and Marriott arrived at Thames Ditton railway station, Marriott suggested that they walk to the police station only half a mile away. Somewhat reluctantly, and surprisingly, Hardcastle agreed.

Arriving at Ditton police station, the DDI, already displeased at having been given a task which rightly should have been Arthur Fitnam's, was about to be confronted by something else that irritated him. It took a good thirty seconds after he had struck the bell on the counter for a police constable to emerge from the inner recesses of the station.

'I think I might have woken someone up, Marriott.'

'Can I help you, sir?' The constable wiped a few crumbs from his mouth, and then did up the buttons on his tunic.

'I'm DDI Hardcastle of A Division, lad.' Hardcastle always called constables 'lad', regardless of their age, and this PC looked as though he was the DDI's age, if not older. 'Is there a sergeant here?'

'Not today, sir. It's his rest day.'

'Heaven help us!' exclaimed Hardcastle. 'Who are you, then?'

'PC Albert Perkins, sir. I'm the station officer – just for the day, like. You're a long way from home, sir, if you don't mind me saying. As a matter of fact, one of the lads has just made a pot of tea. I dare say you could do with one after coming all the way from London.' Perkins made it sound as though London was on the other side of the moon.

'I haven't got time to waste drinking tea, lad,' snapped Hardcastle. 'I'm here to take over Mr Fitnam's job for him.'

Suddenly, the constable straightened up. 'Oh, I see, sir. Welcome to V Division,' he responded half-heartedly. The prospect of this fiery DDI appearing at regular intervals in the tranquil and bucolic setting of Ditton's bailiwick was extremely disturbing. It was apparent from Perkins's reaction that he had mistakenly assumed Hardcastle was replacing Fitnam permanently, and Hardcastle saw no reason to disabuse him.

'What d'you know about a fire that took place recently on this manor, Perkins? It belonged to two former army officers named Stoner and Holroyd.'

'Where is this place, sir?'

'For God's sake, lad, I don't know,' said Hardcastle, his temper shortening by the minute. 'That's why I'm asking. In my young day, a constable was expected to know everything about his manor.'

The PC ran a hand round his chin. 'To be honest, I don't rightly know, sir. You see, sir, I've only just returned to duty after a longish spell on the sick list. I had a touch of pleurisy, you see, sir, and I had to—'

'I'm not interested in your ailments, lad. Just get on with it.'

'Ah, yes, sir. Big investigations like that are dealt with by the CID at Surbiton. We don't have much call for that sort of thing round here, which is why we haven't got a CID. That, and being a sectional station, I mean.'

'Does this sectional station have a telephone, by any chance, Perkins?' enquired Marriott sharply. Although of a more equable disposition than the DDI, he too was becoming increasingly irritated by the relaxed attitude of Police Constable Albert Perkins.

'That we do, sir.' The constable seemed quite pleased that he was able, at last, to give a positive reply.

'Don't call me "sir"; I'm a detective sergeant,' snapped Marriott. 'I suggest you get on the telephone and find an answer to the DDI's question about this fire; otherwise he's likely to have words with the sub-divisional inspector about inefficiency. And that, of course, could result in transfers out and transfers in. A few spells of point duty in Whitehall would soon get rid of your illnesses.'

Perkins looked visibly shocked at the thought of duty in a Central London division, but said nothing.

'Better still,' put in Hardcastle, 'I want a CID officer who knows about this matter to get on his bicycle and come down here a bit tout de suite.'

'It's nigh on three miles, sir,' said PC Perkins, his tone of voice suggesting that Hardcastle had just proposed an impossibility.

'Shouldn't take him long, then.'

The detective who appeared at Ditton police station was in his forties. Hot and breathless, he entered the sergeant's office where Hardcastle and Marriott had, after all, accepted a cup of tea. His suit was ill-fitting, and he wore a flashy tie of which Hardcastle immediately disapproved.

'Detective Constable Mitchell, sir.' The Surbiton CID officer took off his trilby hat and bent down to remove the bicycle clips from the bottom of his trouser legs. 'I understand you're making enquiries about the fire at Ditton Garage.' He tugged at his ragged moustache.

'Ditton *Garage*, Mitchell? Why are you talking about a garage? I'm looking for a farm. At least that's what I was told by Captain Stoner's uncle.'

Mitchell referred to a file that he took from under his arm. 'The premises were owned jointly by Guy Stoner and Rupert Holroyd, sir. Both ex-army captains by all accounts. It was originally run as a chicken farm from about 1922 to 1925, but then it went bottoms up.' The DC paused to glance up from the docket he was reading. 'A lot of 'em did, sir,' he added philosophically.

'Who investigated this fire, Mitchell?' snapped Hardcastle, who was in no mood to discuss the economics of chicken farming.

'Inspector Granger, sir. He's stationed at Surbiton.'

'Is he a Uniform Branch officer?' Hardcastle's voice registered surprise.

'Yes, he is, sir. You see, when the fire happened, there was nothing suspicious about it, and as far as I know, there isn't now.'

'That's where you're wrong,' muttered Hardcastle. 'But where does this business of a garage come into the picture?'

'After the chicken farm went under, those two officers decided that a garage was the best way forward, what with more and more people buying motor cars.'

'Captain Stoner's uncle said something about arable farming after the chicken farm failed,' said Marriott.

'I've no knowledge of that, Sergeant. But as far as a garage was concerned, there were already garages in Esher and Surbiton, as well as in Kingston, and it seemed car owners were more likely to trust the older, established firms for repairs, rather than one in a converted barn run by a couple of ex-officers. And there wasn't enough trade in just selling petrol to keep 'em going, so to speak. What's more, Sergeant,' Mitchell continued, intent on airing his local knowledge, 'the Kingston bypass should be opened later this year, and there'll be a few garages along there in the fullness of time, I shouldn't wonder.'

'When exactly did this fire take place?' asked Hardcastle.

'Monday the fourteenth of March, sir,' said Mitchell, without hesitation. 'The report says that the brigade was called at five thirty-five that afternoon.'

'What sort of damage was done to the premises, Mitchell?' asked Marriott.

'Only two areas of damage, Sergeant. There was a barn that had been converted into a workshop and there was also an office. The office is still structurally sound, but the desk had been completely destroyed, and there was a lot of burnt paper on the floor, which Inspector Granger noted in his report. The old chicken run and another row of barns weren't affected by the fire at all. Funny thing, though, was that the insurance company must've had their doubts about the cause of the fire because they refused to pay out.'

'How far apart are these two places that were burned down – the office and the workshop?'

'Quite a distance, Sergeant. I mean, not a great distance,

but probably too far for one to have caught fire from the other, if you see what I mean.'

'Did the insurance company ask the police to investigate?'

'Not to my knowledge, sir.'

'Where are these two ex-officers now?' asked Hardcastle.

'I don't rightly know, sir,' said Mitchell. 'It seems they left the area, but I don't know where to.'

'Has this place been sold, then?'

'I'm not sure about that, sir. I did hear that an estate agent in Kingston had the place on his books, but I don't know whether he's had any luck selling it.'

'What's the name of this agent? And while you're about it, you can give me the name of the insurance company as well.'

Mitchell referred to his file. 'I think I made a note of them both somewhere, sir. Ah, yes, here we are. The estate agents are called Coates and Company in the High Street, and the insurance company's the Surrey Insurance Company Limited.' He glanced up. 'Their head office is in the City of London, sir.'

'Have they got a local office closer than that?' asked Hardcastle.

'Yes, they have, sir. That's in Kingston, too. I'll give you that address as well.'

'How far away is this garage, Mitchell?' asked Marriott.

'Go to the top of the road and turn right, Sergeant, and it's about twenty yards down, on the other side of Portsmouth Road.'

'In that case, you can show us the way.'

As the three CID officers walked out to the front office of the police station, the acting station officer appeared.

'Everything all right, gentlemen?' asked Perkins, his hands fluttering nervously in front of him. Marriott's cautionary comment about transfers had obviously alarmed him.

'No,' said Hardcastle, thereby causing the constable further distress. 'But what you can do, lad, is get on that telephone of yours and find me a taxi that'll take Sergeant Marriott and me to Kingston, once I've been down to look at this here ruined garage.'

Hardcastle and Marriott, accompanied by Mitchell, walked the short distance to the site of the garage owned by Stoner and Holroyd, but there was little to see. As Mitchell had said, the fire had affected the brick-built, burned-out office and the barn-cum-workshop. The detectives hazarded a guess at the site being somewhere in the region of an acre, possibly an acre and a half.

'We'll get back to Ditton nick, then, Mitchell,' said Hardcastle, 'where Perkins should have arranged a taxi to take us to this estate agent at Kingston. I won't offer you a lift as you've got your bicycle. Anyway, the exercise will do you good.'

'I might see you later, then, sir.'

'I've no doubt, Mitchell. In the meantime, you can tell me of a decent pub in Kingston where Sergeant Marriott and I can get a pie and a pint.'

'There's the Three Fishes in Richmond Road, sir. That's a good pub, and not far from the insurance agent I mentioned.'

'Good afternoon, gentlemen. How may I be of assistance?' An unctuous man crossed the floor of the estate agency the moment that Hardcastle and Marriott entered. He was immaculately dressed in a single-breasted lounge suit, with a double-breasted waistcoat and a red handkerchief that overflowed a little too much from his top pocket. To cover his advancing baldness, he had plastered the remains of his hair across his head in what was known as a 'fold-over' style.

'Are you the manager?' asked Hardcastle, who was unreasonably suspicious of men who wore double-breasted waistcoats.

'Indeed, I am, sir.' The manager revolved his hands around each other in a washing motion. 'Wilfred Chapman at your service, sir.'

'I understand that you are acting for the owners of a garage in Ditton that's for sale,' said Hardcastle.

'That is correct, sir. Allow me to fetch the details. I'm sure you'll find it a most attractive site with great potential for development.'

'I don't want to buy it,' said Hardcastle curtly. 'I'm a police

officer. Divisional Detective Inspector Hardcastle of the
Whitehall Division, and this is Detective Sergeant Marriott.'

'Oh!' Chapman was unable to hide his disappointment, but
that expression quickly turned to one of anxiety. 'Is there a
problem of some sort?'

'That's what I'm hoping you'll be able to tell me,' said
Hardcastle. He was unimpressed by estate agents who seemed
to think that they were in a professional class on a par with
lawyers.

'What exactly did you want to know?' Chapman's original
sycophantic attitude had now been replaced by one of grave
concern. Once the police began to look into the affairs of
this particular estate agency, there was no telling what they
might find. The manager's principal worry was the slightly
illegal way in which he had 'assisted' some of his clients to
obtain a mortgage. And that involved a solicitor of doubtful
repute, who happened to be a member of the same lodge as
the one to which Chapman belonged. He began to 'wash'
his hands again, but this time it was an indication of his
anguish.

'I've been given to understand that the property is owned
jointly by Guy Stoner and Rupert Holroyd.'

'If you'll excuse me for a moment, sir, I need to consult
the file.' Chapman crossed to a cabinet and withdrew a manila
folder. 'You're quite correct, sir,' he said, having quickly
perused the few sheets of paper the folder contained.

'How can I find those two gentlemen, Mr Chapman? I need
to contact them urgently.'

'I don't have an address for them, sir, because they appointed
an agent to act on their behalf, but I do have an address for
him. Well, an address of sorts.' Chapman took a slip of paper
from a nearby desk and scribbled a few lines on it. 'There we
are, sir,' he said, handing the note to Hardcastle.

'But that's a newsagent's shop in Paddington,' protested
Hardcastle. 'What good's an accommodation address?'

'I'm afraid it's all we have, sir. Our instructions are that in
the event of someone showing genuine interest, we are to write
to the agent, a Mr Oliver Talbot, at that address.'

'Most unsatisfactory,' muttered Hardcastle. 'Have any

enquiries been made by the . . .' He paused. 'What was the name of that insurance company, Marriott?'

'The Surrey, sir.'

'That's it. Have any enquiries been made by the Surrey Insurance Company?'

Chapman shook his head. 'Not of this office, sir. I suppose they might have contacted this Mr Talbot, but they certainly haven't spoken to me. Is there anything I should know about?'

'You'll have to ask them,' said Hardcastle. 'Come, Marriott.'

The two policemen left, leaving behind a very worried estate agent. The possibility had suddenly occurred to him that he might be attempting to sell a piece of land that was the property of an insurance company and not the people for whom the mysterious Mr Talbot claimed to be acting. If that turned out to be the case, the police would most certainly start looking into the affairs of Chapman's office, and that worried him considerably.

The manager of the Surrey Insurance Company's branch in Kingston was more helpful. He introduced himself as Dudley Forester, and invited the two detectives to take a seat in his office.

'To cut a long story short, Mr Hardcastle,' Forester began, 'head office sent a fire investigator down from London. Whenever there's an incident like that, the company wants to make sure that everything's above board before they pay out. It's not the first time that ex-officers have invested in chicken farms that have gone bust, and then looked for something else to do. And if the second business goes bankrupt and the third enterprise is followed by a fire, we tend to look at it closely.'

'And *had* the garage business gone bankrupt, Mr Forester?' asked Hardcastle.

'Look at this way,' said Forester in matter-of-fact tones. 'We knew from local information that Ditton Garage did hardly any business in the few weeks it was open. There wasn't enough motor trade to keep it afloat.'

'As a matter of interest, Mr Forester,' asked Marriott, 'how much was the garage insured for?'

'Ten and a half thousand pounds, Mr Marriott.'

'Having visited the site, I'd think that was well in excess of its value.'

'Our view, too,' said Forester.

'What did your fire investigator find that caused your company to refuse to pay out?' asked Hardcastle, getting to the nub of his enquiries.

'Although the fire had been out for nigh on seventy-two hours by the time our man went down there, he's very skilled at his job, and when he found two separate seats of fire a good distance apart, that settled the matter. That's as good an indication of arson as anything you're likely to find.'

'Did your insurance company refer the matter to the police?'

'We sent them a report, Mr Hardcastle, which stated that the company wasn't satisfied that the fire had begun accidentally and left it at that. If they chose not to pursue the matter of arson, it's no concern of ours.' Forester gave an expressive shrug. 'I think those two will have great difficulty getting cover in future, cooperation among underwriters being what it is.'

'What was Holroyd's reaction when he was told that his claim had been refused?'

'No idea,' said Forester airily. 'We sent a letter to someone called Oliver Talbot, whom Holroyd had appointed his agent, but we got no reply.'

'What address did you send this letter to?'

'Some newsagent in Paddington.' Forester laughed. 'Well, that tells you there's something not quite right, doesn't it, Inspector?'

After a pork pie and a pint or two of best bitter at the Three Fishes, Hardcastle and Marriott took a cab back to Surbiton police station. Hardcastle said nothing, but Marriott, from his long experience of working with the DDI, could tell that he was seething with anger that the local police had apparently done nothing about Forester's allegation of arson.

It was DC Mitchell who was the first to receive the brunt of Hardcastle's ill temper.

'I've no idea, sir. I never saw any report from the insurance company. A serious allegation of that sort probably went straight to divisional headquarters at Wandsworth. I've no idea what would have happened to it there. As you probably know, sir, Mr Fitnam's been off sick for some time now. Maybe he was going to deal with it when he got back, or maybe he handed it to Mr Robson.' Ted Robson was the V Division detective inspector who deputized for Fitnam when the latter was away but, as the Chief Constable CID had pointed out, he was heavily involved with a fraud enquiry. Hardcastle knew Robson to be a reliable officer, and he could not imagine him allowing an allegation of arson to be ignored. However, that was not his problem; his concern was the missing Guy Stoner. And, for that matter, the mystery of the absent Rupert Holroyd too. 'Mr Granger was the reporting officer, sir, and he's on duty this afternoon,' continued Mitchell, in the hope of getting this irascible inspector off his back.

Hardcastle found Inspector Granger in his office next to the communications room.

'I understand that you dealt with the fire at Ditton Garage, Mr Granger,' said Hardcastle, having introduced himself and Marriott.

'Yes, sir, I did.' Granger stood up. He was a grey-haired man in his fifties, with a stooped posture and a repetitive cough. The DDI assumed that he had fetched up at Surbiton because he was unfit for the rigours of a Central London division.

'What were the circumstances?'

'I got the docket out ready, sir. Mitchell said you might be coming in.' Granger opened the folder on his desk, donned a pair of spectacles and spent a few moments scanning through it. 'Now then. Ditton Garage fire, Monday the fourteenth of March.' He looked up at Hardcastle. 'I was the reporting officer. It always has to be an inspector who reports a fire, you see, sir.'

'And you had to travel from Surbiton in order to do so, I suppose, Mr Granger.' Hardcastle forbore from pointing out that he was a police officer too and knew the regulations about fire reporting.

'Yes, I did.'

'And so did the fire brigade, I suppose.'

'Oh, no, sir. There's no fire station in Surbiton, although there's talk of building one. I did hear mention that a volunteer steam fire engine was kept somewhere near Victoria Road, but I don't know much about it. No, the station at Ditton dealt with it. But it's a volunteer station, so they had to call out their members from home. Even so, it only took them about twenty minutes to get there after the alarm. They're very keen.'

'Who raised the alarm, sir?' asked Marriott, breaking off his note-taking to glance at Granger.

Granger ran a finger down his report. 'That was Captain Rupert Holroyd, Skipper. One of the owners. He ran to a telephone box at the corner of the road.'

'He was lucky to find one,' said Marriott. 'Most of them are in London.'

'Was there no telephone at the garage, Mr Granger?' asked Hardcastle, cutting across his sergeant's comment.

'I don't know, sir. It may have been that there was one in the office and it was destroyed by the conflagration.'

'Was Captain Stoner present when you arrived, sir?' asked Marriott.

'If he was, I didn't see him.'

'What about Holroyd?'

'He'd returned to the site of the incident after calling the brigade, sir, and when I questioned him, he said he'd no idea how the fire had started. He'd been with a young lady in London, where he'd taken her for luncheon, so he said. When eventually he got back to Ditton, he found the garage on fire.'

'I spoke to the insurance company earlier today and they've refused to pay out,' said Hardcastle. 'The manager talked of the fire being suspicious. Any idea why? Did you see anything suspicious?'

'No, sir, but the fire brigade was there, as I said, and they never said a word about anything being wrong. In fact, their leading fireman put the cause down to possibly a cigarette or a careless flame associated with petroleum spirit fumes – it being a garage, like. And that's what I put in my report.'

'But there were two fires quite a distance apart, Mr Granger,' said Hardcastle. 'Did you not find that a bit odd?'

'Thinking back on it, I probably did, but I was guided by

what the fire brigade said. Unfortunately, they are amateurs, sir, and don't have the same training as the regular firemen.'

'There's one more thing you can do for me, Mr Granger,' said Hardcastle, who was beginning to think that it was not only the fire brigade who were amateurs.

'Yes, sir?'

'Get someone to call me a cab to take me to Surbiton railway station. I've had enough for one day.'

'It'll be a pleasure, sir,' said Granger, and received a sharp glance from Hardcastle.

THREE

On Saturday morning, Hardcastle decided to visit the Paddington newsagent's shop that the manager of the Kingston estate agency had said was the accommodation address used by Oliver Talbot.

An overweight, bald-headed man, with a ragged moustache and finger-marked spectacles, looked up when Hardcastle and Marriott entered.

'Help you?' he asked, wiping his hands down the front of his cardigan.

'Are you the owner of this establishment?' demanded Hardcastle.

'Who wants to know?' The man had initially decided that the two men who had just entered his shop were bailiffs. He had good reason for thinking that – indeed, had been expecting them – but his concerns were about to get worse.

'Police.'

'You won't find anything wrong here, guv'nor.' Suddenly, the newsagent became sycophantic.

'I asked you if you were the owner.'

'Yes, I am.'

'What's your name?' Hardcastle persisted.

'Sam Cox.'

'Would that be Samuel Cox?' asked Marriott, taking out his pocketbook.

'S'right.'

'Where and when were you born?'

'What d'you want that for?'

'I suggest you answer my sergeant's questions, Cox, because you are on the verge of being arrested for committing an offence under the Official Secrets Acts of 1911 and 1920.'

'What are you talking about? I don't know nothing about no official secrets. Anyway, the war's long since over.'

'I think we *will* take Cox into custody, Sergeant Marriott.

He is clearly being evasive,' said Hardcastle, appearing to give the matter great thought.

'I was born on the seventh of January 1865 in Whitechapel, sir.' Cox gave a nervous laugh. 'I'm sorry, guv'nor, it's just you took me aback, going on about official secrets an' that. I thought you was being serious for a moment.'

'I was,' said Hardcastle, 'but now we've got that out of the way, at least for the moment, you can tell me about a man called Oliver Talbot who uses this shop as the address for any letters that are written to him.' He took out his pipe and began to fill it.

A shifty-looking man sidled into the shop, put a penny on the counter and took a copy of the *Daily Mirror*. Belatedly realizing that the two men who were talking to the shop's owner were obviously policemen, he was about to scurry out when he was stopped by Hardcastle's stentorian voice.

'Bates!'

The man turned. 'Oh, hello, Mr 'Ardcastle. I never saw you there.'

'What are you doing on this manor, eh, Bates?'

'I live just round the corner, guv'nor.'

'Well, just you mind you keep your nose clean.' Hardcastle turned to Marriott as Bates hurried out of the shop. 'Spotter Bates was a look-out man for a team of pickpockets who robbed tourists at the Changing of the Guard at Buck House. Got sent down for five years' hard labour about seven years ago.' He turned back to Cox. 'Now then, about this man Talbot, Cox.'

'Mr Talbot's only come in the once since he paid for the arrangement, guv'nor,' said Cox, 'just to see if there's anything for him, but there was only one and there ain't been nothing since.'

'How long has he had this arrangement with you, Cox?' asked Marriott.

'Getting on for a fortnight, I s'pose.'

'So, we can assume that he intends to come in once a fortnight, or maybe once a week,' said Hardcastle, half to himself. 'Did he leave an address where he could be reached if something turned up?'

'No, he never.'

'He didn't?' Hardcastle raised his eyebrows in mock surprise, but it was the answer he had expected. 'Let's have a look at your record book, then, Cox.' He took out a box of Swan Vestas and lit the tobacco in his pipe.

'What record book?' A hunted look appeared on Cox's face.

'When you registered your business as an accommodation address with the police, you were told to keep a book in which to record the name and address of each person who was having mail sent here.' Hardcastle looked around for an ashtray; not finding one, he dropped the match on the floor.

Sam Cox looked decidedly unhappy at Hardcastle's latest revelation. 'Well, I, um . . .'

"So, you're not registered,' said Hardcastle accusingly.

'No, well, I never knew I had to.'

'Ignorance of the law is no excuse, Cox. You'll be reported for a summons, and you could get six months' imprisonment for breaching Section Five of the Official Secrets Act 1920.' There was no need for Hardcastle to quote the statute, but he did so to ensure that Cox would do as he was told from now on.

'Oh, my Gawd!' exclaimed Cox. 'I never knew, guv'nor, as the good Lord is my witness.'

'There's no need to take the oath yet, Cox. Save it for your appearance up the Old Bailey. Now, I'll tell you what you're going to do. If any letter comes for this Oliver Talbot, you won't give it to him. And if he asks, tell him that nothing's arrived for him. Then you'll immediately telephone Detective Sergeant Marriott here, and tell him, and he'll come and collect the letter. Understood?'

'Yes, guv'nor,' said Cox. After a moment's thought, he added plaintively, 'but I haven't got a telephone.'

'Haven't got one?' said Hardcastle. 'I'm amazed. Well, you'd better get one.'

Marriott turned away, almost choking with suppressed laughter at Hardcastle's perverse statement. For years the DDI had expressed his abhorrence of the telephone and swore that it was a new-fangled device that would not last. It's a flash in the pan, like all the other things the Metropolitan Police has tried, he would frequently tell Marriott.

'D'you want me to swear an information and get a summons for Cox, sir?' asked Marriott, as he and Hardcastle left the shop of the distressed newsagent.

'No, Marriott. Just write a brief report and send it to Special Branch. They deal with Official Secrets Act matters. They've got nothing else to do, and while you're at it, you might as well tell 'em how to get to court.' Over the years, Hardcastle had developed an animosity towards Special Branch, mainly as a result of the attitude of Superintendent Patrick Quinn, its wartime chief. Hardcastle believed that Quinn had always treated him like some sort of common-or-garden dogberry. What he did not realize was that Quinn treated everyone in much the same way. And to add to Hardcastle's irritation with the man, Quinn had received a knighthood when he retired.

On Monday morning, Hardcastle made another instant decision. 'We shall go to the Old Bailey, Marriott.'

'The Bailey, sir? What for?'

'To get a warrant under the Bankers' Books Evidence Act, Marriott, that's what for. I want to have a gander at any cheques young Stoner might have drawn on his account. Knowing how sniffy bank managers are about anyone wanting information about a client, it's best to have a warrant.'

Deciding that the weather was warm enough not to bother with an overcoat, Hardcastle seized his bowler hat and umbrella, and made for the stairs. 'Come, Marriott.'

Walking out to Parliament Street, the DDI waved his umbrella imperiously at a cab.

'The Old Bailey, driver.'

The cab driver yanked down the flag on his taximeter. 'You in trouble, then, are you, guv'nor?' he asked jocularly.

'What's that building behind me?' asked Hardcastle, pointing with his umbrella.

'That's the bladder o'lard, guv'nor,' said the cabbie, but a little nervously now.

'Yes, Scotland Yard. We have dungeons underneath it, and if you don't keep your trap shut, you'll finish up in one of them. And you mind you take the most direct route, because I know all about the Cab and Stage Carriage Act of 1907. In fact, you might say that I'm an expert on the subject,' Hardcastle added, as he clambered into the cab.

The two detectives hurried into the Central Criminal Court and pushed their way through the throng of people either surrendering to bail, waiting to give evidence or reporting for jury service.

Hardcastle made straight for the court inspector's office. 'I'm Divisional Detective Inspector Hardcastle, Metropolitan A,' he announced.

'And what can I do for you?' asked the inspector.

'You can tell me who's sitting today,' said Hardcastle curtly. For no good reason, he disliked the City of London Police, regarding them as toy policemen who had only a square mile of territory to worry about. In return, the City Police, who had no officers under six feet tall, referred to the shorter Metropolitan officers as 'Metro-gnomes'.

'See for yourself.' The court inspector turned a sheet of paper on his desk. He did not like Metropolitan officers, regarding them as overbearing know-alls. There was a phrase familiar to City officers, and it came to the court inspector's mind now. *You can always tell a Metropolitan Police officer, but you can't tell him much.*

'Ah!' exclaimed Hardcastle. 'Mr Justice Cawthorne is sitting in Court Three this morning, Marriott.' Addressing the court inspector, he said, 'Perhaps you'd be so good as to ask if His Lordship would be prepared to see me in chambers before he sits, Inspector.'

The court inspector returned a few minutes later. 'Mr Justice Cawthorne can see you now, Mr Hardcastle,' he said. 'His chambers are—'

'I know where his chambers are, thank you, Inspector,' said Hardcastle, and swept from the office with Marriott hurrying behind him.

Hardcastle knocked on the judge's door and was bidden to enter.

'Well, well, Mr Hardcastle, I haven't seen you in a while. What can I do for you?' Mr Justice Cawthorne had a jovial countenance and a reputation for telling amusing anecdotes at bar mess dinners. However, his joviality was readily abandoned when he was sentencing a criminal who had used violence to commit his crime. He abhorred robbery with violence, and those found guilty in his court knew that they would face a substantial sentence of penal servitude, which carried with it hard labour.

'I'd be grateful if you would grant me a warrant under the Bankers' Books Evidence Act 1879, my lord,' said Hardcastle, and outlined the reasons for requiring it. 'I'd also be grateful, my lord, in view of the circumstances, if you could see your way clear to appending a direction for immediate execution rather than waiting for the normal three days.'

'Sounds reasonable,' said the judge. 'I presume you've brought the necessary paperwork with you, Mr Hardcastle.'

'Indeed, my lord.' Hardcastle signalled to Marriott, who immediately produced a number of sheets of paper from his briefcase.

The branch of the bank that held Guy Stoner's account was in the Strand.

Hardcastle asked to see the manager and thwarted the efforts of the clerk who wanted to know why, merely saying that it was police business.

'Rodney Smales, gentlemen,' announced the bank manager, once Hardcastle had introduced himself and Marriott. Smales, tall, slender and suave, was immaculate in morning dress. His greying hair was pomaded and, Hardcastle suspected, his moustache was waxed. 'How may I be of service?' It was a statement of courtesy. He was a bank servant who knew that he was within his rights not to give the police any information about his clients. As he had confided to colleagues on more than one occasion, 'Wild horses would not drag one iota of information from me.' Rodney Smales, however, had not taken account of DDI Hardcastle's possession of a Bankers' Books Evidence Act warrant.

Hardcastle outlined the police's interest in the affairs of Guy Stoner and explained that he would like sight of anything held by the bank that was in his handwriting.

'My dear Inspector,' began Smales smoothly, 'I'm sure that you are aware—' But that was as far as he got.

'I have here,' began Hardcastle, flicking his fingers in Marriott's direction, 'a warrant issued this morning by Mr Justice Cawthorne under the provisions of the Bankers' Books Evidence Act 1879.' Taking the document from Marriott, he handed it to Smales.

'You appreciate, Inspector,' said the discomfited Smales, as he cast a cursory glance over the warrant, 'that I am allowed three days before being required to produce the necessary documents.'

'Normally,' said Hardcastle, 'but on this occasion Mr Justice Cawthorne has waived that requirement, as you will see from the endorsement.'

Smales read the document in greater detail. 'Most unusual,' he murmured.

'It is, Mr Smales, but I'm investigating a case of suspected murder. Captain Stoner's murder, to be precise.'

'Good gracious me! You think Captain Stoner's been murdered?'

'That's what I'm attempting to find out.' Hardcastle took out his watch and made a point of staring at it, as if to emphasize the urgency. Winding it briefly, he dropped it back into his waistcoat pocket.

'What exactly is it you want to see, Inspector?' Smales became a little more accommodating.

'I have here two letters and one of the cheques the bank returned, as is the practice. The cheque and one of the letters are written in Captain Stoner's hand, but the other letter is entirely different, the excuse being that Captain Stoner had injured his hand in a fire and dictated this letter that was sent to his uncle in Norfolk. I'd like to compare the signatures on cheques that Stoner wrote to see if they are the same.'

'D'you have a reason to think that some fraud may have been perpetrated on the bank, Inspector?'

'No reason at all,' said Hardcastle. 'But it's always a possibility, I suppose.'

Smales did not like Hardcastle's response very much, interpreting it as a slur. Nevertheless, he sent for his secretary and instructed her to find any cheques that had not been returned to Captain Stoner.

Minutes later, the woman returned and placed three cheques on the manager's desk together with a letter.

After spending a few moments perusing the documents, Smales handed the letter to Hardcastle.

'That letter, purporting to come from Captain Stoner,' said Smales, 'but claiming that he dictated it due to an injury, asks the bank not to forward any correspondence or cheques until advised of his new address. It goes on to say that due to an unfortunate fire at the place where they lived, he and his business partner are in temporary accommodation. He further undertakes to advise the bank when they have permanent accommodation.'

'A likely story,' muttered Hardcastle, and handed the letter to Marriott.

'I'm afraid you can't keep that, Inspector,' said Smales. 'A certified copy is accepted by the courts.'

'You can have it back,' snapped Hardcastle, who was well aware of the law on the subject. 'That's why my sergeant will make a copy.'

While Marriott began the weary task of making a hand-written copy of the letter, Smales examined the three cheques and compared them with the cheque that Hardcastle had produced. 'Oh, my God!'

'Is something wrong?' asked Hardcastle.

'Have a look, and see what you think, Inspector.' The manager handed both cheques to Hardcastle.

The DDI handed them to Marriott. 'Your eyesight's better than mine, Marriott. Have a look and tell me what you think.'

Marriott spent a few minutes examining the cheques. 'I would say that a clumsy attempt has been made to forge Captain Stoner's signature, sir, and I'm sure that a handwriting expert would agree.'

'These three cheques, Mr Smales, are for a total of forty-five pounds.'

'Yes, Inspector, and I've just been looking at Captain Stoner's account. It would appear that those three cheques have used up the last of his available funds.'

'Were they were cashed at this branch, Mr Smales?' asked Marriott.

'No, at our branch in Chelsea.'

'I suppose that the staff there had no reason to doubt their validity.'

'Obviously not; otherwise they wouldn't have been cashed.' Smales sounded relieved that the onus for cashing three forged cheques, if that was the case, would now fall on the manager of the Chelsea branch.

'It's looking as though there will be a court case, Mr Smales,' said Hardcastle, 'and I would strongly advise you to keep hold of those cheques. If, in fact, your client has been murdered, they will be evidence.'

'You may rest assured, Inspector, that they and all records pertaining to Captain Stoner will be kept in my safe from now on.'

'Well, Marriott,' said Hardcastle, as he walked out to the Strand and hailed a cab, 'it didn't take long to knock Master Smales off his high horse.' The DDI climbed into the cab. 'New Scotland Yard, cabbie.' He turned to Marriott. 'Tell 'em Cannon Row, and half the time you'll finish up at Cannon Street in the City.'

'Yes, sir,' said Marriott wearily, who had received this advice on almost every occasion that he and Hardcastle had shared a cab back to the police station.

When the cab set them down, Hardcastle made straight for the Red Lion in Derby Gate. 'I think, Marriott,' he began, once he had a pint in front of him, 'that I'll get you to apply to the Bow Street beak for a search warrant for Ditton Garage this afternoon.'

'Do we need one, sir?'

'Are you suggesting that we get the owners' consent, Marriott?' Hardcastle emitted a derisive chuckle. 'Because if you are, I suggest you find the owners.'

'That's not what I meant, sir. A further search would be quite legal, even without a warrant, in pursuit of evidence of arson.'

'You might be right,' said Hardcastle, pausing with his glass halfway to his mouth, 'but I'm not much interested in the arson. On the other hand, though, we'd be on safer ground with a warrant in case some clever brief started picking holes in the evidence when we get to court.'

'Court, sir? What are you hoping to find, then?'

'We won't know until we look, Marriott,' rejoined the DDI enigmatically. He glanced along the bar until he spotted the landlord. 'Another two pints, please, Albert.' Hardcastle was not being generous towards his sergeant: Albert never charged Hardcastle for his beer, imagining that it would accord him some sort of preferential treatment if ever he fell foul of the law. He had, however, seriously underestimated A Division's DDI in that regard.

Marriott made his way to Bow Street as soon as he and Hardcastle left the Red Lion.

'I've got the search warrant, sir,' said Marriott, when he arrived back at the police station.

'I should hope so, Marriott.' Hardcastle took out his hunter and glanced at it. Briefly winding it, he dropped it back into his waistcoat pocket. 'We'll go to Ditton and start searching tomorrow morning bright and early, then.'

'Who d'you want to take with you, sir?'

'Who's in the office?'

'Ritchie, Proctor and Vickers, sir. Oh, and the new sergeant's arrived, posted in from Vine Street.'

'Vine Street, eh? He should be all right, then. I served at Vine Street as a sergeant, you know, Marriott.'

'So I understand, sir,' said Marriott diplomatically. Hardcastle had said as much every time mention was made of the C Division police station.

'Who is this new sergeant?'

Metaphorically taking a deep breath, Marriott said, 'Detective Sergeant Henry Catto, sir.'

'What?' Slowly, Hardcastle replaced his pipe in the ashtray. 'It's bloody Posh Bill working one off on me.' Suddenly realizing that he was obliquely criticizing another senior officer, he quickly added, 'Forget I said that, Marriott.'

There had always been a suppressed animosity between Hardcastle and DDI William Sullivan of C Division. In short, Hardcastle detested him, mainly because he regarded

Sullivan as a poseur who dressed like a dandy and wore a monocle. He would never be seen outside Vine Street police station without his curly-brimmed bowler hat and a rattan cane, an outfit that caused villains to refer to him as 'Posh Bill with the Piccadilly window'. As if that was not enough, a rumour was circulating that Posh Bill had a mirror glued inside his bowler hat so that he could check the tidiness of his hair whenever he entered a building. But no one had ever seen it and the tale was put down to malice.

Hardcastle had always doubted Catto's abilities as a detective, despite Marriott frequently telling the DDI that Catto was a good thief-taker. Nevertheless, at some stage, Hardcastle had suggested to Catto that he studied for promotion. There was, however, an ulterior motive: Hardcastle wanted shot of him. But Catto had persevered with his studies and achieved promotion to third-class sergeant. Now he had been promoted to second-class sergeant and posted back to A Division. Hardcastle was in no doubt, unreasonably, that somehow or other William Sullivan had engineered the transfer as an act of spite. The fact of the matter, however, was that Chief Constable Wensley had oversight of promotions and transfers in the CID and thought that he was doing A Division's DDI a favour.

'Fetch him in, then,' said Hardcastle.

'Good morning, sir.' Detective Sergeant Catto beamed at the DDI. Although in the past he had turned to jelly every time the DDI had spoken to him, several years on the C or St James's Division had made him more self-confident.

'I hope you've improved, Catto.'

'Of course, sir. I've been at Vine Street for a few years,' said Catto craftily, knowing that the DDI would not argue with that.

'You haven't taken to wearing a curly-brimmed bowler hat, I suppose?' enquired Hardcastle jocularly.

'No, sir.' A dark-haired, slender man, with brown eyes that seemed to dart everywhere in their search for wrongdoers, Catto was smartly dressed in a dark suit with a double-breasted jacket, which he was slim enough to be able to wear.

'Oh! I thought all the CID officers did on C Division's manor these days. Now then, Catto, tomorrow we're going down to Ditton to search what remains of a garage. You'll be in charge of the search team under Sergeant Marriott's direction and he'll tell you what to look for. Don't make a pig's ear of it.'

Marriott treated that remark with some misgiving. He had not the faintest idea what they were supposed to be looking for.

'Of course not, sir.' Catto beamed again. 'How do we get to Ditton, sir?'

'You're a sergeant, Catto; use your initiative.'

'He seems different,' said Hardcastle grudgingly, once Catto had left the office.

'Yes, sir,' said Marriott, and followed Catto into the detectives' room, not wishing to become involved in a discussion about Catto's qualities or lack of them.

'How many of us are going to Ditton altogether, Skip?' asked Catto.

'There's Ritchie, Proctor and Vickers. And you, of course, Henry.'

'Does this nick have a van?' asked Catto.

'Of course it does.'

'That'll be best way to get to Ditton, then, Skip. And it'll be useful if there's any evidence for us to bring back.' Catto paused. 'Does Mr Hardcastle want to come with us?

'I think that most unlikely, Henry. Nevertheless, I'll ask him.'

FOUR

Hardcastle's answer had been predictable. He had no intention of travelling in a police van with Catto and the constables. Despite Marriott's previous advice, the DDI decided to take a taxi for the journey to Ditton and directed Marriott to travel with him.

When they arrived at the garage, or what was left of it, Hardcastle found that Catto had already organized his search team and they had begun to comb the area.

Looking around, Hardcastle wondered, more even than when he had visited the site of the garage the previous Friday, how it was that Stoner and Holroyd had thought they were going to make a living. There was a single petrol pump, but presumably it had not contained any petrol or it would have exploded. On reflection, he thought that perhaps it had been emptied in order that the petrol could be used as an accelerant. The office and the workshop – a converted barn – were hardly likely to inspire confidence in anyone bringing their precious motor car for repairs to be carried out on it. He also spotted a large heap of rubbish on the far side of the area, not far from the workshop. All in all, it was a sorry attempt to generate a business.

Hardcastle's reflective gazing was interrupted by Detective Sergeant Catto.

'What is it, Catto?'

'I've found what appear to be bloodstains, sir.'

'Where?'

'On the floor of the office, sir.'

'That's that building there, isn't it?' Hardcastle, using his umbrella as a pointer, indicated the brick structure.

'Yes, sir. There also appear to be the remains of two camp beds, so I imagine that Stoner and Holroyd were living here.'

'Better take a look, then.' Hardcastle followed Catto across the uneven ground to the gutted office.

'Just there, sir.' Catto pointed to a dull patch, almost black, that was in front of the ashes that had once been a desk.

'Where did the other fire start, Marriott?' asked Hardcastle.

'In that large barn there, sir, or what remains of it. It was in use, according to DC Mitchell, as a workshop.' Marriott pointed at a building that stood in front of three smaller barns. The only difference was that an attempt had been made to destroy the larger barn, and most of its wooden sides were now just charred debris.

Hardcastle walked towards the workshop and, for a minute or two, stared at the ground. Then he turned. 'Something tells me, Marriott, that it's no coincidence that only two buildings were set fire to. Catto here has found what looks like bloodstains on the floor of the office, and the other fire was started in this workshop. Why?'

'D'you think we might find Captain Stoner's body buried there, sir?' asked Catto, before Marriott had the opportunity of replying.

'It's a possibility,' said Hardcastle, 'but first get someone to take that heap of rubbish apart.'

'Yes, sir.' Catto turned to DCs Proctor and Vickers. 'Right, you heard what the guv'nor said. Get to it.'

'What are we looking for specifically, Henry?' asked James Proctor.

'It's "Sergeant" to you, Proctor,' snapped Catto furiously. 'And you'll know when you find it.'

Hardcastle nodded. 'I think you're right, Marriott,' he said, and then, out of Catto's hearing, added, 'Our new sergeant seems to have benefited from his time at Vine Street, but then I knew he would.'

'Yes, sir,' said Marriott. There was nothing else he could say. He was just grateful that the DDI had not pointed out, yet again, that he had once served there.

Reluctantly, Proctor and Vickers began to dismantle the heap of rubbish. Much of it consisted of oily rags and other waste connected with the abortive garage business set up by the two proprietors.

'There's a shovel here, Sergeant,' said Proctor, after ten minutes' searching, 'but it looks as though the handle's been burned off.'

'Bring it here,' said Hardcastle, who was standing next to Catto.

'I don't know if I'm right, sir, but there's a mark along the cutting edge that could be blood.' Proctor held up his find. The blade was intact, although blackened, but only an inch or two of the wooden shaft protruded above the metal socket. And it had clearly been burned.

'It might be blood,' said Hardcastle, not wishing to commit himself. 'But in this tip of a place, it could be anything. I think it's time we got a scientist to look at it, and at the stain on the floor of what's left of the office, Marriott.'

'I can telephone from Ditton nick, sir.'

'Possibly,' said Hardcastle, 'but we'll finish the search first. Has anyone searched the workshop, Catto?'

'Not yet, sir. That was going to be the next job.'

'Sir!' Vickers, up to his knees in filth and rubbish, was holding a large biscuit tin aloft.

'What are you all in a sweat about, lad? It's an old tin,' said Hardcastle.

'It's heavy, sir.'

'Bring it here, then,' said Hardcastle wearily.

Vickers walked across to where the DDI was standing and placed the tin on the ground.

'Well, don't stand there looking at it, Vickers,' snapped Hardcastle. 'Take the bloody lid off.'

'Good God!' exclaimed Vickers, as he peered closer. The biscuit tin contained a human head.

'If you're going to throw up, Vickers,' said Catto, 'don't do it over the evidence.'

'I was in the bloody war, Sergeant,' said Vickers, 'and I survived the first day of the Somme. You don't think a nice clean head's going to worry me, do you?'

Henry Catto, who had not been in the war, said nothing. He had momentarily overlooked the fact that quite a few policemen had joined after the war as soon as they had been discharged from the army. It was a legacy of that terrible war that too many of them had seen a surfeit of dead bodies, in some cases to the extent that death merely caused a shrug of the shoulders.

'Unless I'm very much mistaken,' said Hardcastle calmly, 'that is the head of Captain Guy Stoner.'

'What's next, sir?' asked Marriott, choosing not to query how the DDI seemed to be sure it was Stoner's head. It certainly bore little resemblance to the photograph that he had obtained from the Reverend Percy Stoner.

'Get down to Ditton nick and arrange for Sir Bernard to come here.' Hardcastle paused. 'No, wait a moment. We'll have a look in the workshop before we bother him.'

Sir Bernard Spilsbury was regarded as the foremost forensic pathologist in the country. In court, his persuasive evidence was rarely disputed and had been instrumental in sending a string of infamous murderers to the scaffold.

Hardcastle led his team of detectives across to the workshop. The fire appeared to have gone halfway up the wooden walls and charred them badly without actually destroying them. The workbench, however, was a different story; it had been completely destroyed, leaving a collection of tools lying among the ashes.

'There is a car-jack handle down there, sir,' said Stuart Ritchie, 'and a machete and a saw. I wonder if the jack handle was used as a murder weapon, and the saw and the machete used to cut off the head Vickers found.'

'You could be right, er . . .' Hardcastle paused. 'What's your name, lad?'

'Ritchie, sir.'

'Of course it is, Ritchie, but we won't touch anything until we can get hold of someone who knows how to move that sort of stuff without damaging any evidence that there might be on it. The dirt floor of this barn could be worth investigating. However, we'll wait for Dr Spilsbury before we do anything else. What's the time, Marriott?'

Marriott glanced at his wristwatch. 'Just gone half past twelve, sir.' It was another of Hardcastle's idiosyncrasies that he frequently asked Marriott the time, despite having a watch of his own.

'Good. In that case, we'll have some lunch, Marriott. There's
what looked like a half-decent pub just down the road. Proctor
and Ritchie, you can take a break. Vickers . . .' Hardcastle
paused thoughtfully. 'You are Vickers, aren't you?'

'Yes, sir.'

'Yes, of course you are. You'll remain here to guard the
site, and one of the other two will relieve you as soon as
possible. Back here by half past one. Catto? Where's Catto?'

'Here, sir.'

'Go to Ditton nick and call Cannon Row. See if they can
get Sir Bernard Spilsbury to come down here as quickly as
possible. Tell them what we've found. Once you've done that,
you can join Sergeant Marriott and me, and you'll have the
privilege of buying me a pint to celebrate your promotion and
return to the Royal A Division.'

It was almost three o'clock when Sir Bernard Spilsbury's
Rolls-Royce drew to a standstill at the entrance to the abandoned land that had once been a chicken farm, then an arable
farm, and finally a garage, all of which enterprises had failed.

Immaculate in morning dress, top hat and spats, he sported
a bloom in his buttonhole. He immediately spotted the DDI.

'My dear Hardcastle. Good to see you. You're rather a long
way away from your customary haunt.'

'Indeed, Sir Bernard, but the DDI of V Division is off sick.'

'Sorry to hear that. Fitnam, isn't it?'

'That's correct, Sir Bernard. So I'm dealing with what's
beginning to look like a murder.'

'You'd better show me what your fellows have found. The
telephone call said something about a severed head in a
biscuit tin.'

'Yes, sir,' said Hardcastle. 'I'll get one of the lads to bring
it over.'

'No, no. Leave it where it is.' Spilsbury looked around.
'What is this place? Looks like a chicken farm.'

'It was to start with,' said Hardcastle, 'but it went
bankrupt.'

'What an extraordinary coincidence,' began Spilsbury,
shaking his head. 'I was concerned with a case in Sussex in

. . . now let me see . . . yes, it was in 1925. Fellow called Thorne ran a chicken farm and murdered his fiancée. He put *her* head in a biscuit tin, too. No imagination, murderers, you know, Hardcastle.'

'You don't suppose this Thorne was responsible for my murder, do you, Sir Bernard?'

'Shouldn't think so.' Spilsbury chuckled at the thought. 'Thanks to my evidence, he was hanged at Wandsworth Prison two years ago. It wasn't in the Metropolitan area, of course, although the police in Sussex called on the Yard for assistance.'

'Couldn't have been him, then,' said Hardcastle in all seriousness. 'The man whose head we think we've found was last in touch with his uncle in Norfolk about three or four weeks ago. Incidentally, Sir Bernard, we've found what appears to be the murder weapon.'

'I'd better make a start.' Spilsbury took off his top hat and tail coat and handed them to DC Vickers. He crossed the yard to where DC Ritchie was standing guard over the biscuit tin.

Spilsbury bent down and lifted the lid. 'That can go up to St Mary's Hospital as it is, Hardcastle. No point in examining it here.' Next, he followed most of the detectives across to what remained of the workshop.

Hardcastle explained about the fire, the fact that the insurance company's investigator found two seats of fire, and finally the apparent disappearance of the two former owners. He also outlined what he had learned from the Reverend Percy Stoner.

'In that case, Hardcastle, I strongly recommend that you dig up the floor of the workshop.'

'Well, Catto, you heard what Sir Bernard said. Get to it.'

'I'll just get a couple of shovels, sir,' said Catto, and before the DDI was able to ask where he would get them, he had sped away to a hardware shop he had noticed a little way down the road.

'I hope you got a receipt for those,' said Hardcastle, when Catto returned with two new shovels.

'Didn't need to, sir. I told him to send his account to Scotland Yard.'

Hardcastle nodded his approval. 'I told you he'd learn a lot by being at Vine Street, Marriott.'

The three DCs, supervised by Catto, began carefully to dig up the floor of the workshop. It was not long before they discovered an arm.

'Take it carefully now, gentlemen,' advised Spilsbury.

Slowly, a second arm, two legs and a torso were discovered over an area of about four square yards.

'I'll send a scientist down here to supervise the removal of these body parts to my laboratory, Hardcastle,' said Spilsbury. 'I really can't understand why the Metropolitan Police doesn't have a scientific laboratory to deal with that sort of routine stuff. However, if you can direct me to a telephone, I'll arrange it immediately. The post-mortem examination will be tomorrow morning.'

'Thank you, Sir Bernard. I shall be there. Of course, the site will be guarded until your man gets here.'

'Excellent. I think your men have found the victim, Hardcastle. All you have to do now is find his killer.'

'It certainly looks like it, Sir Bernard.'

In that regard, however, Hardcastle was to be disappointed. The finding of the body parts in Ditton turned out only to be the start of a complex murder enquiry.

'Come in, Hardcastle, and you too, Marriott.'

The two detectives entered the mortuary room at St Mary's Hospital in Paddington.

'There is evidence of a severe blow with a blunt instrument, Hardcastle, sufficient to have caused a fracture of the skull,' Spilsbury began. 'The injury is compatible with the blow having been struck by the car-jack handle you showed me.'

'I suspect that the victim is Captain Guy Stoner, late of the Royal Field Artillery, Sir Bernard.'

'You may be right, Hardcastle,' said Spilsbury, 'but that, of course, is your department rather than mine. However, there is a complication.'

'Oh! What might that be, sir?' Hardcastle frowned.

'One arm and one leg did not come from the torso that your chaps found.'

For a moment or two, Hardcastle remained in stunned

silence. 'It's likely that there are more body parts at that site, then, Sir Bernard?'

Spilsbury smiled. 'So it would appear, unless for some reason they've been removed to some other place.'

'I suppose so,' said Hardcastle gloomily. It was not an outcome that he had anticipated and was one he could certainly do without. Ever since interviewing the Reverend Percy Stoner and his nephew's bank manager, he had assumed that Captain Rupert Holroyd had plundered Guy Stoner's bank account and then murdered him. But now he had to consider the possibility that Holroyd, too, had been murdered. On the other hand, of course, it could still be the case that Holroyd was the murderer he was looking for. But that, in turn, raised the question: who was the person whose arm and leg had been found?

'I have no wish to distress you further,' Spilsbury continued, 'but I am ninety per cent sure that the other arm and leg are those of a female.'

Oddly enough, Hardcastle's reaction was to laugh. 'I must say, Sir Bernard, I began to wonder if I'd misread the calendar, and that today was All Fool's Day.'

'Well, Marriott, it's time to put our thinking caps on.' Hardcastle reached for his pipe and began to fill it with tobacco.

'Did you have anything particular in mind, sir?' asked Marriott.

'It looks as though we'll have to return to the site and do some more digging.'

'We didn't look at the disused chicken run, sir, and as Sir Bernard mentioned the 1925 Norman Thorne case in Sussex where Thorne buried his woman friend's body parts under his chicken run, it might be an idea to dig that up.'

'Yes. See to it, Marriott. Send Catto and a couple of DCs down there and . . .' Hardcastle paused. 'On second thoughts, I'll get on to the sub-divisional inspector at Surbiton and ask him to send a couple of uniformed men down there to work under Catto's supervision. You know what to tell them, if they find what we're looking for.'

'Yes, sir.' Marriott was amazed that the DDI didn't give him advice on exactly what he should do. It might be that Marriott's impending promotion had led Hardcastle to believe that his sergeant really did not need guidance on such matters. On the other hand, perhaps Hardcastle was getting tired, and was considering retirement. He was, after all, fifty-five years of age, and already had thirty-six years' police service behind him.

'Right, then, d'you two lads know what to do?' Catto addressed the two young constables that the 'sub' at Surbiton had assigned to Hardcastle's investigation.

'Yes, Sergeant,' chorused both constables.

'If you come across any body parts, stop digging straight away, and tell me. Have either of you dealt with bits of a human body before?'

'No, Sergeant.'

'Right, well if you do find any, I don't want to know that you've vomited all over them. That, I can assure you, will make my DDI very cross indeed. Making my DDI cross is a very unwise thing to do, and I speak from experience. Right, lads, get on with it.' Catto found part of a wall to sit on, took out the pipe he had recently taken to smoking, and filled it with Sweet Crop tobacco. Had Hardcastle seen it, he would have dismissed it as boys' tobacco.

It was at about four o'clock when two very tired constables found what Hardcastle had hoped they would find.

'I think you should come and have a look at this, Sergeant,' said the senior of the two constables. 'We've found some more body parts.'

Catto walked across the chicken run and gazed into the depression in the ground where the policemen had been digging. There was another leg and an arm.

'Very good. Now keep going but be very careful. I don't want any of that evidence damaged because one of you has thrust the blade of a shovel into it.'

It took another hour before a torso, this time with the head attached, and a second arm and another leg were assembled at the edge of the dig.

'I wouldn't mind betting that one of those legs and one of the arms belongs to the other body we found yesterday,' said Catto, half to himself.

'It's a very exciting job you've got, Sergeant,' said one of the young constables enthusiastically. 'I'm thinking of applying for the CID when I've got two years' service.'

'It's not all that exciting,' said Catto, knocking his pipe out on the heel of his shoe. 'You'd be surprised how much report-writing you have to do with a job like this. Which reminds me, I'll need reports from you two, and you'll be responsible for handing over those bits of body you found to the scientist who comes to collect them. And don't forget to get him to sign for them; it's called continuity of evidence.'

FIVE

A t Sir Bernard Spilsbury's request, Hardcastle and Marriott returned to St Mary's Hospital in Paddington the following morning.

'No doubt you've already been informed by one of your men, my dear Hardcastle, that the second torso found at Ditton is indeed that of a woman.'

'Yes, Sir Bernard. Detective Sergeant Catto told me as much.'

'Having carried out further tests,' continued Spilsbury, 'the arm and the leg that were found with the first set of body parts are those of the woman whose torso was found in the chicken run.'

'So, now I've got two murders on my hands, and I don't know who either of the victims is.' Hardcastle sounded extremely depressed about the problem facing him. Marriott was also depressed, because he knew who would be doing most of the work.

Hardcastle's gloomy mood was still apparent when he and Marriott returned to Cannon Row police station.

'Holroyd, Marriott.'

'I'm sorry, sir. What d'you mean?'

'That must be Stoner's body we found, and Holroyd's got to be the killer. There's no other explanation.'

'But do we know for certain that the body parts are those of Stoner, sir? And we don't have any idea who the woman is.'

'Have you heard anything from Cox, the man who runs that excuse for an accommodation address?' Hardcastle did not intend to expound on his identification theory, probably because he knew that it was untenable without further evidence.

'No, sir,' said Marriott. 'But might I make a suggestion?' He was always loath to offer opinions to the DDI, although many another DDI was grateful for any assistance offered by his sergeant. But Hardcastle was not like other DDIs.

'Well?'

'Why don't we circulate details of Rupert Holroyd in the *Police Gazette*, sir?'

'We don't know what he looks like,' said Hardcastle dismissively.

'The newsagent Cox has seen the man. We could get a description from him.'

'Waste of time!' Hardcastle was clearly unimpressed by that suggestion. 'What good d'you think that would be? Cox couldn't find his own backside in broad daylight.'

But Marriott's abortive suggestion – at least the DDI thought it was – was cut short when DC Vickers knocked on the DDI's door and entered.

'Excuse me, sir?'

'What d'you want, Vickers?'

'There's a telephone call for Sergeant Marriott, sir.'

'Tell 'em to call again unless it's Mr Wensley's clerk. We're busy trying to solve a murder. Who is it, anyway?'

'It's from someone called Samuel Cox, sir.' Vickers glanced down at the note he had made. 'He said a man called Talbot had been into his shop this morning.'

'That's different. Find out as much as you can, Marriott.'

'Yes, sir.' Marriott tried not to appear irritated but could not help wondering if Hardcastle remembered how much first-class detective sergeants knew when he had held the rank.

When Marriott returned to the DDI's office, he did not look too happy. 'Cox said that Oliver Talbot went into the shop this morning and enquired if there were any letters for him. In accordance with your instructions, Cox told Talbot there weren't any, although one had arrived by the morning post.'

'Did Talbot say anything else to Cox?'

'Yes, sir.' Marriott paused. 'He said, in that case, he wasn't expecting any more and that he wouldn't be in again.'

'Damn the man!' exclaimed Hardcastle. 'I think we might have been a bit too clever, Marriott. I wouldn't be surprised if Cox tipped him off that we were looking for him. If that's the case, it's a rare example of honour among thieves. On the other hand, of course, it might be that we gave that estate agent chap the idea that the garage and the ground it was on might not belong to Holroyd any more, and that the insurance company could be the owners.'

'But that wouldn't be the case, sir. There is no way in which the insurance company would acquire that land as they'd refused to pay out.'

'I know that, and you know that, Marriott, but does that idiot estate agent know that?'

'There's another reason, sir. Holroyd might've got wind of the digging that went on at the site.'

Hardcastle nodded wearily. 'That's a possibility, I suppose. Did you get any sort of description from Cox?'

'Yes, sir, but it would fit a hundred men.'

'Thought as much. Well, put it in the *Police Gazette* all the same, Marriott. Tell them to say that Rupert Holroyd, also known as Oliver Talbot, is wanted for questioning in connection with a fraud, rather than murder.' Hardcastle paused. 'I'm sure that Holroyd and Oliver are one and the same. Even if Talbot is not Holroyd, he might lead us to him. In the meantime, Marriott, send someone up to Paddington to take possession of that letter addressed to Oliver Talbot.'

An hour later, DC Vickers handed Marriott the letter that he had collected from the Paddington newsagent.

Marriott scanned it briefly and took to Hardcastle.

'It's from Wilfred Chapman, the manager of Coates, the estate agency in Kingston, sir.'

'So I see,' said Hardcastle. 'Well, that's no help at all.' The letter merely stated that Coates was no longer prepared to act for Talbot in the sale of Ditton Garage. 'He's taken fright, Marriott. He obviously got wind of the digging, and maybe even the recovery of body parts, and decided that he didn't want anything to do with it. Mind you, I should think it'd be bloody difficult to sell a site where a couple of bodies had been buried after being cut up.'

'It was in today's evening paper, sir.'

'What was?'

'A report about the excavations at Ditton. It was in the early edition of the *Star* this afternoon, sir.'

'It wasn't in the *Daily Mail*.' Hardcastle made it sound as though that omission was Marriott's fault. 'Did they mention that we'd found anything?'

'No, sir. It merely said that police were taking an interest in the site, and there were suggestions that it was in connection with the arson.'

'That's all right, then,' said Hardcastle, 'so long as they keep on thinking that. In fact, we might just encourage the press to think that's what we're up to. At least, until we lay our hands on Holroyd.'

In fact, Hardcastle did not have to wait very long before Rupert Holroyd was in police custody.

It was pouring with rain the following Saturday afternoon, but, undaunted by the weather, crowds of racegoers made their way to Kempton Park. Most had arrived at the nearby railway station and were getting soaked; others had come by specially chartered charabancs. They were a cheerful lot and, despite the weather, were looking forward to the race meeting, optimistic that they might leave a few shillings the richer.

But they were to be disappointed. Two days previously, nearly five inches of rain had fallen and the course was waterlogged. There would be no racing that day.

Mingling with the racegoers were teams of pickpockets, as well as elements of the criminal classes intent upon robbing bookmakers of their day's takings. These cutpurses were formed into sophisticated gangs and resented any interlopers. In 1927, turf war was prevalent at most racecourses, and many of the pickpockets carried cut-throat razors or razor blades in pieces of wood, known as chivs, with which to ward off the opposition. This anticipated criminal activity led to the presence of a third group – members of the Flying Squad were there in strength. Existing in one form or another for the past eight years, the Squad had only recently been confirmed as a permanent unit of the Metropolitan Police.

The cancellation of the racing had inflamed tempers, more so because no one had learned of it until arriving at the course.

Bookmakers, racegoers and the teams of pickpockets and assorted robbers saw themselves being deprived of rich winnings, legal or illegal.

Several fights broke out but were dealt with swiftly and firmly by the uniformed police officers for whose presence the racecourse owners had paid.

It was not long before one of the Flying Squad officers saw the flash of a blade as a habitual pickpocket threatened a well-dressed man who, presumably, he thought was rich enough to be worth robbing.

The victim, realizing that the Queensberry Rules would not be observed by a man armed with a cut-throat razor, had been backing away from his attacker until he was up against a bookmaker's stand and could go no further.

At this point, one of the Flying Squad officers, who played rugby in what little spare time he had, sped towards the razor-wielding would-be robber. He threw himself forward and brought the pickpocket crashing to the ground with a classic flying tackle. At that point, he was joined by one of the Squad's sergeants, and together they hoisted the pickpocket to his feet.

'Well, well, well! If it's not Tommy "The Weasel" Flynn. You're privileged to have been nicked by the Flying Squad, Tommy . . . again,' said the sergeant, a statement that did little to encourage Flynn to think he might be able to talk his way out of his latest bit of trouble. 'Attempted armed robbery, carrying an offensive weapon, and anything else we can think of . . . like breathing.'

'It's a mistake, guv'nor. I was only going to ask this gent for the time.'

'What, so you could pinch his watch? Don't worry, Tommy, the judge will give you the time. About five years of it, I should think.' The sergeant turned to the DC who had made the arrest. 'Take him to Teddington nick, Charlie, and I'll join you as soon as I've taken this gentleman's particulars.'

'Righto, Skipper,' said the DC and, with the aid of a uniformed constable, put the prisoner into a police van.

'I can't begin to thank you enough, Officer,' said the man, as the Flying Squad sergeant turned his attention to the victim.

'All in a day's work, sir,' said the sergeant. 'Now, I need your name and address for my report.'

'Of course, Officer. I'm Captain Rupert Holroyd, and at the moment I'm living at the Ritz in Piccadilly.'

The sergeant was a conscientious officer and always read the *Police Gazette* on the day of its publication. Yesterday's edition had contained details of a Captain Rupert Holroyd, believed also to be known as Oliver Talbot, who was wanted for questioning regarding fraud. The sergeant had quietly chuckled when he had read the name of the officer in the case.

But Rupert Holroyd knew little of the way in which the police circulated information, and firmly believed that his cheque frauds in London could not possibly be known to a police officer at Kempton Park racecourse, and he had furnished his name and address without hesitation. Another thing that he did not know was that the Flying Squad had a roving commission and had been responsible for a prestigious record of arrests during its short history.

'Rupert Holroyd, I'm arresting you on suspicion of committing fraud. You do not have to say anything, but anything you do say will be taken down in writing and may be given in evidence.'

Desperately, Holroyd looked around, seeking a way of escape, but with his back still against the bookmaker's stand, he realized there was no way in which he could make a run for it. Apart from anything else, he had witnessed the somewhat violent arrest of his attacker and had no wish to tangle with one of that detective's colleagues. Nevertheless, he felt that a denial would be in order.

'I'm afraid you're making a terrible mistake, Officer.'

'They all say that,' said the sergeant wearily.

'We've just received a telegraph message from Teddington police station, sir.' Marriott entered the DDI's office clutching a piece of paper. 'Holroyd has been arrested at Kempton Park racecourse by a Flying Squad officer.'

'Has he, indeed? And who was this resourceful and observant officer, Marriott?'

Marriott pretended to read the telegraph message again.

'It was a Detective Sergeant Walter Hardcastle, sir,' he said, looking up with an innocent expression on his face.

'Send two officers to Teddington to bring Holroyd back here, Marriott.' Hardcastle did not react to the news that his son had effected the arrest of a man the DDI wanted to speak to about the goings-on at Ditton Garage, and more particularly what had been found there.

It was half past five on that same Saturday afternoon when Holroyd was brought to Cannon Row by Detective Constables Vickers and Proctor. Normally, Hardcastle would aim to go off-duty at about five o'clock on a Saturday, but he was not prepared to leave interviewing Holroyd any longer than necessary. And that meant that Marriott was also kept from going home.

By the time Holroyd had been brought to London, he had recovered sufficient of his self-confidence to convince himself that he could talk his way out of any trouble. After all, the police would be no match for a former officer who had fought in the war. But then Hardcastle and Marriott had entered the room and sat down.

'When exactly did you murder Guy Stoner, Holroyd? Was it before or after you drained his bank account of every penny?' Without pausing, and without any preamble whatsoever, Hardcastle had made the accusation.

'Are you telling me that Guy is dead?' Holroyd appeared to be shocked at both the suggestion that Stoner had been murdered and that he stood accused of being his killer. Above all, he was shaken that this detective should talk about murder when Holroyd was expecting to be questioned about fraud.

'I am Divisional Detective Inspector Hardcastle, Holroyd, and this is Detective Sergeant Marriott. A word of caution – don't take me for a fool.' For once, and for good reason, Hardcastle did not mention that he was the DDI in charge of the CID for the A or Whitehall Division of the Metropolitan Police.

His instruction to DCs Vickers and Proctor had been to make sure that Holroyd was removed from the police van *outside* the police station rather than in the station yard. In that way, he could not fail to see the forbidding edifice of New Scotland Yard opposite, constructed in 1890 from Dartmoor granite hewn, fittingly, by the inmates of Dartmoor Prison. Many members of the public entering Cannon Row police station firmly believed that it was a part of the Yard. Some criminals had also believed that it was the headquarters of the Metropolitan Police, and the reputation of the Yard's detectives was such as to plant in a suspect's mind the belief that there must be more than enough evidence with which to convict him.

'I didn't know he was dead,' said Holroyd. 'I couldn't possibly have killed him. He was my friend, and we'd been through the war together. How on earth can you think I'd have killed him?' He needed desperately to convince this policeman that he was innocent; otherwise he could see himself facing the hangman at eight o'clock one morning.

'Your friend, was he?' Hardcastle posed the question in scathing tones. 'So much of a friend that you didn't hesitate to present fraudulent cheques and take every penny he had out of his account. Is that what you call friendship, Holroyd? Is that the sort of wartime camaraderie you were talking about?'

'Now look here—'

'Did you or did you not present several cheques upon which you had forged Guy Stoner's signature, Captain Holroyd?' asked Marriott mildly.

Holroyd turned his gaze on Marriott. The quietly spoken way in which the sergeant had posed the question had more effect on him than Hardcastle's hectoring approach. He decided that Detective Sergeant Marriott was a force to be reckoned with. The manner of the two detectives put him in mind of the difference between the attitude of his commanding officer and that of the battery sergeant major.

'I admit that I did forge one or two cheques, Sergeant, but I was desperately short of money and, to be perfectly honest, I didn't think Guy would notice. You see, the difference between Guy and me was that he came from a good family, a family with old money. I, on the other hand, had hardly any spare cash. With my background, I was damned lucky to be commissioned, and I really couldn't afford the expense that went with it.'

'Now that you've admitted to the forgery, Captain Holroyd,' Marriott continued, 'I probably won't be able to ask you any more questions about it, but you will be charged with that offence contrary to the Forgery Act of 1913.' He followed this announcement by cautioning Holroyd.

'You told the officer who arrested you,' began Hardcastle, 'that you were living at the Ritz Hotel in Piccadilly. Is that true?'

'No.' Holroyd spoke in almost a whisper.

'Would you repeat that, Holroyd? I didn't quite hear you.'

'I said no, Inspector.' This time Holroyd almost shouted his reply.

'Why, then, did you lie to the officer?'

'I was trying to avoid being arrested by making out I was a person of some substance.'

'Didn't work, did it?' said Hardcastle, almost dismissively. 'Now then, the police have found a body at the garage in Ditton of which, as I understand it, you are, or were, a part owner. We believe that to be the body of Captain Guy Stoner.'

'We were trying to sell the site.'

'Who is Oliver Talbot, Captain Holroyd?' asked Marriott quietly, but so suddenly that it caught Holroyd off guard.

'I, er, well, it was a name that I used.'

'Why?'

'It's difficult to explain.' Holroyd was beginning to perspire.

'Let me explain it for you, then,' said Hardcastle helpfully. 'You murdered Guy Stoner, dismembered his body and then attempted to sell the site of the garage as if it was all yours. Your attempt to hide the evidence by setting fire to the office and the workshop failed, because we still found both bodies.'

'Both bodies? What on earth are you talking about, Inspector? I don't know anything about any of this.' But Holroyd had good reason to worry about just how much the police *did* know.

'The second body was that of a woman.' Hardcastle continued to press the ex-army officer. 'Who was she?'

'I've no idea. I know nothing about a woman.' Holroyd paused, frowning. 'Just a moment, though. Guy was running about with a girl. He'd hooked up with her a couple of months previously.'

'What was her name?'

'I don't know, I'm afraid. Guy didn't introduce us, and I only saw her a couple of times when she picked him up from the garage.'

'Are you saying that she had her own car?'

'I suppose it *was* hers,' said Holroyd thoughtfully. 'On the other hand, it could have been her brother's or something like that. It looked brand new – come to think of it, it was a model that only came out this year. It was a Triumph Super Seven. A dinky little two-seater in black with white mudguards and wheels. Wish I could afford something like that.'

'Have you any idea where she lived or where she came from?' asked Marriott.

'No, no idea. Sorry.' But Holroyd was lying and had been lying for most of the interview in a desperate attempt to avoid the inevitable charge of murder.

'I don't suppose you took a note of the registration number of the car.'

'No. Sorry.'

Hardcastle took out his watch and gazed at it thoughtfully.

'You'll be detained here until you appear in court on Monday morning. At that appearance, I shall seek a remand in police custody while further enquiries are made in connection with the double murder that you deny having committed. Take him down, Marriott.'

'D'you think he did commit those murders, sir?' asked Marriott, when he had finished arranging for the station officer to put Holroyd into a cell.

'I'm bloody convinced of it, Marriott. He's too smooth by half. All the old ex-officer la-di-da. On his beam ends? No, he fancied a bit of the high living. Which reminds me. Send Catto up to the Ritz to find out if Holroyd was staying there. He might have denied it because he had left incriminating evidence in his room there.'

*   *   *

It was eight o'clock by the time that Hardcastle put his key in the lock of his house at 27 Kennington Road, where he and his wife, Alice, had lived since their marriage thirty-four years ago. Pausing in the hall, he took out his hunter and checked the time of the longcase clock that had stood there for years. Satisfied that it was keeping good time, he pushed open the door of the parlour.

'You're late for a Saturday,' said his wife. 'I've got your supper, but it just needs warming up.'

'I'm sorry, love, but I had a murder suspect to deal with. It was one that Wally arrested at Kempton Park. He's got the makings, has that lad.'

Alice laughed. 'Praise indeed, coming from you, Ernie.'

'Would you like a sherry, love?'

'Please, Ernie.'

Hardcastle poured an Amontillado for his wife and a whisky for himself before sitting down in his armchair opposite Alice.

'Well, are you going to tell me about it?' Alice stopped knitting and pushed the needles into the ball of wool. 'Clothes for Wally's new baby,' she explained.

'There's not much to tell,' said Hardcastle, taking a sip of his Scotch. 'We'd put the name of the wanted man in the *Police Gazette* and young Wally spotted him at Kempton Park.' He made it sound as though Walter had recognized Holroyd on description, but he saw no harm in making his son appear smarter than he had been. He was secretly very proud of him.

'Oh, well, if that's it, I'll go and put your supper in the oven.' Alice placed her knitting on a side table and took her glass of sherry with her as she went through to the kitchen.

Hardcastle picked up the *Daily Mail* which had arrived after he had left for work that morning. Its late delivery was, in Hardcastle's view, another example of slipping standards brought about by the effects of the war, a war that had ended nine years ago.

About the time that Hardcastle arrived home at his Kennington Road house, his son Walter put his key into the door of his terrace house in Ewhurst Road, Brockley, in south-east London.

He had moved into the rented property shortly after his marriage to Muriel Groves on the sixteenth of January 1924. On the first of July 1925, she gave birth to Edward and was now pregnant with the couple's second child.

Walter crossed the room to where his wife was seated awkwardly in an armchair and gave her a kiss. 'How's number two?' he asked, patting his wife's stomach affectionately.

'Kicking like mad,' said Muriel, 'and Edward's been up to mischief all day. But he's a Hardcastle, and my mother-in-law said I should never have married a Hardcastle, especially if he's a copper. How was your day, Wally?'

'Run of the mill,' said Walter. 'I was down at Kempton Park all afternoon, but the racing was rained off. However, I did manage to arrest a bloke that Dad had been looking for.'

'I bet that pleased him,' said Muriel.

'Very likely,' said Wally. 'Not that he'd ever tell me. Would you like a cup of tea?'

'Yes, please. But what about you?'

'I'll just have a bottle of beer.'

'No, I meant what d'you want to eat?'

'Oh, nothing, thanks. I grabbed a bite in the canteen at Teddington nick while we were processing our prisoners.'

Muriel shook her head. 'It's not good for you, all that canteen food, darling. I suppose you had a fry-up.'

'It's all they'd got left,' said Walter, lying convincingly, and walked through to the kitchen to make his wife tea.

'Kitty popped in to see me this afternoon,' shouted Muriel.

'Kitty who?'

'Good heavens, Wally, your sister Kitty.'

'That was nice of her.'

'She gave me lots of advice about bringing up children.' Muriel chuckled.

'She's got a cheek,' said Walter. 'What does she know about it? She's not married.'

'Hardly her fault, Wally.'

'No, I suppose not.' Walter returned to the sitting room and handed his wife a cup of tea. He opened a bottle of beer and sat down opposite her, stretching his legs out.

Right at the end of the war, Kitty had fallen in love with a staff sergeant in the Royal Engineers and had accepted his proposal of marriage. He had been killed in the last week of the war, and Kitty vowed that she would never marry. Instead, she travelled every year to the military cemetery where her fiancé was buried and laid flowers on his grave. In the aftermath of the war, it was a familiar story.

SIX

Catto had returned from the Ritz Hotel and reported that Holroyd had never stayed there, as he had claimed when arrested by Detective Sergeant Walter Hardcastle of the Flying Squad.

Catto could not understand why Hardcastle had sent him there. Holroyd had already admitted that he had lied to the DDI's son when he was arrested. But Hardcastle was known to his subordinates as a 'belt and braces' detective.

'Just as I thought.' Hardcastle had been in no doubt that if Holroyd were to be released on bail, he would disappear without trace, and the lie about staying at that prestigious West End hotel confirmed it. Consequently, the DDI ordered that the former artillery captain should be kept in custody over what remained of the weekend.

On Monday morning, Holroyd was collected by a prisoner-transport van and conveyed to Bow Street police court.

Hardcastle made a point of seeing Sir John Hanbury, the Chief Metropolitan Magistrate, in his chambers before the court sat. He did not want to explain, in open court, the reasons for his application, mainly because of the presence of the press.

'Good morning, Mr Hardcastle.'

'Good morning, Sir John.'

'What can I do for A Division's chief thief-taker this morning?' Hanbury asked jocularly.

'I have a Captain Rupert Holroyd appearing before you this morning, Sir John, and I should be much obliged if you could see your way clear to remanding him into police custody, if you would be so kind. He has admitted uttering a number of forged cheques to the detriment of Captain Guy Stoner and that's what he's been arrested for. However, we have discovered two dismembered bodies, one male and one female, at the site of a garage he and Stoner jointly owned. I strongly suspect that Holroyd has committed both murders, and I would like the opportunity to question him further in connection with this matter.'

Hanbury considered Hardcastle's application seriously for a moment or two, his fingers steepled together and touching his pursed lips. 'I see no problem there, Mr Hardcastle,' he said eventually. 'I'll remand him into your custody until his next appearance at this court on . . .' He paused to examine a calendar. 'Tuesday the nineteenth of April. In the circumstances, I shall not take a plea this morning in respect of uttering forged cheques.'

'I'm much obliged, Sir John,' said Hardcastle, and returned to the courtroom. Five minutes later, the Chief Magistrate took his place on the bench.

'Put up Rupert Holroyd,' said the clerk of the court.

A PC ushered Holroyd into the dock of Number One Court.

'State your full name,' said the clerk.

'Rupert Holroyd, sir.'

'And your address?'

'The Salvation Army refuge at Vandon Street, London SW1, sir.'

'Thank you,' said the clerk. Dipping his pen in the inkwell, he wrote *No fixed abode* in the court register.

'Remanded to police custody until reappearance at this court on Tuesday the nineteenth of April,' said Sir John Hanbury. 'Next!'

As Hardcastle was leaving the court, a reporter sped across the room from the press box. 'Hargreaves, *Surrey Advertiser*, Mr Hardcastle. What was that all about?' he asked optimistically. 'Has Holroyd got something to do with what's been going on at Ditton?' But his hopefulness was cut short by Hardcastle's curt response.

'If I'd wanted the world to know, Hargreaves, it would have been revealed in open court. Good day to you.'

After Hardcastle and Marriott had enjoyed their usual lunch at the Red Lion, they made their way down to the cells. 'You're going to St Mary's Hospital this afternoon, Holroyd,' announced Hardcastle.

'What for? There's nothing wrong with me.'

'That's a matter of opinion,' retorted Hardcastle, standing at the door to Holroyd's cell, 'but the purpose of your visit will be to look at a severed head. I want to see if you recognize it.'

'How d'you want to do this, sir?' asked Marriott, once he and Hardcastle had returned to the DDI's office.

'A couple of DCs can take him up there in the van, and you and I will take a cab and meet them there.'

Ritchie and Proctor were the two officers selected by Marriott to act as escort.

'Out you come, Holroyd,' said Ritchie, as the gaoler opened the cell door.

'It's *Captain* Holroyd to you, *Constable*,' said the prisoner irritably. 'I was an officer, you know.'

'So was I,' said Ritchie mildly.

'Oh!' That surprise response left Holroyd momentarily speechless. Although aware that many ex-servicemen who had fought in the war had joined the police after the conflict was over, he had not realized that some of them had been officers. 'What regiment?' he asked lamely.

'Not that it's any of your damned business, because the bloody war's been over for nearly nine years now,' said Ritchie, 'but I was a captain in the Grenadier Guards.'

'Oh!' said Holroyd again, and remained silent for the entire journey to Paddington.

The mortuary attendant had been alerted by Sir Bernard Spilsbury that Hardcastle would be arriving to examine the remains that had been found at Ditton.

'All ready for you, sir.' The attendant led the party across the room to a side bench and, with a proprietorial flourish, removed the covering from the male severed head, rather like a magician who had just performed a particularly difficult illusion. He then removed the covering from the female sufficient to display the head, but not the torso. 'There we are, gents.' He appeared disappointed that there was no reaction, no cries of horror and no turning away from the grisly sight.

'Have a look at this one, Holroyd.' Hardcastle pointed to the male head.

'Good God!' exclaimed Holroyd. 'It's Guy.'

'Guy who?' demanded Hardcastle, a stickler for accuracy. After all, it might not have been Stoner, but another man called Guy.

'That's Guy Stoner, Inspector. Ye gods! Who would have done such a thing?'

'You, perhaps?' suggested the DDI drily.

'It most certainly was not,' asserted Holroyd. 'We might have had our disagreements, but nothing that would warrant my murdering him.'

'Disagreements about what?' Hardcastle thought that was probably a slip of the tongue or, perhaps, referred to minor tiffs, but he was on it in a moment.

'Guy had started running about with a young married woman, Inspector, and I told him that it was distracting him from getting the garage business up and running. He was never there when a joint decision needed to be made; instead, he was indulging himself and his floozy in the fleshpots of London. He was besotted with the woman. Apart from anything else, of course, it was damned bad form. It was what in the army we called conduct unbecoming an officer and a gentleman, but he wouldn't listen.' In view of what Marriott learned later about Holroyd, that remark was pretentious, to say the least.

'Is that her?' asked Hardcastle, pointing at the female head.

'I've no idea,' said Holroyd. 'I never met her.' He glanced at the head again. 'Pretty, wasn't she? And quite young, as far as you can tell.'

'What was her name?'

'I don't know, Inspector. Guy never mentioned her name. All I can tell you is that one day he remarked that she was married and that her husband was much older than she was.' Holroyd shrugged. 'I suppose that's why she took a shine to the dashing, monied Captain Stoner.' There was an element of envy in Holroyd's comment.

'Monied until you emptied his bank account,' commented Hardcastle. Marriott frowned at the DDI's continued flouting of the Judges' Rules, but he knew it would be pointless to mention it now or later.

'Is this the woman you mentioned who had the sports car?' Hardcastle kept pressing Holroyd for every last piece of information.

'No!' Holroyd answered the question very quickly. Too quickly, perhaps. 'As I told you, I've never seen this woman before,' he said, gesturing at the female head.

There was no respite for anyone once Hardcastle had some evidence that needed following up. Back at Cannon Row police station, he and Marriott continued their attempts to unravel the mystery of the dead woman who, it now appeared, could have been Stoner's lady friend, or at least one of them.

'When did Stoner meet this woman you say was married to an older man, Holroyd?' persisted Hardcastle.

'I'm not absolutely sure.'

'D'you know where?'

'No, I'm afraid not. Guy was very secretive about the whole affair.'

'Where did they conduct this affair? Did Stoner have a room somewhere that he kept for these meetings? Or perhaps a friend whose apartment he used? You must know something about it, or are you being deliberately obstructive?' Hardcastle was beginning to lose his temper.

'He took her to a hotel, I think.' Holroyd was beginning to get annoyed, too.

Recognizing the signs, Marriott stepped in to see if he could extract some vital information.

'As I understand it, Captain Holroyd, Guy Stoner was your friend.'

'Yes, he was. We served together in the war. Both of us were in the Ypres Salient, which was a pretty uncomfortable place to be, I can tell you.'

'So I've heard,' said Marriott. 'My brother-in-law was there for a while.'

'Oh, who was he with?'

'The Middlesex Regiment.'

'The Diehards. That was their nickname.' Holroyd nodded slowly as though recalling that trying and dangerous time: the constant shelling, the unique sound of falling masonry and the cries of the wounded. 'Did he survive?'

'Yes, he stayed on. He's a regular officer now.'

'Rather him than me,' said Holroyd derisively. 'I couldn't wait to get out and enjoy myself in the fleshpots of London.'

'Ah, the nightclubs,' said Marriott, as though dreaming of some youthful escapades. In fact, he detested the places. 'I can imagine that you and Guy had a whale of a time.'

Holroyd laughed. 'That we did, Sergeant Marriott. We reckoned we'd earned it. We'd fought hard and then we played hard.'

Hardcastle was about to intervene, believing that his sergeant was wasting time, when Marriott's next question revealed his strategy.

'I suppose it was to those familiar haunts that Guy took this lady friend of his.'

'Yes, I'm sure it was. There were times when he came to work looking absolutely exhausted. On one occasion, I asked him where he'd been, and he told me that he and his lady friend had spent the night dancing and drinking at the Black Cat in Wardour Street.'

'Is that somewhere that you and he had been in the past?'

'Yes, it was one of our favourite spots, as a matter of fact. On one occasion, Guy told me, he went out with one of the chorus girls from there, but he always had plenty of money to flash about. There's nothing that impresses a girl so much as a chap who's willing to spend money on them.'

'Any idea who she was?'

'No, I'm sorry, I never met her. But I told you that before.'

'Now, Holroyd, tell me about the fire at your so-called garage. That presumably was to disguise the fact that it never stood a chance of being a success.' Once again, Hardcastle took a gamble, as he had so often done in the past, usually with a successful outcome. But not this time.

'I know nothing about that.'

'What d'you mean, you know nothing about it? You tried to claim off the insurance, and you put the land on the market, using the name of Oliver Talbot to cover your tracks.' This time, Hardcastle had more luck.

'I didn't make myself quite clear, Inspector,' said Holroyd. 'I was away the weekend of the fire.'

'Where did you go?'

'I was coming to that, Inspector,' said Holroyd wearily. 'I went to my folks in Rutland, to Oakham. It's about twenty miles from Leicester. Anyway, I got back to Ditton in the late afternoon of Monday the fourteenth of March to find the place ablaze. What was left of it. I promptly called the fire brigade.'

'Where did you live when you were in Ditton, Captain Holroyd?' asked Marriott.

'In the office. It was quite spacious, and we had camp beds and that sort of thing. It was cheaper than taking rooms and it meant that we were on site all the time.'

'When did you leave Ditton to visit your people?' asked Marriott.

'It was the Friday before the fire. That'd be the eleventh. I caught a train at around noon from St Pancras.'

'And you stayed in Oakham the whole weekend, did you?'

'Yes, I did.'

'When you say you saw your folks, are you talking about your parents?'

'Not exactly. My father died some six years ago, and my mother now lives with my sister and her husband. It was at my sister's place that I stayed.'

'So they can vouch for you, can they?' asked Hardcastle.

'They'd jolly well better,' said Holroyd with a laugh.

'Make a note to get the Rutland Constabulary to check Holroyd's alibi, Marriott.'

'Yes, sir.' Marriott was looking forward to his promotion so that he would, at last, escape Hardcastle's overbearing and constant need to tell him how to do his job.

'Why did you decide to use the name Oliver Talbot when you put the land up for sale with Coates of Kingston?'

'My word, you have been doing your homework, Inspector,' said Holroyd, with a tinge of sarcasm.

'We tend to make a lot of enquiries when dealing with a double murder, Holroyd,' said Hardcastle drily, even though he had known nothing of the murders when he spoke to the estate agent. 'Perhaps you'd answer my question.'

'Well, once I'd found that the place had burned down, and having milked Guy's bank account – not something I'm proud of – I thought that suspicion might fall on me for setting fire to the place.'

Hardcastle was about to point out that in one of the letters, purporting to be from Stoner, Holroyd wrote that Stoner had burned his hand. It was a curious coincidence and Holroyd might have been careless in mentioning it. However, Hardcastle was prevented from questioning Holroyd on the matter, remembering, somewhat belatedly, the Judges' Rules. Holroyd had been cautioned in connection with that offence, and could not, therefore, be asked anything further about it. The DDI was not altogether sure on that point as he had only a passing knowledge of those rules of procedure that had been brought in as late as 1918. He thought them to be an unnecessary impediment to the investigation of crime, but he erred on the side of caution nevertheless.

'Why should anyone think that, Captain Holroyd?' asked Marriott.

'It looked as though it was deliberate. I mean, a fire in the office and another in the workshop, some distance away. That wasn't an accident.'

'How do you know such things, Holroyd? Were you in the fire brigade?' asked Hardcastle sarcastically.

'You don't only learn how to fire a gun in the Royal Field Artillery, Inspector,' said Holroyd.

'No, I suppose not. Do you also learn how to burn things down?'

'If I'd been responsible for that fire, Inspector, I'd have made a far more efficient job of it.'

'Take him down, Marriott.' Hardcastle was fast becoming exasperated at his lack of progress. 'And then come and see me.'

'He's a crafty bugger, Marriott.' Slowly, Hardcastle began to fill his pipe. 'How the hell are we going to prove that he killed Stoner and the woman Holroyd reckons he was running about with?'

'If he did, sir.'

'What d'you mean by that?' Hardcastle lit his pipe and leaned back in his chair. 'Sit down, Marriott.'

'I don't think he murdered either of them, sir,' said Marriott, taking a seat. Hardcastle's one acknowledgment of his sergeant's forthcoming promotion to inspector was the frequent invitation for him to sit down in the DDI's office. 'If his alibi checks out, then I don't see that he could have murdered them.'

'Well, who did?' It was typical of Hardcastle to expect that a statement of denial should be followed up with an alternative solution.

'It would help if we could discover the identity of this woman friend of his, sir. Enquiries at the Black Cat might be a start.'

'I was just going to suggest that, Marriott.'

'I'll get up there this evening, then.'

'No, don't you go. Send Catto. I seem to remember that he's quite good at getting information out of reluctant nightclub owners. Anyway, he'll probably know most of them, having served on C Division for a few years.'

Hardcastle had been right. Henry Catto was in his element when persuading the owners or managers of nightclubs to part with information they would rather keep to themselves. Especially when they were labouring under the misapprehension that such information was in some way privileged.

Catto's first victim was the doorman at the Black Cat, who was left in no doubt that any attempt to prevent Catto from entering or to advise his boss of the presence of police would result in the doorman's instant arrest for obstructing a police officer in the execution of his duty.

'There ain't no trouble 'ere, guv'nor.' The doorman rehearsed the well-worn mantra of nightclub doormen throughout the West End of London when confronted by the police.

The moment that Catto passed into the main area of the club, he was met by a suave individual in immaculate evening dress.

'Good evening, sir. I'm Dudley Savage, the owner,' he began effusively. 'If you're intending to become a member, I must point out that black tie is de rigueur.' Savage described a circle

with his hand that encompassed the small crowded dance floor
and a number of closely packed tables. The rather seedy club's
clientele appeared to consist of giggling women and chinless
young men quaffing champagne, all attired in accordance with
Savage's dress code.

'I'm a police officer.'

'Oh, I see. Am I to take it that you are seeking
membership?'

'Good God, no!' exclaimed Catto. 'I'm making enquiries
about certain of your members,' he said loudly, and was pleased
to see an apprehensive reaction not only from Savage but from
those patrons close enough to have heard.

'Perhaps it would be better if we talked in my office,' said
Savage nervously. Without waiting for a reply, he led the way
around the edge of the small dance floor. 'Are you from
Marlborough Street?' he enquired, once they were in his small,
cluttered office with the door firmly shut, 'because if you are,
you must know that Station Sergeant Goddard inspects the
club and the books quite regularly.'

'Does he really?' Catto was unimpressed by Savage's
mention of Goddard. Rumours of corruption had been circulating for some time, and Goddard always seemed to be at the
centre of them, together with Mrs Meyrick of the famous 43
Club in Gerrard Street. 'No, I'm Detective Sergeant Catto,
attached to the Whitehall Division, and I'm investigating a
murder.'

'A murder? I see. Well, it can't be anything connected to
my club, surely?'

'That's what I'm here to find out,' said Catto, taking a seat
adjacent to Savage's desk.

'May I offer you a drink, Sergeant?' Savage's hand waved
nonchalantly across a table laden with bottles of whisky, gin,
brandy and a variety of mixers.

'No, thank you.'

Savage helped himself to a whisky and then sat down behind
his desk. 'Now, what seems to be the trouble, Sergeant?'

'Captain Guy Stoner, late of the Royal Field Artillery.'

'Oh, Guy. Yes, he's one of our members.'

'Not any more,' said Catto, in a dismissive tone that would

have merited a nod of approval from Hardcastle. 'He's the murder victim whose death we're investigating. Well, one of them, anyway.'

'Good grief!' exclaimed Savage, visibly shocked by Catto's revelation. 'But, regrettable though it is, how is that anything to do with the Black Cat?'

'Our enquiries have indicated that he frequently brought a young lady to your club, and we are anxious to discover her identity.'

'Has the young lady disappeared, then?' Savage had regained his sangfroid and took on a slightly bantering tone.

'Not exactly. We believe her to be the woman whose body was found – in several pieces – not very far from where we found Stoner's body, also in pieces.'

'Ye gods!' exclaimed Savage. 'It sounds like something out of a Hollywood horror movie.'

'Have you any idea who this woman might be?' said Catto, rapidly tiring of Savage's false emotions.

'I have no idea of her name, Sergeant, but I can tell you that she was about twenty, I should think. A long-haired blonde with a ravishing figure. She moved well on the dance floor, almost as if she were a professional dancer, and she was clearly taken with Guy. She could hardly keep her hands off him.'

'But you've no idea of her name.'

'I'm sorry, no. Much as I always like to assist the police, I'm afraid I can't do so on this occasion.'

'You say that she danced like a professional. D'you think she might've been a showgirl or a chorus girl?'

'It's possible. I'd have been very happy to take her on for the cabaret.'

Catto returned to Cannon Row somewhat vexed that he had progressed little further. He could visualize an unending round of visits to nightclubs, of which there were many, in an attempt to discover if any of their showgirls or cabaret artistes were missing. Even then, it might turn out that the dead woman was neither the one nor the other.

SEVEN

DI Hardcastle received Catto's report stoically. 'No more than I expected,' he said gloomily. 'What I want you to do now, Catto, is to find out whether any young married woman possibly seen in the company of Stoner has been reported to the police as missing. You can follow that up if there has been such a report, and if there ain't, then you'd better start round the clubs just to see if they've lost any showgirls. But whatever you do, don't speak to that Station Sergeant Goddard on C Division. I don't trust him.'

'There's no chance of that, sir,' agreed Catto, who knew Goddard better than Hardcastle, even though Goddard might be able to provide the answer. Catto was not at all happy with the potentially endless assignment that Hardcastle had just given him, but he had to admit that he would have given the same orders had he been in the DDI's place.

The first part of Catto's search started immediately and took very little time. Crossing the narrow road from the police station to the main building of New Scotland Yard, he eventually found a small room, several floors up, staffed by an elderly clerk who introduced himself to Catto as Mr Powter. Mr Powter had the appearance of someone who was permanently downtrodden, an impression heightened by his shabby suit which hung on him as though it had originally been the property of someone of a much larger build.

'How can I help you, Sergeant?' Powter coughed and pulled at his ragged moustache as though fearful he was about to be presented with an unanswerable query.

'I'm wondering whether you have any missing showgirls, dancers or actresses listed, Mr Powter.'

'A name would be useful.' Powter took off his wire-framed spectacles and polished them with a colourful handkerchief, playing for time while he thought about Catto's request.

'I'm afraid we have yet to discover her name, Mr Powter,

although it's possible we will find it out in the next few days.'

'Ah!' Powter replaced his spectacles and peered afresh at Catto. 'Showgirls, showgirls. I don't remember any being reported, Sergeant, but I will have a look through my records. You never know what might turn up,' he said optimistically. The clerk turned towards a long tray full of small index cards. 'This one has all the missing females in it,' he said. 'We've found it useful to separate the men from the women. Just for the card index system,' he added, with a laugh that eventually became a rattling cough, powerful enough, it seemed, to threaten to eject his dentures. 'It helps to speed up the search,' he added, once he had recovered his breath. Fortunately, his dentures had remained in place.

'Yes, I imagine it would,' said Catto.

Mr Powter began to thumb through the cards with such speed and dexterity that Catto wondered if he was a professional card player in his spare time, possibly even a card sharp. After several minutes, he ceased his search and glanced up. 'You say the young lady was a showgirl, Sergeant?'

'Yes.' Catto looked hopeful.

'There's no one who's been listed as a showgirl, I'm afraid, but it's possible the informant didn't know that's what she did for a living when he filed the report.'

'Oh! That's a pity. But then I didn't hold out much hope anyway,' said Catto, a comment that clearly upset Mr Powter.

'I do my best, Sergeant,' he wailed, 'but we can't perform miracles.'

'My dear Mr Powter, that is not a criticism.' Catto was a past master at sweet talk when occasion demanded it. 'I think you've taken a great deal of trouble. But perhaps there is one other thing you can do for me . . .'

'Of course, Sergeant, of course.' A relieved Powter indulged in a short session of hand-wringing.

'If you do get notification of a missing showgirl, possibly married, I'd be most grateful if you'd let me know as soon as possible. It's a murder we're investigating, you see.'

'You have my word on it, Sergeant Catto. If you'd care to give me your telephone number, I'll inform you the moment we receive anything that might assist.' Powter hesitated. 'Of course, we only work office hours, and if such a notification was made at, say, eleven o'clock at night, I wouldn't know about it until nine o'clock the following day when the morning despatch arrived.' Looking at Catto with a pensive expression, he added, 'There again, if it was a Saturday evening, I wouldn't be aware of it until nine o'clock on the following Monday morning.'

'I think I can live with that,' said Catto, picking up his bowler hat. He had known, right from the start, that he was unlikely to have found the dead woman's details as easily as visiting Mr Powter's office, but it had to be done.

There was one other possibility that Catto tried before beginning enquiries in the West End, and that was to contact the Salvation Army's Family Tracing Service which had lately widened its operation to include missing persons in general. Catto realized that a showgirl, who might not be a showgirl, and whose name was not known, was going to be extremely hard to trace. Helpful though the Sally Ann's staff were, they could not come up with an answer, but promised to let Catto know if anyone fitting that rather vague description should be reported to them.

Marriott assigned Detective Constable Stuart Ritchie to assist Catto in the search for the identity of the woman whose body had been found at Ditton. Until that happened, finding her killer would be nigh on impossible. Both Marriott and Catto were of the view that Ritchie, the former Grenadier Guards captain who had so effectively silenced Holroyd, was unlikely to accept any obstruction by nightclub owners, many of whom had been commissioned during the war, and who mistakenly believed that their members' details were not open to police inspection.

It was an unrewarding task. Working methodically, street by street, the two officers trudged wearily from club to club. They discovered showgirls, cabaret dancers and hostesses who had vanished from one club only to turn up at another or in the chorus line of a revue at a West End theatre. A telephone enquiry had even located one missing London dancer alive and well in the chorus line of the Sheffield Empire, such was the thoroughness of Catto's enquiries.

Detective Constable Proctor, who had been assigned to search all the records held at Scotland Yard, even learned of two so-called nightclub hostesses who had appeared at Marlborough Street police court charged with soliciting. But nowhere did the detectives discover a missing married show-girl, and Catto was beginning to believe that perhaps the dead woman had not been connected with show business at all.

On the third day, however, the two detectives discovered a more promising lead at the Twilight Cabaret Club in Brewer Street, the last club they intended visiting that day.

Unlike many of the sleazy dives that Catto and Ritchie had visited in the course of the last two days, the Twilight Cabaret Club appeared to cater for the upper echelons of the market. As if to emphasize this, the door to the club was opened by a tall man attired in a dress suit that actually fitted and had probably been made to measure by a West End tailor. The man was courteous to a fault, even when Catto told him who they were. In Catto's experience, it was a good indication that this club had nothing to hide.

'Please come in, gentlemen.' The doorkeeper admitted them to a large, carpeted entrance foyer. To one side was a cloak-room, staffed by a young woman.

'I'd like to speak to the manager. I'm Detective Sergeant Catto.'

'There isn't a manager per se, sir. Major Craddock is the owner and he runs the club. If you'd be so good as to wait one moment, gentlemen, I'll telephone him and tell him that you are here.' After a brief conversation, the doorman said, 'The major will be with you shortly, sir. If you care to go in and take a table, please feel free to order a drink. On the house, of course,' he murmured.

'Thank you,' said Catto, 'but we'd rather wait here.' It was his policy never to accept a free drink until he had assessed the calibre of the person offering it.

The man who appeared some minutes later was tall and immaculately dressed, and probably aged around the mid-thirties.

He walked with a limp and was aided by a black walking cane
that he held in his right hand.

'Leo Craddock, gentlemen. My admissions manager tells
me you're from the police. Would that be the Marlborough
Street station by any chance?'

'No, Major.' Catto immediately sensed that Craddock had
had dealings with Station Sergeant Goddard and had been
unimpressed. 'I am Detective Sergeant Catto from the Whitehall
Division, and this is Detective Constable Ritchie. We are
investigating a murder, and it's possible that you may be able
to assist us.' It was the same request that Catto had made on
countless occasions since his enquiries had begun. In fact,
Hardcastle was investigating two murders, but as far as the
nightclubs were concerned, it was the identity of the woman
in which Catto was interested.

'A murder, eh?' Craddock brushed his guardee moustache
with the back of his left hand. 'Perhaps you'd care to come
up to my office. It's more private to discuss such things
there.' He took a gold half-hunter from a fob pocket in his
cummerbund, stared at it and replaced it. 'Given that the sun
is over the yardarm, I dare say I could persuade you gentlemen
to accept a drink.'

'That's very kind of you, Major,' said Catto, as he and
Ritchie followed Craddock. It was particularly noticeable that
the major's right leg remained stiff, making his climb up the
stairs a slow and difficult one. His richly carpeted, oak-lined
office was well appointed, and there were several framed prints
on the walls that depicted cavalrymen clad in a variety of
uniforms, on horseback or dismounted and striking various
poses.

'I take it you were in the cavalry, Major,' said Ritchie, as
he and Catto sat down.

'Yes, I was with the Sixteenth Dragoons, but we were
deployed as dismounted infantry on several occasions, the last
in November 1918. And, would you believe, at eleven o'clock
on the tenth of November – exactly twenty-fours before the
end of the bloody war – I got a Boche bullet through my right
knee.' Craddock shrugged. 'Fortunes of war, eh? But it put
paid to my army career. I was a regular officer, you see.

However, to get our priorities right, let me get you a drink and then we can talk about this murder.' Having poured three generous measures of Laphroaig, Craddock took the armchair adjacent to the two detectives, sitting down awkwardly. He dropped his walking cane on the floor.

'We have discovered the body of a young woman buried on the site of a burned-out garage at Ditton in Surrey, Major Craddock,' began Catto. 'The only clue to her identity came from an informant who said that he believed her to be young and married. We have no name and no description. Unfortunately, the body had been dismembered and a photo-graph would not be of any use for identification, there having been some putrefaction already.'

Craddock nodded, but otherwise did not react. He had seen too many dismembered bodies to be affected by such a grue-some description of the police find.

'One source,' Catto continued, 'suggested that the young lady was a showgirl or actress. The pathologist put her age at somewhere between seventeen and twenty-three. Another informant thought she was about twenty and danced like a professional. She was sometimes in the company of a Captain Guy Stoner, late of the RFA.'

'I'm afraid dancers come and go, Sergeant Catto. There are always girls who think they've got a better job somewhere else, and others who come knocking at the door seeking employment. As the club's name implies, we have a cabaret every evening and we've employed quite a few girls in the years since I opened. As for this Stoner, I've never heard of him. Have you tried asking him?'

'I'm afraid he's been murdered, too, Major,' said Catto.

'Great Scott! You're being kept busy, then.' Craddock stopped and appeared to be thinking. 'I'm damned sure that all the girls who have worked here always left after giving the proper notice, usually a week, and I don't think we had one who just disappeared without telling me – or rather without telling Marjorie.'

'Who is Marjorie, Major?' asked Ritchie.

'Marjorie Hibberd, my right arm. Mrs Hibberd is first and foremost the show's choreographer. But she's more than that.

She's a sort of mother hen who makes certain the costumes are right, makes sure the band is present and correct, the piano is tuned, and generally keeps an eye on the girls to ensure that none of the members takes advantage of them. She's very good at it, too. I suppose she must be at least fifty now, but she was quite a dancer in her day, so I'm told. She would know about any girl who disappeared. Would you like a word with her?'

'That might well be helpful, Major,' said Catto. 'Thank you.'

Reaching across his desk, Craddock lifted the earpiece of his pedestal telephone and requested that Marjorie be asked to come to his office.

The woman who entered some five minutes later wore a sleeveless black dress that came to mid-calf, and an expensive but discreet string of pearls. She had kept her figure and was clearly still very fit, and she moved with the sort of grace one would expect of an accomplished dancer.

'You wanted me, Major?'

'Marjorie, these two gentlemen are police officers.'

'Oh?' Marjorie glanced suspiciously at Catto and Ritchie. 'You're not from the Vice Squad at Vine Street, I hope.'

'No, ma'am,' said Catto, sensing that Marjorie Hibberd had also had dealings with that particular unit and did not much care for the attitude of its officers. 'We're from the Whitehall Division.'

'Oh, that's all right, then.'

'Sit down, Marjorie,' said Craddock. 'Would you like a drink?'

'Not right now, Major, thank you. So, how can I help the police?' she asked, keeping her eyes fixed on Craddock.

'We're trying to identify a young woman who has been murdered, Mrs Hibberd,' said Ritchie.

'And you think it's something to do with the Twilight Cabaret Club?' Marjorie Hibberd's comment sounded more like a criticism than an enquiry.

'Not necessarily,' said Catto, 'but Major Craddock wondered if you knew of any showgirl who had disappeared without giving notice.'

Marjorie appeared to give the matter some thought, but then shook her head. 'I honestly can't recall any of the girls having left without giving notice,' she said eventually.

'Well, thank you, Marjorie,' said Craddock. 'It was a bit of a long shot, anyway.'

'I'll give it some thought, Major,' said Marjorie, as she rose to leave. 'If anything comes to mind, I'll let you know.'

'If anyone is likely to remember, it's Marjorie,' said Craddock, once the woman had left the room. 'Of course, she's not infallible and she does have quite a lot on her plate. As I implied earlier, there's a brisk turnover of dancers and it's sometimes difficult to keep track of—' The club's proprietor stopped suddenly. 'Celine Fontenau,' he said, and turned to take a foolscap-sized book from his desk. 'It's an old army habit,' he continued. 'I always kept an unofficial roll of my chaps. My parade state, I called it. Made it much easier when it came to identifying their remains.' For a moment he looked immeasurably sad as he recalled the number of trench burial services he had conducted in the mud and under threat of constant shelling and sniper fire.

'The name Celine Fontenau sounds French,' said Catto. 'Was she French or was that just a name she used for show business?'

'Oh, she was French all right,' said Craddock as he found the entry in his book. 'As I recall, she was rather full of herself. More confident than the average showgirl of her age. In fact, she looked more like a Parisian model than a dancer, but I asked to see her passport and that showed that she was born in Marseilles. I wanted to make sure that she wasn't under the legal minimum age for the job. One has to be very careful in this business, and you get all sorts of young women coming to Soho in search of what they think is the high life. For the most part, they're silly little girls hoping to find a rich husband.' He chuckled. 'And if he's got a title, that's a bonus. Marjorie was off sick for a few weeks about that time, so I'm not surprised she didn't remember the Fontenau girl. I considered sacking her at one stage because she was inclined to cause trouble among the other dancers. Anyway, I decided to leave it until Marjorie came back to work, but by then the girl had walked out.'

'Did you happen to make a note of her date of birth, Major?'
Catto took out his pocketbook, ready to make a note.

'Twentieth of July 1907.'

'When was it she disappeared?' asked Ritchie.

Craddock referred to his book again. 'Friday, the eleventh
of March,' he replied, without hesitation.

'You're sure of that?' Catto wanted to be certain. The fire
at Ditton had taken place just three days later.

'Yes,' said Craddock. 'It made me short of a girl for the
show, and in the absence of Marjorie, I had to get the senior
dancer and the band leader to revise the whole routine in the
space of about an hour. I don't know whether Celine Fontenau
got a job anywhere else in the West End, but there are more
unemployed showgirls in London than you can shake a stick
at, Sergeant Catto.'

'Do you happen to have an address for her, Major?' asked
Ritchie.

'No, I'm afraid not. Even if I had, she'd probably be long
gone by now.'

'D'you know of any men friends Celine Fontenau might
have had?' Catto asked.

'We discourage liaisons between our girls and the members,
Sergeant,' said Craddock. 'But that said, it's virtually impossible to prevent them meeting away from the club. A substantial
tip to a waiter from a member will ensure that a discreet note
is passed to one of the girls.'

'But you don't know of any men Celine might have been
seeing, Major.'

'No, I'm afraid not.' Craddock shook his head. 'Sorry I
can't be more helpful. She was a flighty little piece, was that
Celine, and it doesn't really come as a surprise to hear
that she's been murdered.'

'We don't know it is her, Major,' said Catto, surprised at
Craddock's ready assumption. 'That's what we're trying to find
out.'

Next morning, Catto and Ritchie went to the Aliens
Registration Office. Although convinced that making
enquiries about Celine Fontenau would lead them nowhere,

it was an enquiry that had to be made, if only to avoid Hardcastle's wrath.

The constable manning the counter was probably fifty years of age and, as he was nearing the end of his service, had acquired a soft billet bullying foreigners who were seeking refuge in the United Kingdom. Without asking any questions, he slapped two forms on the counter.

'Fill 'em in, and then bring 'em back along with your passports.' The constable then made the mistake of turning his back.

'Come back here, you, and move a bit bloody smartly,' said Ritchie, in what Catto presumed was his best parade-ground voice.

The startled constable, taken aback by the sound of an authoritative and educated English accent, returned to the counter.

'I'm Detective Constable Ritchie of the Whitehall Division, and this is Detective Sergeant Catto. If I were in your position, cully, and wanted to stay in that position, I'd be very careful what you say next, and that you do everything possible to assist my sergeant. Understood?'

'Oh, I'm sorry. I didn't know you was in the Job.'

'You didn't bloody well ask, did you?' responded Ritchie.

'I want you to show me everything you have on record for a Frenchwoman named Celine Fontenau,' said Catto. 'She was born in Marseilles on the twentieth of July 1907, and I want it now.'

'Yes, Sergeant. I'll attend to it immediately.' The constable, now fearing that he would be back walking a beat come Monday, scurried away to do Catto's bidding.

Once the PC had disappeared to a back office, Catto turned to Ritchie. 'Next time, Ritchie, if there is a next time, just remember that I'm quite capable of dealing with bloody-minded constables. I don't need you to fight my battles for me.'

'Sorry, Skip, but blokes like that make my blood boil. They let the Job down.'

Five minutes later, the PC, now an obsequious shadow of his former self, reappeared clutching an index card. 'There's not a great deal to help you, Sergeant. Not that I know what you're looking for.'

The card showed that Celine Fontenau was born on the date that Major Craddock had given Catto and Ritchie. She had arrived in England on Monday the fifth of October 1925 and had registered with ARO on the twentieth of that month. Her address was a dwelling house in Balls Pond Road in Islington, North London, where she was employed as a house parlour-maid. The card also showed that she was unmarried. Attached was a photograph of an attractive blonde, but whether it was of the person whose dismembered body had been found at Ditton was open to conjecture.

'Thank you,' said Catto, returning the card. 'I take it you've received no further information since the date she registered.'

'No, Sergeant.'

'So, with any luck, she'll still be at that address,' said Catto, musing aloud.

'If she's not, she'll have committed an offence under the Aliens Registration Act of 1914, Sergeant,' volunteered the helpful constable.

'Bit difficult to prosecute her if you don't know where she is,' Ritchie pointed out. But the logic of his argument escaped the constable.

EIGHT

I t was half past two when Catto and Ritchie called at the Balls Pond Road address in Islington, the details of which they had obtained from the Aliens Registration Office.

The butler who answered the door was skeletally thin, and what remained of his greying hair manifested itself as little tufts on either side of his head. But his most noticeable feature was his rounded shoulders, as though the burden of his office, or perhaps the weight of his faded morning coat, was too much for him to bear. He gazed at the two police officers as if they were strange beings who had just arrived from another world. Experience told him that they were not guests of the master and mistress, but neither did they appear to be itinerant salesmen.

'Yes?'

'I'm Detective Sergeant Catto of the Whitehall Division of the Metropolitan Police, and this is my colleague, Detective Constable Ritchie.'

The butler's attitude softened, albeit slightly. 'I'm afraid that the master and mistress are away,' he said, hoping that the police officers would go away, too.

'I presume you're the butler.' Catto noticed that his speech was slightly slurred.

'That is correct.'

'In that case it's you I wish to speak to, Mr . . .'

'Parker's my name.'

The arrival of the police wanting to speak to him appeared to have disconcerted Parker more than a little, and Catto wondered what dark secrets the man was hiding. In his experience, a butler was always fiddling something, and it was, more often than not, the wine book that recorded his master's cellar stock. And judging by Parker's slurred speech, he was also drinking some of it.

'It concerns a house parlourmaid by the name of Celine Fontenau, Mr Parker.'

'Oh, that little French trollop!' The butler looked relieved that, after all, it was not him in whom the police were interested. 'You'd better come in, gentlemen.' He opened a door leading off the hall and conducted the two officers down the stairs, across the kitchen and into his pantry.

'I take it, from your reaction, that Miss Fontenau is no longer in employment here.'

'No, she ain't, and good riddance, too. She got herself a job as a dancer at some Soho dive. At least, that's what I heard she was doing, but I had my doubts about that.'

'How did you hear that, Mr Parker?' asked Catto.

'We butlers stick together, Mr Catto. It's like a secret society. Intelligence what's likely to be useful to those of us in the profession gets passed around, see?' Parker reached across for a bottle of sherry. 'Fancy a drop?' he asked, as he poured a large measure into a glass near at hand.

'No, thanks,' said Catto, and Ritchie shook his head. 'When did Miss Fontenau leave here?'

'She never left in the sense that she gave notice. She just pushed off without a word. But just to make sure, I'll look at my day book.' Parker moved a large leather-bound book from the edge of his desk and opened it in front of him. 'I make a note of everything that goes on in this household,' he explained, as he donned a pair of spectacles and began to thumb through the pages. 'You never know when it might come in handy.' Given that the butler appeared to be over sixty years of age, he must have made a great number of entries in his book. Perhaps he was intending to write his memoirs one day, thought Catto. 'Here we are, gents. She started work as a house parlourmaid on the fifth of October 1925.'

'When did she leave, then?' asked Ritchie.

Parker turned a page and ran a finger down the entries. 'She weren't in her room on the second of August.' He glanced up. 'That'd be 1926, the August bank holiday. Just as well that the master and mistress was away at their country estate. Put me in a right two-an'-eight, being one short. I shouldn't have been surprised, mind you; I'd had to reprimand her on more than one occasion for slovenly work. Anyway, all her stuff was gone from her room, and we never saw hide nor hair of her again. Like I said, I did hear through my contacts that she'd got herself a job as a dancer or some such thing up one of them nightclubs in the West End.' The butler closed the book and placed a hand on it. 'And that's all I can tell you, gents.'

'Did you report her missing, Mr Parker?' asked Ritchie.

Parker laughed, although it was more of a grating cackle. 'Not likely,' he said. 'They might've found her and brought her back.'

'D'you know which nightclub it was that she went to?' asked Catto.

'No, that's the one thing I never bothered to find out. Of course, I wasn't much interested after she'd gone.' To which Parker added once more, 'Good riddance, if you ask me.'

'What about references?' asked Ritchie, somewhat naively.

'I shouldn't think getting a job as a dancer would depend on how you shaped up as a house parlourmaid, would you?' Parker smirked. 'Unless you'd been providing services to the master that was a bit more than dusting and polishing.' He winked at the two officers and drained his sherry glass before filling it up again. 'Although . . .' he began pensively.

'Although what?' asked Catto, sensing that Parker was about to betray what he thought was a confidence.

'Well, I shouldn't really say this, but I think there might have been a bit of hanky-panky between her and the master. Of course, the mistress tolerated the master's carryings-on up to a point, but there came a limit, if you know what I mean. If the mistress and the master hadn't both been away that weekend, I'd have thought her ladyship had given Fontenau her marching orders.' Parker gave an expressive shrug. 'Who's to know, eh?'

On Saturday morning, Catto took his seat in the detectives' room and stretched his arms above his head. 'We've got two choices now, Ritchie,' he said. 'We can keep on doing the rounds of the nightclubs, or we can investigate this Celine Fontenau a bit more. But we might be wasting our time.'

'Couldn't we ask the guv'nor for advice, Skip?' asked Ritchie.

Catto leaned forward and rested his arms on the table, his hands linked. 'I can see you don't know Mr Hardcastle as well as I do, Ritchie. I'll tell you exactly what he'd say. He'd say, "You're a sergeant, Catto. Use your initiative. It's what you're paid for."'

'But supposing you did that and it all went wrong, Skip?'

'Then he'd want to know why we hadn't asked him for advice in the first place. You can't win.'

'Well, what *are* we going to do?' asked Ritchie.

'I'm going to do something the guv'nor would never think of: I'm going to ask the press for help.'

'Ye gods!' exclaimed Ritchie. 'The old man hates the press. He'll blow his top if he finds out.'

'Only if it doesn't get a result,' said Catto. 'Anyway, he won't find out.'

'Well, which papers are you going to pick?'

'I'm going to pick one with a large circulation – come the day following publication, the others will have picked it up.' Catto gave the matter a few moments' thought. 'I think I'll have a word with the *Daily Mail*. I read the other day that they've got a circulation of about one and a half million.'

'Doesn't the guv'nor read the *Mail*?' asked Ritchie. 'Could be trouble if it's the first thing he sees on his way to work.'

Catto shook his head wearily. 'Ritchie, you might've been a very good officer in the war, but you've still got a lot to learn about coppering.' He reached for the telephone and asked to be connected to the *Daily Mail* office in Carmelite Street in the City. After a brief conversation with someone he obviously knew, he took his bowler hat and coat from the stand in the corner of the office and made for the door. Ritchie was about to hurry after him, but Catto stopped him. 'That's something else, Ritchie – when you speak to a reporter and impart certain confidential information in exchange for assistance, you don't take a witness with you.'

'But supposing this chap has got someone with him?'

'He won't have, but if he has, the conversation won't even start. And he knows that.'

* * *

The pub that Frank Harvey, the *Daily Mail* reporter, had selected for their meeting at twelve noon was some distance from Carmelite House, and one that he knew was not generally frequented by other members of the fourth estate.

'What are you having, Henry?'

'A pint of Boddington's, please, Frank.'

'I thought you were a Guinness drinker?'

'Not at midday; it's too heavy. And I've got work to do this afternoon.'

Harvey bought the drinks, and ushered Catto to the other end of the bar where there was no chance of them being overheard. 'Well, Henry, old son, what breathtaking snippet have you got that's going to make my name for me?'

'I need some help,' admitted Catto, taking the head off his beer. He went on to explain about the unidentified female body that the police had found at Ditton Garage. 'The male body was identified as Guy Stoner by Rupert Holroyd, Stoner's partner in the enterprise.'

'So, that's what the excavations were all about. We got a whisper that your chaps were doing some poking about at the site of a garage in Ditton, but we thought it was something to do with arson as there'd been a fire there. Looks like you've got a puzzle on your hands, Henry.' Harvey drank the last of his whisky. 'How come you're investigating a murder at Ditton? You're on C Division, aren't you?'

'I was, but now I'm back at Cannon Row on A Division.'

Harvey laughed. 'Back with Ernie Hardcastle, eh? Well, good luck, Henry. But what's A Division doing investigating business that's on V Division?' As the crime reporter of the *Daily Mail*, Harvey knew his way around the labyrinthine organization of the Metropolitan Police.

'Arthur Fitnam is off sick, so the Elephant put Ernie Hardcastle on the job.'

'So, *he's* in charge of the investigation, I suppose, but you're doing all the legwork. Is that it? *Plus ça change!*'

'You obviously know my guv'nor as well as I do, Frank.' Catto signalled to the barman for another round of drinks. 'D'you think you can help?'

Harvey appeared to give Catto's request some consideration,

but he knew a good story when he heard one. 'I suppose you don't want this story attributed, do you, Henry?'

'Not bloody likely,' said Catto vehemently. 'If Ernie Hardcastle thinks I've been talking to the press, he'd hang me out to dry.'

'What do I get out of it, Henry?'

'Confirmation of the name when we've formally identified her, and details of any arrest. All right?'

'You'd better give me the details of this French girl you think it is, then. No point in running this story if we get the bloody name wrong.' Harvey produced a small notebook and began to record details of what Catto had just told him. 'It'll be in Monday morning's edition, Henry. Did you say that Hardcastle reads our prestigious journal?'

'Yes, he does.'

'In that case, old boy, I'd take the day off, if I were you.'

'He won't know it's me that gave it to you, Frank, but I'm surprised our press department didn't put it out,' said Catto reflectively. 'Someone from Fleet Street must've asked.'

Harvey laughed. 'In Fleet Street it's known as the *suppress* department, Henry.'

On Monday morning, Hardcastle arrived in a foul mood and immediately shouted for Marriott.

'Sir?' Marriott appeared in the doorway of the DDI's office.

'Have you seen this?' Hardcastle gestured at his somewhat crumpled edition of the *Daily Mail*, the open broadsheet pages of which almost covered his desk.

'What is it, sir?'

'The *Daily Mail* has somehow got hold of the story about that damned woman whose body was found at Ditton. How the hell did they get hold of that?'

'May I see, sir?' Marriott always read the *Daily Chronicle* and, naturally enough, there was nothing in that paper about the case, as it was the *Daily Mail*'s scoop. He scanned the article and returned the paper. 'I think they've followed up on that newspaper report about police activity over the arson at Ditton, sir.' He did not know that the information had been provided by Catto, and Ritchie had been promised a brand-new helmet and a far-flung beat to go with it if he told anyone of Catto's meeting with the *Daily Mail* man. There were, after all, careers at stake. 'I reckon you can blame one of the night-clubs that our people visited, sir. If you tell them why you want to know about any missing showgirls, they'll start putting two and two together, and before you know it, they'll be blab-bing to one of their newspaper friends. These people have all got contacts with Fleet Street.'

'Why should they have contacts with the press, Marriott? You're not making a lot of sense.'

Hardcastle's naivety amazed Marriott, but only momen-tarily. 'It's always worth a few quid to let the press know if someone of note has been out on the town in a nightclub, sir,' he explained. 'For instance, any news of the Prince of Wales's appearances at one of these places is probably worth a fiver. And if he's got someone else's wife with him, it's probably deserving of a tenner.' Marriott was beginning to believe that Hardcastle really was getting past it. The nightclub scene that Marriott was describing was common knowledge among the younger detectives but was alien territory to Hardcastle.

'Yes, that's as maybe, but how the hell did they know it was me investigating it? It would make more sense if they'd said Arthur Fitnam was. He's the DDI on V Division, after all.' Hardcastle's perplexity continued unabated.

'It might actually turn out to be helpful, sir,' said Marriott, making an attempt at placating the DDI. It was obvious that the article had put him in a bad mood, made worse by appearing on a Monday morning and thus boding ill for the rest of the week. 'By the way, sir, we received a reply from the Rutland Constabulary late on Saturday evening.'

'What did they want?'

'We asked them to confirm that Holroyd stayed with his sister and her husband over the weekend from the eleventh to the fourteenth of March, sir, and they did confirm it.'

'Very convenient,' said Hardcastle. 'But I think we'll do some checking of our own when we have the time.'

*   *   *

In the event, Marriott was right that the newspaper article might help, although even then it was not without another outburst from Hardcastle.

A man giving the name of Gerald Walker called at New Scotland Yard on Tuesday morning, after he had read the report about the missing showgirl in that day's *Morning Post*, his newspaper of choice.

Unfortunately for Mr Walker – and the constable on duty at the Back Hall of New Scotland Yard when Hardcastle learned of it – he was directed to Ditton police station, some twenty miles away. There, he was told that the matter was being dealt with by DDI Hardcastle whose office was to be found at Cannon Row police station immediately opposite New Scotland Yard.

'Excuse me, sir.' The station constable hovered in the doorway of Hardcastle's office.

'What is it, lad?'

'There's a Mr Gerald Walker downstairs asking to see you, sir. He said it's something to do with his missing wife.' The PC glanced at a slip of paper. 'A Mrs Selina or Celine or Cecile Walker, I think he said, sir. Anyway, it was some sort of foreign name.'

'I expect police officers to be efficient in what they do, lad,' snapped Hardcastle. 'So, any time in the future you come up here with a message, make bloody sure it's not some half-baked story. Show this Mr Walker up, a bit *jildi*, and on your way down, ask Sergeant Marriott to step in.'

Moments later, Marriott came through the door, fastening the last button of his waistcoat as he did so.

'I think we might be getting somewhere, Marriott. Where's Catto?'

'In the detectives' room, sir.'

'Better bring him in. He seems to know more about this job than I do,' said Hardcastle in a rare admission of his own fallibility. 'But don't tell him I said so.'

'Mr Walker, sir.' The station constable ushered Hardcastle's caller into the DDI's office, followed by Henry Catto.

'Come in, Mr Walker, and take a seat.'

'Thank you very much, sir.' Walker's slightly wavy, neatly trimmed hair was parted in the centre, and he was wearing a three-piece suit that was clearly not a recent acquisition. A sober tie and polished black shoes completed the picture of someone who could be an impecunious clerk. There was a neatly folded raincoat over his left arm, and he held a greying bowler hat in his right hand. 'I'm sorry to bother a busy man like yourself, sir, but I am worried about my wife, you see.'

Hardcastle was somewhat mollified by the man's deference. 'It's what the police are here for, Mr Walker.'

'I had a bit of a setback to start with, sir.' Walker sat down but held on to his raincoat and his hat.

'Take the gentleman's hat and coat, Catto, and hang them up.' Hardcastle waited until that was done before continuing. 'Now tell me about this setback, Mr Walker.'

'Well, sir, I thought that Scotland Yard would be the proper place to go in order to lodge my concern. As a result, I obtained the day off work, but once I'd told the officer at Scotland Yard this morning that I was enquiring about a missing dancer called Celine who the police were interested in, he told me to go to Ditton police station. But when I got there, the officer sent me back here. So, here I am, sir.'

'I'm sorry you've been inconvenienced, Mr Walker,' said Hardcastle, only containing his rising bad temper with difficulty. He turned to Marriott. 'I want to see the Back Hall PC and the Back Hall inspector who were on duty this morning, sooner rather than later, Marriott.'

'I'll arrange it, sir.'

Walker looked somewhat concerned at this turn of events. 'I have no wish to make trouble for anyone, sir,' he said hurriedly. 'I imagine it was a genuine mistake.'

'You leave that to me,' said Hardcastle. 'Now then, let's start at the beginning. I understand from what you were saying that your wife is Celine Walker.'

'That is so, sir.'

'What was her maiden name?'

'Fontenau,' said Walker. 'She's French, you see.'

Hardcastle glanced across to ensure that Marriott was taking notes. 'As a matter of interest, Mr Walker, what is your profession?'

Walker gave a weak smile. 'I'd hardly call it a profession, sir. I'm a clerk.'

'And where do you work as a clerk?'

'At Hudson and Peartree Limited, sir, in Vauxhall. Installers of bakers' ovens. Twenty years I've been there.'

'And do you live locally, Mr Walker?'

'I have a bachelor flat in Chapter Street, Westminster, paid for by my employers. That is to say, it was a bachelor flat until I married Celine and she came to live with me.'

'How did you meet your wife?' asked Marriott.

Walker turned in his chair. 'At the Twilight Cabaret Club, sir.' For the first time since his arrival, Walker appeared embarrassed by this admission. 'My colleagues treated me to a night out there to celebrate my fortieth birthday.'

For a moment or two, Hardcastle pondered the incongruity of Gerald Walker being at the Twilight Cabaret Club. He also wondered, given the state of the man's suit, where he would have acquired a dinner jacket – obligatory in most nightclubs – because Hardcastle doubted that the clerk seated in front of him owned one. But Walker himself answered that unasked question.

'My friends paid for the whole evening, but I had to hire a dinner suit from Moss Brothers in Covent Garden. Cost me two shillings and sixpence, sir – a sizeable part of a clerk's weekly wage, I can tell you.'

'But how did you meet your wife?' persisted Marriott.

'At the Twilight Cabaret Club, sir.'

'I think Sergeant Marriott means how exactly did you make contact with Miss Fontenau, given that you were a guest, so to speak, and she, presumably, was on the stage.' It was the first time that Catto had spoken, and Walker had to turn in the opposite direction from where Marriott was sitting.

'Oh, I see, sir. I'm sorry, I didn't quite understand the question. Well, my friends are very generous and bought several bottles of champagne. I have to admit that I got a little bit tipsy, but it's not every day you have a fortieth birthday, is it?'

'That's true,' said Catto, whose own fortieth was still some years away.

'Anyway, to answer your question, sir,' Walker continued, 'one of my friends said that Celine, who was in the centre of the chorus line, kept looking at me and smiling, and he dared me to send her a note asking her out for a meal. I must admit I was tempted as she was such an attractive girl. Then my other friends started daring me, and before I knew what was happening, I'd given a note to one of the waiters, and another of my friends gave him a Bradbury to slip my note discreetly to Celine.'

'Your friends seem to have plenty of money, Mr Walker,' said Catto. From his visit to the Twilight Cabaret Club, he knew that champagne there did not come cheap.

'I think they'd been saving up, sir. As I said, they're very good friends, and one of them seems to have good luck on the horses. Anyhow, to my surprise, I received a letter from Celine by Monday morning's post. In the letter, she said that she'd be delighted to go for a meal with me and asked me to suggest a date, bearing in mind that she worked all week, but had Monday evenings off.'

'And you and she met, I suppose.'

'That we did, sir, the very next Monday. I tell you, sir, I couldn't believe my luck. This beautiful young lady wanting to go out with an old duffer like me, but I suppose being French she didn't worry so much about the age difference.'

'Where did Miss Fontenau live, Mr Walker?' asked Hardcastle.

Walker swung back to face the DDI. 'D'you know, I've no idea, sir. I suppose she had accommodation at the club, but as soon as we were married, she moved in with me.' He said nothing further for a few seconds, and then added, 'Actually, she moved in with me before we were married.' He sighed. 'Well, it is the nineteen twenties, isn't it? Things have changed.'

'Thank you for coming in, Mr Walker,' said Hardcastle, standing up. 'I'll contact you the moment I have any information. Just give your full address to my sergeant, will you.'

'It might be easier for you if you were to telephone me at work, sir. The number comes through to my desk because I deal with orders and appointments and the like. I wouldn't like my employers to know that I was having to deal with the police. I didn't tell them that I'd got married, and they might think I was up to something.'

'Your firm sounds very old fashioned,' said Hardcastle.

'Oh, it is, sir. It hasn't changed one little bit since I started there in 1907.' As Walker stood up, Catto fetched the man's hat and raincoat and handed it to him. 'I hope I've not taken up too much of your time, sir.'

'Not at all, Mr Walker,' said Hardcastle. 'As I said when you came in, that's what the police are here for.'

NINE

'The question I have to decide now,' said Hardcastle, once Walker had left the office, 'is whether to ask him to identify the remains of the woman we think is Celine Walker née Fontenau.'

'It might be a bit harrowing for him, sir,' suggested Catto.

'I think we'd have to ask Walker if he was willing, sir,' said Marriott, 'although there's always the possibility that the woman we found at Ditton is *not* Walker's wife.'

'We could get Parker, the butler at Balls Pond Road, to view the remains, sir,' said Catto, 'although he might be too drunk. On the other hand, a much more reliable person would be Marjorie Hibberd, the choreographer at the Twilight Cabaret Club. If she remembers her. According to Major Craddock, Mrs Hibberd was off sick at the time of Celine's disappearance. But I don't suppose that she would be too distressed by the sight of a dead body.'

'If she was off sick at the time the girl was at the club, I very much doubt she'd remember her,' said Hardcastle. 'No, we'll start with Walker. Get on that telephone machine first thing in the morning, Catto, and see what he says.'

'Won't he wonder why we didn't ask him when he was here, sir? I mean, what do I tell him?'

'Good God, Catto, use your initiative.'

At eight thirty on Wednesday morning, Catto rang the number Walker had given him. It was Walker who answered the phone, as he had said he would.

'It's Detective Sergeant Catto from Cannon Row police station, Mr Walker.'

'Do you have some news, sir?' asked Walker hopefully.

'It's not so much news as the need for us to make certain arrangements, Mr Walker. Would it be possible for you to get some time off to come to the police station?'

'Yes. I sometimes have to go out to meet clients and suggest the best sort of oven they might need. It often takes quite a while because I have to look at where they want them installed. Consequently, I'm often out of the office for long periods of time, especially if I have to travel a distance. I had to go to Scotland once. It's quite a responsibility, you know, but I combine being a clerk with an estimator and general sort of salesman.' Walker paused. 'I just wish they'd pay me a little more than I'm getting.'

Gerald Walker arrived at a quarter past nine and was shown straight up to Hardcastle's office where Marriott was already waiting with the DDI.

'I'm sorry to drag you back so soon, Mr Walker,' Hardcastle began, 'but I needed to think whether to pose my next question.'

'You make it all sound very mysterious, sir.' Walker stood in front of the DDI's desk with his hands linked in front of him.

'Do sit down, Mr Walker.' Hardcastle signalled to Marriott to get a chair. 'We have found a body—'

'Oh no! Are you suggesting that Celine has met with an accident?'

'We are not sure if it is your wife, Mr Walker, but if it is, I'm sorry to tell you that she was murdered.'

'May the good Lord have mercy on her soul!' said Walker, with a sharp intake of breath that sounded almost like a sob. For a moment or two it appeared that he might break down completely.

'We are by no means sure that this is your wife, Mr Walker,' said Marriott hurriedly. 'That is why Mr Hardcastle asked you to come in.'

Walker stared at Marriott for what seemed to be an endless period of absolute silence. 'It can't be true,' he said eventually. 'It can't.'

'If you're willing to view the body at St Mary's Hospital in Paddington, Mr Walker, that would resolve the matter one way or the other. But I appreciate that it might be too much of a shock for you.'

'How do I get there, sir?' asked Walker plaintively.

'Sergeant Marriott and I will take you by cab,' said Hardcastle.

The mortuary attendant at the hospital had been instructed by Sir Bernard Spilsbury to arrange the parts of the unidentified woman's remains so that they presented the semblance of a complete body beneath the shroud. The task was made slightly easier for the attendant in that the woman's head remained attached to the torso.

'Are you still willing to go through with this, Mr Walker?' asked Marriott, one last time.

'Yes, sir, I am,' said Walker reluctantly. 'It is my duty.'

The attendant drew back the shroud, sufficient to reveal the head.

'It's her. May the Lord have mercy on her soul.' With that repeated appeal to the Almighty, Walker collapsed to the floor in a dead faint.

'Excuse me, gents,' said the attendant, as he bustled officiously towards the recumbent Gerald Walker. 'It happens all the time, you know.' He knelt down and held a small phial under Walker's nose until the man began to show signs of recovery.

'What's that you're giving him?' demanded Hardcastle, concerned that the attendant might be administering some noxious substance.

'Ammonium carbonate,' said the attendant, without looking up. 'Better known as smelling salts. It irritates the nose and lungs and sets off a reflex action that makes the patient inhale.'

'All right, I don't want a lecture,' said Hardcastle testily, as the attendant, aided by Marriott, helped the unsteady Walker to his feet and took him out to the anteroom, where they sat him on a chair. The attendant fetched him a glass of water.

'I have to ask this question formally, Mr Walker,' began Hardcastle. 'Can you identify the body you just saw?'

Walker stared at the DDI with a baleful expression on his face. 'It's my wife, Celine,' he said, the tears welling up in his eyes. 'I'm sure it is.'

'We'll take you back to the police station, Mr Walker,' said Marriott, 'and once you feel a bit better, I'll ask you to make a short statement.'

'I dare say you could do with a cup of tea, Mr Walker,' suggested the DDI once the three of them were settled. 'Marriott, ask Mrs Winstanley if she would bring in three cups of tea.' Agnes Winstanley was the police station matron who had replaced Bertha Cartwright. A year or so after the end of the war, Mrs Cartwright had retired and gone to live in Aldershot where her son Jack, now a major in the Royal Artillery, was stationed.

'I've prepared a short statement in which you identify the body you saw as that of your wife, Celine Walker née Fontenau, Mr Walker,' said Marriott. 'Perhaps you'd read it while we're waiting for the tea and tell me if you disagree with anything it contains.'

Gerald Walker produced a pair of spectacles from an inside pocket and placed them carefully and precisely on his nose. Accepting the single sheet of paper from Marriott, he gave it but a cursory glance. 'Yes, sir, that's it exactly. Do I sign it?'

'Just there,' said Marriott, leaning across to indicate the exact place on the official form. 'Do you have a pen?'

'I do, sir, thank you.' Walker produced a fountain pen, unscrewed the cap and signed the form.

'I presume that your wife gave up working at the Twilight Cabaret Club when you were married, Mr Walker?' suggested Hardcastle casually.

Walker did not answer immediately, as though unwilling to admit the truth, but eventually he said, 'No, sir, she carried on. She loved her job, and it seemed a shame to deprive her of so much enjoyment. Apart from which,' he admitted, with apparent reluctance, 'it helped with the finances. After all, women worked in the war, and we even had some female staff at the factory working on the shop floor.' He continued in his attempt to justify his decision. 'Mind you, they've all gone now, but to my way of thinking it seems a shame. Some of the ladies we had were very good at the jobs they were doing.'

Hardcastle made no comment about that. Despite his objections, his own daughter, Kitty, had worked as a conductorette for the London General Omnibus Company during the war. But such were his outdated views that he firmly believed that, after the war, women should have returned to their peacetime occupations of bringing up children and keeping house. Events, however, were overtaking his old-fashioned ideas of what women should do.

'May I come in, sir?' Mrs Winstanley had opened Hardcastle's door with one hand while balancing a tray on the other.

'Of course, Mrs Winstanley.'

The matron placed the tea tray on the edge of Hardcastle's desk and handed a cup of tea to each of the people in the room.

'Very kind of you, miss,' murmured Walker.

'It's a pleasure, sir,' said Agnes, and left the room, closing the door behind her.

'Mrs Winstanley's predecessor always wanted to talk about her son who was in the army, Mr Walker,' said Marriott, giving the impression of making banal conversation while they were drinking their tea. But there were deeper reasons. 'Were you in army or the navy during the war?' he asked casually.

'No, sir, unfortunately I wasn't privileged to be allowed to go. On two counts, as a matter of fact. I suffer from asthma, which apparently could be fatal in the event of a gas attack, and secondly, my employers, Hudson and Peartree, switched from making bakers' ovens to manufacturing field kitchens for the army. Consequently, sir, I was deemed to be in a reserved occupation.'

'Oh, I see.' Marriott refrained from saying that a lot of men died from gas attacks, whether they had asthma or not. 'I hope you don't mind me asking you one or two personal questions, but we need to know as much as possible about your late wife, and that can only happen by discussing matters with you.'

'I quite understand, sir.' Walker stirred his tea absent-mindedly.

'Had you been married before you met Celine?'

'No, sir. I never met the right young woman. I have to say I thought a miracle had come to pass when Celine agreed to become my wife. She was such a beautiful girl that I couldn't believe my luck. And now fate has snatched her away from me.' Walker took a sip of tea, before continuing. 'You said she'd been murdered, sir,' he said, directing the comment at Hardcastle.

'That is so.'

'Where did you find her body?'

'I'm afraid I'm not at liberty to say at the moment, Mr Walker; not until we have completed our enquiries. It's the coroner's decision.' The truth had nothing to with the coroner but was simply that Hardcastle had no wish to go into the sordid details of where, and in what condition, Walker's late wife had been found. 'You may rest assured that we'll find whoever was responsible, and he'll be dancing on the hangman's trap at eight o'clock one morning.'

Walker nodded sagely. 'It's God's will, sir. An eye for an eye.' He paused. 'I make no excuse for my frequent references to the Almighty, sir, but it's become something of a habit. I'm a lay preacher, you see, and I even considered taking holy orders at one time, but the war put paid to that, as it put paid to so many things. But in a strange sort of way, the war strengthened my belief in God.'

'Well, I think that's all, Mr Walker,' said Hardcastle, who had no great belief in religion of any sort. 'We'll be in touch with you once we have further details. And we will, of course, let you know the moment we make an arrest.'

'Thank you, sir, you've been very considerate.' Walker stood up, put his cup and saucer on Hardcastle's desk, and accepted his raincoat and bowler hat from Marriott.

Once Marriott had shown Walker the way out, he returned to the DDI's office.

'Poor devil. You can't help feeling sorry for him, can you, sir?'

'He must've thought his luck had changed when he found Celine,' said Hardcastle, 'but then she was murdered. He's a bit like a man who thinks he's won the football pools only to find his coupon had got lost in the post.' After a moment's thought, he added, 'Horace Boxall, the newsagent at the bottom of my road used to take the coupons for the pools companies. Saved them getting lost. Still, old Horace is dead now . . . I don't know if his daughter still takes them.'

'What's next, sir?' asked Marriott who, after all the years he had worked with Hardcastle, had never quite grown accustomed to his cynicism. But what worried him more was Hardcastle's recent habit of rambling on about irrelevancies.

'The one thing we've not established, Marriott, is whether Celine Walker is the same woman who Stoner was carrying on with – at least, according to Holroyd.'

'But surely, sir, the fact that both bodies were found at the same site indicates that Celine was the girl.'

'Not necessarily, Marriott. I gather from talking to Holroyd that Guy Stoner was a bit of a ladies' man. He was apparently good-looking, had plenty of money – at least until Holroyd emptied his bank account – and frequented nightclubs. I reckon he had the pick of available women. And even some who weren't really available on account of 'em being married.'

'Like Celine Walker, sir,' said Marriott, determined not to let the DDI have the argument all his own way.

'Even so, Marriott,' continued Hardcastle, leaning forward to take his pipe from the ashtray, 'we're no nearer finding out who killed her and Stoner. And that reminds me: have we heard from the police in Norfolk?'

'Yes, sir, they confirm that they informed the Reverend Percy Stoner of his nephew's death, but they did not tell him that he'd apparently been murdered.'

Hardcastle lit his pipe and leaned back in his chair. 'I suppose we'll have to go up there again and tell him the truth, Marriott. It's possible he might be able to throw some light on our investigation. He might even know more about the business with young Stoner bedding this here showgirl Celine. If he did.' He placed his pipe in the ashtray. 'On second thoughts, I think I'll send you up there. You can take Catto. Be good experience for you as you're very nearly an inspector.' He glanced at his desk calendar. 'Tomorrow's Thursday,' he said, uttering a truism. 'Be as well if you set off nice and early. Warn Catto.'

'Yes, sir.' Marriott had mixed feelings about the assignment. On the one hand, he liked Norfolk no better than Hardcastle did, but to go out without Hardcastle breathing down his neck the whole time was a bonus. An example of that overbearing and constant advice was the implication that Marriott needed the experience. He determined, not for the first time, that once he became an inspector he would never treat a sergeant like that.

It was half past eleven the following morning when Marriott knocked on the door of the Southfork vicarage.

Once again, the door was answered by Mrs Rudge, the vicar's housekeeper.

'Oh, it's you,' Mrs Rudge said, making it sound like an accusation. 'I s'pose you'm come to see the vicar.'

'Yes, we have,' said Marriott.

'You'm better come in, then. His reverence is in the drawing room. The death of the captain's took him bad.' Without offering any more homespun comments about Stoner's mental state, she led the way through the house to a room at the rear. 'Them policemen's come again, sir,' she announced.

'Thank you, Mrs Rudge.' Percy Stoner rose from his armchair and took a pace towards the two detectives. 'Mr Marriott, it's good to see you again. I hope you had a pleasant journey.'

'Yes, thank you, sir. This is my colleague, Detective Sergeant Catto.'

Stoner shook hands with each of them. 'I dare say you wouldn't be averse to a drop of whisky, gentlemen. It does help to keep out the cold.' Without waiting for confirmation, he crossed to a cabinet and poured three tumblers of Scotch.

'Very kind of you, sir.' Marriott thought that the vicar had been imbibing already that morning, if the slight slurring of his speech was anything to go by. He wondered if he was drowning his sorrow.

'I'm not quite sure why you've come all this way, Mr Marriott,' said Stoner, once the three of them were settled in the comfortable armchairs with which the drawing room was furnished. 'I had a policeman from the Norfolk Constabulary call to tell me that Guy had been killed, although he didn't know the circumstances.' For a moment or two, the vicar stared into the blazing fire. 'I think he was more upset at having to break the news than I was at receiving it,' he said, looking up once again. 'But he was very young. Probably the first time he'd had to do it.'

Waiting until Stoner had put down his glass, Marriott said, 'I'm sorry to have to tell you that your nephew was murdered, sir.'

Rather than appear shocked at this news, Stoner just nodded. 'I can't say I'm surprised, Mr Marriott. I thought it would be something like that. It's ironic when I think about it. Guy went right through the war without a scratch, only for this to occur. What happened to him?'

Without elaborating, Marriott went on to tell the vicar about the garage, the arrest of Holroyd for fraud, the finding of the bodies and the discovery that the other body was that of a young married Frenchwoman. He thought it unnecessary to mention that the bodies had been dismembered.

Once again, Stoner just nodded. 'I think it must be something to do with the war, Mr Marriott. All the standards of common decency seem have gone to the winds. The survivors of that terrible conflict appear to think that they can behave just as they like. I'm not suggesting that liaisons with married women didn't occur before the war; of course they did – but discreetly. This almost flagrant display of unashamed adultery is something quite new. I shouldn't say this really, being a staunch royalist, but I do believe that the Prince of Wales has much to answer for with his quite blatant carryings-on with married women.'

'You said just now, sir, that you weren't surprised that your nephew had been murdered, and that you thought something like that may have happened. Did you mean that his death was something to do with a woman?' asked Catto.

Stoner scoffed. 'He always had a girl on his arm, Mr Catto. He used to tell me in his weekly letters that he'd just met a wonderful new girl, but it was a different girl each time, and, as far as I was aware, most of them were single young women. You see, he had plenty of money,' he said, confirming almost word for word exactly what Holroyd had told the police about Guy Stoner. 'I met one or two of them, when he brought them up to Norfolk, and I had high hopes of him marrying and settling down, but then I realized that he was little more than a philanderer and that these women were merely playthings.' He took another sip of whisky and spent a few seconds staring, once again, into the fire. 'You said just now that you'd arrested this chap Holroyd. Are you charging him with Guy's murder?'

'He's only been charged with fraud, sir, but we're keeping an open mind,' said Catto, 'and we're confident of finding the killer of both Captain Stoner and the young lady.'

'I have no wish to teach you your job, Mr Catto, but it seems to me that if Holroyd defrauded my nephew, and my nephew took him to task over it, surely that's a very good motive for murder.'

'I don't suppose you know the names of any these young women your nephew was friendly with, do you, sir?' asked Marriott, not wishing to say that Holroyd had been ruled out of the investigation, mainly because, in his view, Holroyd was still a suspect.

'He mentioned one,' said Stoner. 'She was called Lavinia Quilter. I think Guy said that she was the daughter of an earl, so she would've been correctly styled Lady Lavinia Quilter.' He paused for a moment. 'He said he'd met her at a party, but I don't know if it ever went any further.'

Marriott decided that he had obtained all that he could from the Reverend Percy Stoner, and he stood up, followed by Catto. 'Thank you for the whisky, sir, and I'm sorry that we had to be the bearers of bad news. Rest assured that when we make an arrest, we'll inform you.'

Stoner struggled to his feet, carefully avoiding the tabby cat asleep on the hearth rug, and shook hands. 'Thank you for coming all this way, Mr Marriott, and you too, Mr Catto. It's much appreciated,' he said, as he opened the drawing-room door. 'I'll show you out.'

TEN

On Friday morning, the day after their visit to see the Reverend Percy Stoner, Marriott and Catto reported the result of their meeting to Hardcastle.

The DDI did not sound in the least surprised when he learned of the vicar's views of his late nephew, Guy Stoner. 'I wonder why he didn't mention it when you and I went to see him, Marriott.'

'Probably because he hoped Guy was still alive, sir, and would rather not have mentioned what he believed to be character defects. You know what clergymen are like about adultery.'

'Only half of them,' muttered Hardcastle. 'The other half are doing it.'

'He mentioned that Guy Stoner had once met a girl by the name of Lady Lavinia Quilter, sir,' said Catto, 'but the vicar didn't know whether they became close.'

'From what Sergeant Marriott was saying, it sounds as though he had a lot of girlfriends, Catto.'

'Is it possible that this is the woman that Holroyd was referring to, sir – the woman with the Triumph Super Seven motor car?'

'You're forgetting something, Catto. Gerald Walker has already identified the remains as those of his wife Celine. And Holroyd said he'd never met the girl.'

'Walker did faint at the sight of the dead body, sir,' Marriott reminded Hardcastle. 'I think he would have said anything just to get out of that room and leave the smell of it behind. And if you think about it, Walker only gave the face of the female victim a cursory glance.'

'Perhaps Stoner had so many girlfriends that he got them mixed up, sir. It must've been very difficult for him.' Catto chuckled at the thought.

'This double murder is no laughing matter, Catto,' said

Hardcastle sharply. 'But in order to clear up your doubts, I suggest you follow it up. According to Holroyd, the model of motor car this woman possessed was new this year. It shouldn't be too difficult for you to trace the owner, and then you can satisfy yourself that she's still alive. Don't forget, however, that Holroyd is a liar and a thief. He could have made the whole thing up.'

Detective Sergeant Henry Catto was an officer who did not believe in physical exertion if it could possibly be avoided, but that did not make him a bad detective. On the contrary, it was indicative of an officer who used his time economically and was therefore more productive. Consequently, he dismissed, as too time-consuming, the idea of contacting the car's manufacturers to get a list of purchasers.

Instead, his first act, in complying with Hardcastle's direction, was to consult *Burke's Peerage*, which listed the aristocracy, their forebears, their spouses and offspring. It did not take him long to discover that Lady Lavinia Quilter was the eldest daughter of the Earl of Wilmslow. The publication also revealed that the earl's country seat was at Durlston Park, Kings Worthy, just outside Winchester in Hampshire.

Enquiries of the General Post Office were disappointing. The earl did not have a telephone at his place in Kings Worthy, nor did he have a telephone in the London area which would have indicated that he had a residence there, too.

There was no alternative, therefore, but for Catto to journey to Kings Worthy.

Following an uncomfortable train ride from Waterloo that took nearly an hour and a half, Catto emerged from Winchester railway station only to find it was pouring with rain. Unlike Hardcastle, however, Catto never carried an umbrella.

His inclination was to find the police station which he understood from the *Police & Constabulary Almanac* to be in the Guildhall in Colebrook Street. He was, however, saved from what promised to be a rather wet journey when he spotted a constable of the Winchester City Police sheltering under the overhang at the front of the railway station.

'Excuse me, can you tell me how I can get to Kings Worthy. I'm trying to find Lord Wilmslow's place.'

'Are you now?' The constable, a man at least six feet and six inches tall, stuck his thumbs into his leather belt and looked down at Catto. 'And why would a young man like you want to go and see His Lordship? Are you one of them reporters?'

'No, I'm Detective Sergeant Catto of the Metropolitan Police.'

'Is that a fact?' enquired the policeman sarcastically. 'And how do I know that?'

'Will this do?' Catto produced his warrant card.

'Ah!' exclaimed the policeman and brushed at his heavy moustache as he examined the document. 'Begging your pardon, Sergeant, but you can't be too careful.'

'That's all right, cully. But why should you think I was a reporter?'

'We've had a few reporters sniffing about, most of 'em from up London, all wanting to know where His Lordship lived. O'course, we don't tell 'em nothing.'

'Did they say what they wanted, these newspaper people?'

'No, they'd never let on. Muttered something about it being confidential, which usually means they're hoping for a scoop. What's more, we haven't heard a dicky bird down at head-quarters.' The constable paused and brushed his moustache again. 'Mind you, there was some whisper about His Lordship's daughter having gone missing, but I don't know if there was anything in it. If you hear anything about it that might be helpful to us, Sergeant, I know the inspector would be very grateful.'

'Yes, but that rather depends upon me finding out how to get to this place,' said Catto, with a wry grin.

'Bless me, o'course it does, Sergeant. Here's me chatting away and I quite forgot what you asked me in the first place. It's about two miles from here, is Kings Worthy, and the place you want is called Durlston Park. I reckon you could walk it in about twenty minutes.'

'Good grief, I'm not walking,' said Catto. 'I'll get one of those taxis to take me.' He waved a hand at the rank where four or five cabs were waiting.

'You London policemen do all right, I must say, Sergeant,' exclaimed the constable, running a hand around his chin. 'Will your force pay for that, then?'

'Definitely,' said Catto.

Durlston Park was a huge Georgian house, set in rolling grounds with an ornamental garden designed by Capability Brown. It seemed to take ages to travel from the open gates to the house, such was the length of the drive.

Catto dismissed the taxi and ascended the steps leading to the front door. He tugged at the metal bell pull but heard no corresponding sound from within. Guessing that there would be some indication of his arrival in the servants' hall, he viewed the immaculate garden while waiting. He turned as the front door was opened, creaking on its hinges.

'Good morning, sir,' said the butler, as he cast a critical eye over the caller.

'I'm Detective Sergeant Catto of the Metropolitan Police. Is it possible to speak to His Lordship?'

'Thank God! At last,' said the butler, with a rare breach of his self-imposed professional reserve. 'If you care to come in, I'll tell His Lordship that you're here.' It was a statement that made a refreshing change from the somewhat fatuous pretence of enquiring if the master of the house was at home.

It was less than a minute before the butler returned and conducted Catto into the drawing room.

'Detective Sergeant Catto, my lord.'

Catto guessed that the Earl of Wilmslow was about fifty years of age. The agility with which he leapt from his chair and sped across the room to shake hands testified to his physical fitness.

'Come and sit down, m'boy.' Wilmslow glanced at his butler. 'Bring in some whisky, Patterson. I'm sure this officer could do with some fortification on a miserable day like today.'

'Very good, my lord.'

'Well, Catto, found my daughter, have you?'

'I think there must be some confusion, Lord Wilmslow. I came here today to see if you could tell *me* where I could find her. I presume we're both talking about Lady Lavinia Quilter.'

Further conversation was briefly stemmed by the arrival of the butler bearing a decanter of whisky, tumblers and water on a salver. He had arrived so quickly that Catto assumed he had prepared the tray of Scotch in readiness.

'Oh, put it over there, Patterson.' Wilmslow waved a hand in the general direction of a sofa table, before returning his attention to Catto. 'Now then, let me see. Ah, yes. I spoke to some fellow in the Winchester City Police about my daughter going missing. Seemed to be an important sort of chap, if the amount of silver braid on his uniform was anything to go by, don't you know. God knows what he did about it, because I never heard another peep out of the fellow. When Patterson told me you'd turned up, I naturally thought he'd done the sensible thing and called in Scotland Yard to do something about finding the girl.'

'When did Lady Lavinia go missing, sir?' asked Catto, once Patterson had served him and the earl with a tumbler of whisky each and left the room.

'Week beginning March the seventh,' said Wilmslow promptly, and took a sip of his whisky.

That was the week that ended with the fire at Ditton Garage, resulting in police finding the body parts that had been identified as those of Guy Stoner and Celine Walker. But Catto refrained from remarking on the fact, since the earl's comments seemed to throw doubt on Gerald Walker's identification of the body as that of his wife. Catto tended to agree with Marriott that Walker was so overcome at probably his first sight ever of a dead body that he would have said anything just to escape from the mortuary.

'When you say she went missing, sir, d'you mean that she didn't tell you or anyone else where she was going?'

'Exactly. Mind you, Catto, it wasn't the first time she'd gone off somewhere. Lavinia's become something of a free spirit since her mother died three years ago. Never takes a damned bit of notice of me. Just smiles sweetly and carries on as if I hadn't said a blasted word, don't you know. I even bought her a car, but it didn't make any difference. Yes, bit of a free spirit is Lavinia.'

'Did she have any particular friends, sir?' Catto was finding it difficult to extract any meaningful information from the earl.

'She was running around with some ex-army captain for a while, I believe. She brought him to see me once. He was only a temporary wartime officer, mind you,' said Wilmslow, in a vaguely disparaging sort of way. 'She said something about wanting to marry him at one stage, but then she found out that his only living relative was some pestilential priest living in Norfolk who would probably insist on them having a church do. Well, Lavinia was dead against that sort of thing. I think she wanted to bunk off and get married on some tropical beach.' He shook his head. 'I sometimes wondered, Catto, if she had a screw loose. I blame the bloody war, you know – it's changed everything.'

'D'you happen to know the name of this man, this ex-army captain, sir?'

The earl weighed up the question for a moment or two before replying. 'Lavinia said he was called Stoner,' he said eventually. 'Guy Stoner. Seemed to have plenty of money. Took the girl to nightclubs in the West End, don't you know. All the sort of loose behaviour the younger generation gets up to these days. Dancing the night away and all that sort of palaver.'

'Did this Guy Stoner have a moustache by any chance, sir?'

'Yes, he did. Damned great bushy thing.'

That interested Catto greatly and, on reflection, he wondered why he had asked that question, because it merely served to complicate the investigation to a greater extent. According to the Reverend Percy Stoner, his nephew did not have a moustache. *But Rupert Holroyd most certainly did.* And, to quote the earl, it was indeed a 'damned great bushy thing'.

Catto was on the point of taking his leave when the door of the drawing room opened and a woman entered – he guessed she was about thirty-five years of age – elegantly attired in a green dress that just covered her knees. She wore a long string of beads, and her hair was bobbed in what was known as an Eton crop.

'Hello, love,' she said, addressing the earl in coarse tones. 'Thought I 'eard voices.'

'Ah, Catto, this is my wife,' said the earl.

Catto stood up and took the woman's proffered hand. 'How d'you do, Lady Wilmslow?'

'I'm doin' all right, thanks, love, but do call me Dolly. Everyone does.' She held on to Catto's hand for a little longer than necessary, before turning to the earl. 'Where did you find this 'andsome young blade, Monty?'

'He's a police officer, Dolly,' said Wilmslow, smiling. 'He's here making enquiries about Lavinia.' It was apparent that Wilmslow felt he owed Catto an explanation. 'The countess is my second wife, Catto. She was in a revue at the Chiswick Empire when I found her a year ago. She gave a very good rendition of "I Wish I Could Shimmy Like My Sister Kate", didn't you, Dolly?'

'Yeah,' said the countess, and laughed loudly. 'I ain't bad when I get goin', even though I says it meself.'

Catto was aware that, in the enlightened nineteen twenties, members of the aristocracy were known occasionally to marry actresses and others in 'the profession', something that had been going on since before the turn of the century. But the new Lady Wilmslow, although possessed of a good figure, needed to work on her elocution. There again, he thought, perhaps it was one of the characteristics that had attracted the earl in the first place.

'I'll make some enquiries about Lady Lavinia, sir,' said Catto, 'and inform you of any developments. I understand that you're not connected to the telephone.'

'Certainly not. Wouldn't have one of the damned things in the house.' Wilmslow stood up and shook hands. 'Thank you, Catto, and I look forward to hearing from you. By the way, how did you get here?'

'Train from London, sir, and cab from Winchester station.'

Wilmslow tugged at the bell pull, and when Patterson appeared, he said, 'Get Tuppen to take Mr Catto to Winchester station, Patterson.'

'Very good, my lord.'

'Cheerio, love,' exclaimed Lady Wilmslow. 'Don't do anything I wouldn't do,' she added, and emitted a ribald laugh. 'That ought to give you plenty of leeway.'

When Catto alighted from the Earl of Wilmslow's Rolls-Royce at the railway station, he spotted the Winchester City policeman, who had just completed a circuit of his beat and had finished up back at the railway station.

The policeman shook his head and muttered a few words about the privileged officers of the Metropolitan Police.

Catto walked across to the constable. 'How do I get to your headquarters, cully?' he asked. 'I think I might have a bit of information for your chief.'

'It's in the Guildhall in Colebrook Street, Sergeant. Inspector Culkin is the officer on duty.'

'How far is that?'

'Walking distance? Just under a mile.' The constable gave directions.

'I'd get lost in no time at all,' said Catto dismissively, 'apart from which I'm a detective. I gave up walking when I handed in my uniform. I'll take a cab. Thanks, cully.' He strode across to the cab rank and hired a taxi.

The Winchester policeman shook his head. 'I think I joined the wrong police force,' he said, to the astonishment of a passing pedestrian who thought the constable was addressing him.

The sergeant manning the front office at police headquarters was probably nearing retirement age. He was overweight – his straining leather belt testifying to that – and his double chin seemed to spread over the stiff collar of his serge tunic. His moustache was even more luxuriant than that of the constable whom Catto had met at the railway station.

'Yes, young man? What can I do for you?'

'I'd like to speak to Inspector Culkin, Sergeant.'

'Would you now?' The sergeant appeared to puff himself up, as though this physical action would give weight to his authority. 'Well, my lad, you can't just walk into this here police headquarters like you was someone important and demand to see the inspector.' The station sergeant turned away as though dismissing the caller and his request.

'Let's get one thing straight, cully,' snapped Catto, irritated by what he saw as a country bumpkin dressed up as a policeman. 'I'm not "your lad".'

'Is that a fact?' The Winchester sergeant turned back again as Catto began to speak, doubtless annoyed by the sharpness of his voice, and fully prepared to make an arrest for causing a disturbance in a police station.

'I'm Detective Sergeant Catto of the Metropolitan Police,' Catto continued, 'and I'm involved in the investigation of a couple of murders.' He laid his warrant card on the counter. 'Either I see the inspector or I return to Scotland Yard and explain to my chief that the Winchester City Police weren't interested in what I had to say.'

'Hang on a mo, Sarge, I'll get the inspector.' Having puffed himself up, the sergeant now appeared thoroughly to have deflated, and promptly disappeared into the depths of the headquarters.

Catto picked up his warrant card and grinned at a constable who, having witnessed an unprecedented exchange between two sergeants, was standing at the back of the room with a bemused expression on his face.

'Detective Sergeant Catto?' The inspector who appeared proved to be possessed of a superior attitude. A slender man, at least by comparison with his sergeant, he seemed to be a few years younger, and had a neatly trimmed moustache. 'My name's Inspector Culkin. Come into my office.' He lifted the flap that allowed access to the administrative part of the head-quarters and led the way down a dank corridor.

'I understand from the station sergeant that you may have some information for us, Sergeant Catto,' said Culkin, as the two of them sat down.

'Yes, sir. I saw the Earl of Wilmslow this morning in an attempt to trace his daughter.'

'Did you now? And did you advise the head constable of this force that you were making enquiries in our force area?' Culkin, although apparently more amenable than the station sergeant, was clearly jealous of his police district. In common with officers of smaller forces, there was always an element of resentment when officers of the much larger Metropolitan Police arrived in their bailiwick intent on finding things out.

'No, sir.'

'Well, you should have done, Sergeant. It's common

courtesy, apart from the fact that it may result in subsequent enquiries that we can't deal with because we didn't know you were here. Anyway, how did you know where the earl lived?'

'I was given orders directly by the Chief Constable CID at Scotland Yard, sir, and the earl's address was, of course, in *Burke's Peerage*.' Catto did not want to get the helpful constable at the railway station into any sort of trouble and was sure that the inspector would have neither the courage nor the facilities to question a chief constable at Scotland Yard. 'However, sir, I'm willing to share what little information I obtained from Lord Wilmslow.'

'D'you mean you actually *spoke* to the earl, Sergeant Catto?' Inspector Culkin seemed quite taken aback that an earl should indulge in a conversation with a mere sergeant, but an even more startling revelation was about to be disclosed.

'Oh, yes, sir. He insisted that we should have a glass of whisky together, and he introduced me to Dolly, the new countess.'

'Good grief!' exclaimed Culkin, unable to take it all in.

'However, the information, sir . . .' Catto went on to tell Culkin what little he had learned from the earl about his missing daughter, Lady Lavinia Quilter, but forbore from suggesting that she might have been murdered. That would be much too much for the inspector to take in. 'My divisional detective inspector would, I'm sure, be grateful for any further information that you may come across.'

'Well, of course, Sergeant. We're always happy to assist other forces. Perhaps you'd leave his telephone number with me before you go.'

ELEVEN

Immediately following Catto's departure for Kings Worthy, Hardcastle had made a snap decision to send Marriott to Oakham in Rutland. Although the local police had assured him that they had checked Holroyd's alibi, and that he had stayed with his relatives over the weekend of the fire at the Ditton garage, Hardcastle intended to have it confirmed by one of his own officers. The decision surprised Marriott. It was not long ago that the DDI would have made the enquiry himself, trusting no one to do the job as well as he could. It was, to Marriott, a sign that Hardcastle was beginning to slow down.

Marriott arrived at Leicester railway station at five past eleven, about the time Catto was arriving at the Earl of Wilmslow's seat. Unlike Hardcastle, who would have taken a taxi to Oakham, Marriott caught a train for the half-hour journey. However, he did take a cab from the railway station to Cornhill Street, where Holroyd's sister lived with her husband and her widowed mother in a terrace house.

The woman who answered the door was probably about thirty, but her careworn face belied her age.

'If it's about the rent, my husband won't be in from work until gone six o'clock.' It was a statement that was spoken so automatically that she must have said it many times.

'I'm not a rent collector,' said Marriott, as he raised his bowler hat. 'I'm a police officer. Mrs Ethel Barton, is it?'

'Whatever's happened? It's not one of the boys, is it? I mean, the school would have told me if there'd been an accident.'

'It's regarding your brother's statement to the police that he stayed here one weekend in March, Mrs Barton.'

'But a copper has been here about that already, mister.' Suddenly aware that one of the neighbours was listening to their conversation, Ethel Barton quickly ushered Marriott into the house and, unlocking the door to the parlour, showed him into what she called the 'best room'. Despite it being late April and still chilly, there was no fire in the grate, just a newspaper folded, clearly with great care, into a fan shape.

'So I understand, Mrs Barton, but I'm Detective Sergeant Marriott of the Metropolitan Police, and I'm one of the officers investigating the fire at the garage your brother part-owned. He told us that he stayed here between the eleventh and the fourteenth of March this year. Is that correct?'

There was some hesitation before Ethel Barton answered, but then she said, 'Yes, I think he did. I'm not very good with dates. I remember he came up here for a few days last month, but I'm not sure what the dates were. My husband, Harold, would know for sure.'

'Is he here, then? I thought you said your husband was at work until after six o'clock.'

'That's right, but if you want to talk to him, he works at Springett's. It's the butchers in the High Street.'

The parlour door opened and an old woman shuffled slowly into the room with the aid of a walking stick upon which she leaned heavily. Her straggly grey hair was matted and uncombed, and her appearance suggested that she had dressed herself in the first items of clothing that had come to hand, regardless of their colour and without considering whether they were clean. 'What's going on, Ethel?' she demanded, casting a malevolent glance in Marriott's direction.

'This gentleman's from the police in London, Mother. It's about the weekend that Rupert spent up here last month.'

'Rupert's in the army, fighting for King and Country,' declared Mrs Holroyd. She stared more closely at Marriott. 'And why aren't you in the army, a fit young man like you?'

'The war's over, Mother,' said a clearly exasperated Ethel Barton. Marriott imagined that this conversation was one that took place quite frequently.

'Why hasn't my Roy come home, then, eh? It's all lies. That Lloyd George ain't to be trusted. It can't be over or my Roy would have come home.'

Ethel sighed. 'Roy's not coming home, Mother. Roy was killed at Passchendaele.' She turned to Marriott. 'His name's on the back wall at Tyne Cot cemetery in Belgium. They never found his body, you see. Of course, Mother doesn't believe it, even though we took her there to see the memorial just after the war. Roy was only a private, unlike his brother Rupert.'

'Some bobby from the local cop-shop come here about that,' said Mrs Holroyd, glancing at Marriott as she suddenly switched back to the present day and the reason for his being there.

'D'you recall the dates, Mrs Holroyd?' asked Marriott hopefully.

'No, I don't, mister. Anyhow, what's this all about? My son is a war hero, you know. He's a captain in the army in Belgium. He ain't no criminal, I can tell you that for nothing. And he ain't had leave for years.'

'I've met your son, Mrs Holroyd, and he's helping us to find out who set fire to his garage.' Marriott thought it impolitic to mention that Holroyd was in custody awaiting trial for forgery and was, at least in Marriott's view, a suspect for the murder of Guy Stoner and the woman whom Gerald Walker had identified as his wife, the former Celine Fontenau.

'You can't have done, mister. He's fighting in Flanders. Hasn't been home on leave for years.'

'Rupert left the army nine years ago, Mother. The war's over.' Ethel emitted a sigh of sheer frustration.

'You better speak to my son-in-law, Harold, mister,' said Mrs Holroyd, ignoring what her daughter had said. 'He's got a head on him, that one. He'll remember.' She ferreted about in the pocket of the shapeless woollen cardigan she was wearing and produced a white feather. Handing it to Marriott, she said, 'You should join up today, young man. If my two sons can fight, then so can you.'

'Yes, I think that's a good idea,' said Marriott, who had quickly realized that he was unlikely to make any progress with Ethel Barton and even less with her mother. 'I'm sorry to have troubled you, Mrs Barton. I'll let myself out.'

'It's no trouble,' said Ethel, as she followed Marriott out to the tiny hall. 'Speak to my husband; he'll remember. And I'm sorry about my mother, mister. Her mind's gone. It was losing my brother Roy that did it. She's never been the same since.'

*   *   *

It was only a short distance from Cornhill Street to the High Street where Harold Barton worked for Springett the butcher, and Marriott decided to walk.

There were three assistants working behind the counter of the crowded shop when Marriott entered, one of whom moved along the counter until he was facing the sergeant.

'Can I help you, sir?'

'I'm looking for Mr Harold Barton,' said Marriott.

'I'm Harry Barton. What's this about?' Barton was a big man, probably about forty years of age. He was a red-faced individual with a jovial countenance that gave the impression he would be a boisterous and amusing companion.

'Perhaps we could speak somewhere that's more private, Mr Barton.' Marriott discreetly displayed his warrant card in such a way that the other shoppers would be unaware that he was a police officer.

'Just a minute.' Barton turned to another man. 'There's a copper here who wants to talk to me, Mr Springett,' he said quietly. 'Can I use your office?'

'Yes, but try not to be too long, Harry. You know what Fridays are like. They'll be lining up out of the door in a minute.'

Barton led Marriott up a short flight of stairs and into a tiny office overlooking the High Street. There was only one chair and that was behind a small desk. The two men remained standing.

'Now what's this all about?' demanded Barton truculently, his voice changing to a hostile pitch. 'I told one of your blokes last month about Rupert staying up here, and I don't want you lot badgering me and my family. We gave your bloke the answers, so why are you back here again? Anyway, how did you know where I worked?'

'Your wife told me, Mr Barton.'

'Stupid bitch. I think having that batty mother of hers living with her is affecting her brain an' all. Anyway, you had no right to go calling at my house. It upsets the pair of 'em. An' I told that young copper of yours the same. I sent him off with his tail between his legs.'

'The officer who spoke to you last time wasn't one of my officers. I'm Detective Sergeant Marriott of Scotland Yard.'

Barton obviously needed to be brought down a peg or two, and Marriott decided unashamedly to gild the lily by stating he was from the Yard. It had the desired effect.

'Oh, I never knew that. Rupert's not in any sort of trouble, is he?' Barton was at once deferential, the mention of Scotland Yard having unnerved him more than a little. The headquarters of the Metropolitan Police had an awesome reputation that had spread throughout the world.

'That rather depends,' said Marriott. 'We have two cases under investigation, and it's possible that your brother-in-law may be involved in both of them.'

'Cases of what?' Barton began to fidget nervously with his wedding ring.

'I'm not at liberty to say at this stage, Mr Barton, but it's essential that you're honest in what you say to me; otherwise you may find yourself in trouble.'

'I don't think I should say anything else until I've spoken to my solicitor,' said Barton.

'Your unwillingness to confirm something that apparently you confirmed to the local police leaves me wondering why.' Marriott very much doubted that Barton had a solicitor or even knew how to get hold of one. 'Did you lie to the police officer from Rutland who came to see you and your wife?'

But Barton remained silent and it was obvious to Marriott that the butcher was not going to say another word.

Once Marriott and Catto had returned, Hardcastle sent for them. To their surprise, he invited both of them to sit down.

'What have you to report?' asked Hardcastle. 'You first, Marriott.'

'I'm not altogether sure that the police in Rutland did their job properly, sir. Holroyd's mother is suffering from senile dementia as a result of her youngest son being killed at Passchendaele, and is completely useless as a witness. Ethel Barton, Holroyd's sister, was uncertain about the dates that Holroyd was supposed to have stayed there. Either that or she was being deliberately vague, although frankly I don't think she's clever enough to be that devious. But then we come to Harold Barton. He's a butcher, and when I suggested—'

'A butcher, did you say?' Hardcastle suddenly became interested. 'I must have a word with Sir Bernard and find out if he thinks the dismembering was done by a professional. Go on, Marriott.'

Marriott considered the evidence that had been accrued so far. There was no indication that Harold Barton had a motive for murdering Guy Stoner or the girl, nor could he see any reason for him to travel to Ditton from Oakham – a distance of at least a hundred and fifty miles – to be complicit in one. On the other hand, he may have been covering for Rupert Holroyd, who possibly had not been in Oakham that weekend at all. But he did not share those thoughts with the DDI. 'I spoke to Barton at his place of work, sir, but the moment I told him who I was and why I was there, he clammed up. He refused to say anything until he'd spoken to his solicitor – not that I think he's got a solicitor.'

'Did he indeed! We find two dismembered bodies and then we come across a butcher who doesn't want to talk to the police.' Hardcastle took his pipe from the ashtray and teased the remains of the tobacco from it with the point of a paperknife. 'I think, Marriott,' he continued thoughtfully, as he began to fill his pipe with St Bruno, 'that we'll have to speak to Mr Barton, preferably at a police station. And that means that we'll have to involve the Rutland Constabulary, which is a nuisance.'

'Couldn't we have them arrest Barton on suspicion of murder, sir, and then fetch him down here for interview?'

'D'you know, Marriott, I do believe you're beginning to think like an inspector.' Hardcastle lit his pipe and, with a satisfied smile on his face, emitted a plume of smoke towards his nicotine-stained ceiling. 'Well, Catto, and what did you find out in the wilds of Hampshire?'

'Far from learning the present whereabouts of Lady Lavinia Quilter, sir, the Earl of Wilmslow was under the impression that I was looking for her on behalf of the Winchester City Police. He reported Lady Lavinia missing to that force on Monday the seventh of March, sir.'

'Did he, be damned!' exclaimed Hardcastle. 'That's the week that the fire took place, and I'm beginning to think that it's also the week when Stoner and the girl were murdered.'

'There's a further complication, sir . . .'

'Yes, there always is when you're involved, Catto,' muttered Hardcastle. 'What is it?'

'The earl said that Lady Lavinia had been going around with Stoner, and that they'd visited West End nightclubs and the like. On one occasion, the earl said, her ladyship had taken Stoner to Kings Worthy to meet him. But the earl was adamant that the Stoner he met had a large, bushy moustache. If you remember, sir, the vicar gave you a photograph of Guy Stoner in uniform, and he was clean-shaven. Sergeant Marriott told me that, according to the vicar, young Stoner had shaved off his moustache in 1916 after the army had rescinded the order requiring officers to grow one.'

'Yes, dammit, I do remember,' said Hardcastle.

For a few minutes, the DDI sat in silent contemplation, and Marriott knew what was about to happen. On so many occasions in the past, he had witnessed one of Hardcastle's thoughtful moods, after which he would come up with some bizarre course of action that very often resulted in solving the case. Marriott had only one reservation: he believed that Hardcastle's renowned detective abilities had started to diminish with age, and that he might now make a wrong decision.

At last, Hardcastle moved forward in his chair. 'We'll get a warrant for the arrest of Harold Barton, Marriott, and bring him down here for a talk. See to it, will you.'

'Yes, sir,' said Marriott wearily.

'What do we know about this here Rutland Constabulary?'

'It's very small, sir – only a handful of officers.'

'Oh dear!' exclaimed Hardcastle, with mock concern. 'Small forces are always jealous of their bailiwick, but that won't stop us seeking their assistance.'

On the Saturday morning, Hardcastle decided that he would go to Bow Street himself to obtain the warrant for Harold Barton's arrest. It was not that he distrusted Marriott, but the application for the arrest of a man in Rutland was unusual in that Hardcastle merely wanted to question him. That the application was made by a divisional detective inspector rather than a detective sergeant lent weight to the importance attached to the matter.

The warrant was granted, and Hardcastle returned to his office at Cannon Row.

'Marriott, get on that telephone machine and tell the Rutland Constabulary to arrest Harold Barton and that we'll send two officers up to Oakham to collect him.'

'It'll be quicker to send a message by telegraph, sir.'

'Well, do it,' said Hardcastle tetchily. 'You know I can't abide all this modern equipment they keep foisting on us, Marriott. It'll not last; you mark my words.'

'Yes, sir.' Marriott refrained from pointing out that the telegraph system had been installed in every Metropolitan Police station some sixty years before.

Marriott sent his message requesting that the Rutland Constabulary arrest Harold Barton and asked them to inform the Metropolitan Police when this had been done.

The result, however, was not quite what either he or Hardcastle had expected.

'Excuse me, sir,' said Marriott, entering Hardcastle's office.

'What is it?'

'The Rutland Constabulary is not prepared to arrest Barton, sir. They suggest we send two officers to Rutland with the warrant and have it backed by a local magistrate. The arrest should then be carried out by the officer named on the warrant.' Marriott hesitated before adding, 'That's you, sir.'

'Hell's bells and buckets of blood!' yelled Hardcastle. 'Don't they know anything about the bloody law up there in Rutland? I've never heard such damned claptrap in all my service. That warrant was issued by the Chief Metropolitan Magistrate. Who was the jack-in-office who sent this reply?'

'The Chief Constable of Rutland, sir.'

'Was it indeed? Well, I shall arrange for him to have a conversation with the Chief Constable of the CID at Scotland Yard.' Hardcastle stood up and seized his bowler hat and umbrella.

Returning twenty minutes later, he shouted for Marriott as he passed the door to the detectives' room.

'Mr Wensley explained the status of Sir John Hanbury, the

Chief Magistrate, to the Chief Constable of Rutland, Marriott, and he eventually understood. Rutland officers will make the arrest, but Mr Wensley suggested that it would save time and trouble if you and I went up there rather than waiting for Barton to be brought down here. Rutland will arrest him as soon as possible and advise us when they've done so.'

'When do we go to Oakham, sir?'

'Tomorrow,' said Hardcastle, as though that were obvious. 'You didn't have anything planned for Sunday, did you?' He posed the question airily, as though CID officers should never make plans for anything of a social nature, even on a Sunday.

'No, sir,' said Marriott wearily, wondering how he was going to explain to Lorna, his wife, the cancellation of a family day out to the Regent's Park zoo.

'Good. How do we get there?'

'From St Pancras, sir. It'll take about an hour and a half to Leicester. And then there's a train from there to Oakham that takes a further half an hour.'

'One train ride will be quite enough. We'll take a cab from Leicester to Oakham. While you're waiting for Rutland to tell you they've arrested Barton, you'd better make some enquiries about local hotels, Marriott, in case we have to stay overnight.'

It was at six o'clock in the evening that the call from Rutland Constabulary came through. Harold Barton was in custody at Oakham police station where he would be held overnight pending the arrival of the Metropolitan Police officers. There was a caveat, however. If officers from London did not arrive on Sunday, Barton would be released without charge.

'Damn it!' explained Hardcastle. 'The sooner that pygmy police force is taken over by the Leicestershire police the better.' But it was to be another twenty-four years before that amalgamation took place.

'There's a very good pub in the Market Place at Oakham that does accommodation, sir.'

'Well, at least there'll be some benefit coming out of this fiasco, I suppose, Marriott. I hope they sell decent ale.'

TWELVE

Sunday morning did not start well for Hardcastle. Having reminded Marriott to purchase second-class train tickets and to buy him a copy of the *News of the World*, Hardcastle was annoyed to discover that the St Pancras station bookstall had run out of the DDI's favourite Sunday paper, and only copies of the *Sunday Pictorial* remained.

And as if that was not enough, the newspaper's front page carried a two-year-old account of the murderer Norman Thorne's lovers, one of whom he had killed and dismembered at his chicken farm in Sussex in 1925. Sir Bernard Spilsbury had given telling evidence in the case, and Thorne had been hanged. Sir Bernard had mentioned it when examining the grisly remains of Stoner and the woman found at Ditton, and he had drawn a comparison between that and the Thorne case. The newspaper account also had the effect of reminding Hardcastle that he was no nearer finding the murderer's identity than he had been at the outset.

It was nearing eleven o'clock when the two detectives arrived at Oakham police station.

'Can I help you?' asked the station sergeant.

'I'm Divisional Detective Inspector Hardcastle of the Metropolitan Police. You have Harold Barton in custody at this station.'

'Yes, sir, that's correct. He's not very happy about it either, protesting that he's done nothing wrong. He also asked if he could go to church, it being a Sunday like.'

'I'm not interested in whether he's happy or miserable, Sergeant, or whether he missed out on having a pray. He'd be better off talking to a solicitor than a priest. Do you have an interview room here?'

'Yes, sir, we do.'

'Be so good as to show me where it is, and then have the prisoner Barton brought up.'

'Well, sir, but I—'

'Thank you, Sergeant,' said Hardcastle, in such a way as to stem any further discussion of the matter.

Harold Barton, not only annoyed at what he saw as an unjustified arrest, but intent on making a protest, irritably shook off the restraining hand of the constable who brought him to the interview room. It was made more difficult because he was holding up his trousers, a conscientious sergeant having removed the prisoner's belt, braces and necktie, for fear that he might be tempted to hang himself.

'I want to complain about being dragged in here last night as if I was some common criminal,' protested Barton loudly. 'I'm going to write to my MP and I'm going to—'

'Sit down and shut up,' said Hardcastle mildly.

For a moment or two the butcher stared aggressively at Hardcastle, but then, sensing that the DDI was a man whom it would be unwise to cross, sat down on the chair opposite the two detectives. At that point, he recognized Marriott. 'Oh, it's you,' he said, as if blaming the sergeant for his present predicament.

'I'm Divisional Detective Inspector Hardcastle of New Scotland Yard,' began the DDI, unwittingly following Marriott's example in enhancing his status, 'and I'm going to ask you some questions. I strongly advise you to answer them truthfully; otherwise I'll remove you to London where you'll probably be charged with conspiracy to murder.'

'*What?*' Barton went white in the face and gripped the sides of the table. 'I never done no murder, mister, as God's my witness.'

'Sir Bernard Spilsbury,' continued Hardcastle, as though Barton's outburst had not occurred, 'is the best forensic pathologist in the world. He has examined two bodies that were found at the site of a garage in Ditton, Surrey, which was part-owned by your brother-in-law, Captain Rupert Holroyd.' He paused to give his next statement impact. 'The bodies had been dismembered and Sir Bernard's professional opinion is that whoever was responsible for that dismembering had received professional training. *Like a butcher!*'

It was enough. Barton began sweating, little rivulets of

perspiration running down his red face. Taking his handkerchief from his pocket, he started to dab at his face and neck.

'It's not what you think, Inspector,' Barton was eventually able to gasp. Even though he had been deprived of his tie, he felt almost as if he was choking.

'Well, that's original,' said Hardcastle, leaning back in his chair and taking out his pipe and tobacco. 'But I'll tell you what I *am* thinking. I'm thinking that your brother-in-law murdered his partner and his partner's girlfriend in a fit of rage and then realized that he'd have to get rid of the bodies. Enter Harold Barton, *the butcher of Oakham*.' The DDI made it sound as though Barton was a psychotic mass murderer. 'The weekend Rupert Holroyd told me that he was in Oakham, staying with you and your family in Cornhill Street, he was really in Ditton committing a double murder. He probably then sent you a telegram – or got in contact somehow – pleading with you to go south and help him out. Which you did, no doubt for a handsome fee – money he'd actually stolen from Captain Guy Stoner, one of his victims.'

Hardcastle began to fill his pipe, and Marriott took over the questioning. 'The situation is this, Barton. My inspector is of a mind to charge you with murder or conspiring to commit murder.'

'And it'll give me great pleasure to see you dancing on the hangman's trap at eight o'clock one morning, Barton,' put in Hardcastle, as he was lighting his pipe.

'Even if my inspector goes down the scale a bit and instead charges you with being an accessory after the fact or even disposing of a corpse with intent to obstruct or prevent a coroner's inquest, you'll still be facing the rest of your life in prison.' That was unlikely, but Marriott felt that emphasizing the gravity of Barton's situation would encourage him to tell the police exactly what did happen.

'Could I have a drink of water?' pleaded the sweating Barton, only just managing to get the words out. For a moment, it looked as though the butcher might fall off his chair in a dead faint.

Marriott went to the door of the interview room. 'Constable!'

'Sir?' The policeman outside responded immediately.

'Would you get some water for the prisoner, please.'

'Yes, sir, right away, sir.'

Moments later, the officer returned with an enamel jug of water and a tin mug that he placed on the table. 'Will that be all, sir?'

'Thank you, yes,' said Marriott, wondering if the policeman had ever been a footman or a butler as his deferential attitude seemed to suggest. He could not be bothered to correct the PC's assumption that he was an inspector. He watched as Barton gulped down a full mug of water. 'Well, d'you have anything to say, Barton?'

'It didn't happen like that, sir.'

'Then tell me how it did happen, Barton,' said Hardcastle, now taking a renewed interest.

'Rupert spent the whole of that weekend bedding some doxy in Hampshire, and when he got back on the Sunday afternoon, he found two bodies in the office of the garage what him and Mr Stoner owned. Well, he must've panicked because he'd told me before that he'd been stealing money from Mr Stoner's bank account and that the law would think he'd done him in because he was going to peach on him.'

'It had already happened,' said Hardcastle quietly. 'We know all about the forged cheques, but do go on with this fascinating story.'

'So, first thing on Monday morning, Rupert is on the phone to the shop where I work – Springett's in the High Street – in a right panic. He said I'd got to get on the next train straight away and get down there as soon as I could. He said he'd make it worth my while. And that's what happened. I told my boss that my missus had been taken to hospital, and he said to take as much time off as I needed.'

'So, what did you do?'

'I caught the next train from Leicester and met Rupert at the garage. I cut up the bodies and Rupert buried them, some bits in the old workshop and some others in the chicken run, and I think he put one of the heads in an old biscuit tin and chucked it on a pile of rubbish in the corner of the yard. Then Rupert set fire to the office and the workshop. I pushed off back here straight after that, and Rupert said he was going to

call the fire brigade like he'd just arrived and found the place
burning. But before he left, he said that if the bogeys come
asking if he'd been at Oakham that weekend, I was to tell 'em
yes, because that was going to be his story.'

'What a wonderful tale,' said Hardcastle, relighting his pipe,
'and I don't believe a word of it.'

'But it's the God's honest truth, sir. I swear it. You've got
to believe me.' Barton's tone of voice had now been reduced
to a whining supplication, a radical change from the truculent
attitude he had adopted upon entering the interview room. But
it was to no avail.

'Where were the bodies when you arrived, Barton?'

'In the workshop. It's where I did the cutting up.'

'Sergeant Marriott and I will take you back to London today,
and you'll be charged with the offence Sergeant Marriott
mentioned just now – disposing of a corpse with intent to
prevent an inquest. But I warn you, Barton, that's only a
holding charge. I've no doubt that more serious charges will
follow.'

'But what's going to happen to Ethel and the bairns?'

'You should have thought of that before you rushed down
to Ditton and took your handful of dirty gold,' said Hardcastle.
'Incidentally, what did you use to dismember those bodies?'

'I took my own set of saws and knives down there with me.
Every butcher worth his salt has his own set. Rupert had told
me what I had to do, so I knew to bring my own kit.'

'Going equipped,' muttered Hardcastle. 'Evidence of intent.'
But he meant intent to murder. 'And I suppose you used those
tools of your trade to cut up someone's weekend joint when
you went back to work.'

'Yes, sir.'

'God help us!' exclaimed Hardcastle.

It was late evening by the time Hardcastle and Marriott got
back to London and charged Harold Barton. At nine o'clock,
Hardcastle sent Marriott home, and Hardcastle went home
himself. Straight into a heated discussion about telephones.

'If only you'd have a telephone connected, Ernie,' said his
wife, Alice, 'you could ring me up and I could have your

supper ready for you when you walk through the door. As it is, I have to wait till you're here and then start cooking.'

'For the last time, Alice, I'm not having one of those things in this house, and that's final. Just imagine what would happen if someone at the station didn't know what to do. They'd be straight on it, ringing me up and asking my advice.'

'They wouldn't dare,' said Alice drily. 'But you never give a thought for me, do you, Ernest?'

'I think about you all the time, Alice, my dear,' said Hardcastle apprehensively. Whenever Alice used his full Christian name, he knew that some criticism was about to be directed at him.

'Maud and Charles are back in Aldershot now, as you well know. And they have a telephone.' Their daughter Maud had married Charles Spencer, an army officer, back in 1919.

'Yes, but he's a lieutenant colonel, Alice, and he's in command of the battalion.'

'Exactly. That is so his officers can telephone him whenever there's something he needs to know about. And you're a divisional detective inspector and you're in command of all the CID officers on A Division – so what's the difference? Apart from anything else,' Alice continued, before her husband was able to mount a counter-argument, 'it would very nice if I could ring Maud from time to time. Much more personal than exchanging letters every week, and I'd like to know how the children were getting on at school, for instance, or if Maud wanted to ask my advice if they had any health problems, she could just ring me. I would have thought that you'd take a greater interest in your daughter and son-in-law and your grandchildren.'

'I speak to Walter every so often.' The moment he had spoken, Hardcastle realized that in attempting to defend himself, he had made a mistake.

'Yes, and I'd like to speak to him, too,' said Alice triumphantly. 'But you use the police telephone at Cannon Row to talk to Wally on his police telephone at the Flying Squad, don't you? It doesn't cost you a penny. And that's the truth of the matter, isn't it, Ernest? You're too mean. Aren't you interested in your grandson Edward or how Wally's wife is?

In case you'd forgotten, her name's Muriel and she's expecting another child two months from now. Or had you forgotten that, too?'

'I'll look into it, Alice,' said Hardcastle reluctantly. He knew that his wife would keep on and on until eventually he capitulated.

'I've already looked into it,' announced Alice. 'It's perfectly simple. You go and see the GPO telephone manager in Lambeth and apply to have a line installed. It's not expensive, either,' she said, forestalling Hardcastle's next question. 'What's more, because you're an important police officer, they'd probably install it the very next day.'

'How did you find out about all that?' Hardcastle felt he was fighting a rearguard action.

'I met Mrs Burns in Boxall's, the newsagents. She had a telephone installed just before Christmas, and she told me all about it and how easy it was.'

'Who's Mrs Burns?'

'She's the wife of a station sergeant at Nine Elms, and they live in Lambeth Road, just round the corner from us.'

'You've been talking to a station sergeant's wife about things like that?' Hardcastle sounded outraged and incredulous that his wife should do such a thing.

'And why shouldn't I, Ernest? You might be in the police force, but I'm not, and neither is Mrs Burns.'

'What's for supper?' asked Hardcastle.

On Monday morning, Hardcastle was back at Bow Street police court.

'Put up Harold Barton,' said the clerk of the court.

Barton, whose appearance accurately portrayed a man who had not slept at all, gazed around Number One Court, his face expressing a combination of awe and fear.

Hardcastle stepped into the witness box. 'Ernest Hardcastle, Divisional Detective Inspector A Division, Your Worship.'

'Yes, Mr Hardcastle?' The Chief Magistrate fingered his regimental necktie and acknowledged the DDI with a slight inclination of his head.

'Yesterday, Your Worship, Harold Barton was arrested in

Oakham in the County of Rutland on a warrant granted by
you. He is charged with conspiring with another person or
persons, not in custody, of disposing of a corpse with intent
to prevent a coroner's inquest, against the peace.'

'I take it there is more to this matter than meets the eye,
Mr Hardcastle.'

'Indeed, Your Worship.'

'In that case, I shall not take a plea. The prisoner is remanded
in custody to appear at this court again on Tuesday the third
of May at ten o'clock in the forenoon.'

'Now all we've got to do is interview Rupert Holroyd,
Marriott, and get his side of this fanciful yarn that Barton
came up with,' said Hardcastle as he stepped down from the
witness box. But that proved to be more difficult than he had
imagined.

It was late on the Monday afternoon, after Marriott had spent
a fruitless hour making numerous calls on the telephone, that
he broke the news to Hardcastle.

'When Holroyd appeared before the Bow Street magistrate
on the nineteenth of April, he was released on bail of his own
recognizance in the sum of twenty-five pounds, sir.'

'Good God! Well, where is he now?'

'Nobody seems to know, sir. He was remanded to appear
again on the twenty-third of May, when it was proposed depos-
itions would be taken.'

'And I suppose they'd like me to be there. It would have
been nice if they'd told me,' said Hardcastle sarcastically.
'Where is Holroyd living, then?'

'The address he gave to the court was the Langham in
Portland Place, sir, but when I made enquiries at the hotel, he
wasn't there, never has been, and has not made a booking for
any time in the future.'

'And I suppose the court didn't bother to check whether he
was there or not.'

'That would appear to be the case, sir.'

'Well, I'm not waiting until the twenty-third of May to see
if he turns up at court,' said Hardcastle furiously. 'No, you
mark my words, Marriott: the bugger's done a runner. Surely

to God it wasn't Sir John Hanbury who let the damned man out on bail, was it?'

'No, sir, it was one of the more junior stipendiaries.'

'How on earth are we expected to maintain law and order if magistrates go around letting criminals out?'

'Apparently, the magistrate took the view that forging a couple of cheques was not a grave enough charge to warrant keeping Holroyd in custody, sir.'

'I'll put money on him still being in London, Marriott. Send out an All Stations message on that telegraph thing you're so fond of and arrange for his details to be circulated in the *Police Gazette*. Again! Maybe my son will find the bloody man for us for a second time. The Flying Squad must wonder if we know what we're doing.'

It was reasonably early, at least by CID standards, when Charles Marriott parked his bicycle in the hall of his police quarters in Regency Street, Westminster.

He walked through to the kitchen where his wife Lorna was preparing supper.

'Any news, love?' Lorna asked the same question every evening. She was, of course, keen to know whether his promotion to inspector had been announced.

'Not yet, pet. Ernie Hardcastle keeps telling me that it could be years yet, but he's only being his awkward self.' He took his wife in his arms and gave her a lingering kiss.

'Oh, please!' Doreen, the couple's sixteen-year-old daughter, appeared in the doorway. 'Aren't you two a bit too old for canoodling in public?'

Lorna broke away from Marriott's embrace. 'It's what keeps a marriage going, young lady, as you will find out one day, if you're lucky enough to find a man as decent as your father.'

'Are you an inspector yet, Dad?' Doreen asked, realizing that there was no point in pursuing that particular discussion, albeit light-hearted, with her mother.

'No,' said Marriott, 'but you'll know as soon as I am.' He turned to Lorna. 'I've been thinking, pet, that it's time we thought about moving house.'

'Where to?'

'There are some nice little properties in Catford. There are some on the market for about three hundred pounds.'

'Where on earth would we find three hundred pounds, Charlie Marriott?' Lorna turned from the cooker and placed her hands on her hips.

Marriott knew that stance and laughed. 'We'd get a mortgage, pet.'

'And what would that cost?'

'I've priced it. When my promotion comes through, my pay will go up to about four pounds a week. We could easily afford it and, quite frankly, pet, I'm sick of living in police quarters.'

'Don't you think we should wait until we find out where you're posted to, love? It's no good buying a house in Catford if you finish up somewhere like Staines.'

Marriott laughed. 'Ever the practical one, eh, pet?' He took her in his arms and kissed her once more.

'Oh, God! Not again,' exclaimed Doreen. 'I'm going to my room.'

THIRTEEN

London is a big place when you are looking for someone who probably does not wish to be found. Although a population of about eight million made searching for Rupert Holroyd rather like looking for a single needle in several haystacks, Hardcastle's men did their best.

The DDI had already lodged a request with the Assistant Provost Marshal for details of Rupert Holroyd's service in the army. Two days later, he received a call to say that the records were now available.

Hardcastle and Marriott entered the APM's office by way of Horse Guards Arch. As was so often the case, the dismounted sentry, rather than risk being reprimanded for failing to salute an officer, assumed that Hardcastle was an army officer, came to attention and brought his sword to the salute. Hardcastle solemnly raised his bowler hat in acknowledgment of a compliment to which he was not entitled.

The APM's clerk, Staff Sergeant Turner, looked up as Hardcastle entered the anteroom. 'Go in, Inspector, the colonel's expecting you.'

Lieutenant Colonel Roland Patmore was an officer of the Royal Fusiliers seconded to the Corps of Military Police. He was a tall, slim and distinguished man with a full head of jet-black hair, a neatly trimmed moustache and a hook nose.

'Ah, Inspector. How d'you do? Not met before. Patmore's the name. Just been sent here from the Tower. Tower of London, of course. Regimental headquarters, don't you know.' The APM shook hands with the two police officers. 'Have a seat, me dear fellah, and you too, er, Sarn't Marriott, is it? Yes.' He sat down himself and reached for a manila docket. 'Captain Rupert Holroyd. Late of the Royal Field Artillery. Hostilities-only commission. Temporary gentlemen, we called 'em. Applied to stay on. Unsuccessful.' The APM had a tendency to speak in short staccato sentences. Hardcastle assumed it resulted from issuing orders during intervals in the gunfire during the war. 'Reading between the lines of his personal reports, not exactly top drawer, eh, what?' He turned over a page in the docket. 'Was a clerk in a water company before the war. Somewhere called Oakham, wherever that is. Still, we had to take what we could get. Such a dreadful drain on officers, don't you know. Getting killed left, right and centre.' He closed the docket. 'Anything else, Inspector?'

Detective Sergeant Henry Catto was particularly diligent in his attempts to track down the errant Holroyd. He went to the Langham Hotel to make certain that they had not been mistaken when they told Marriott that Holroyd had not stayed there. But the head receptionist was adamant that Holroyd had never been a guest of the hotel. He also revisited the Ritz where Holroyd had claimed that he had once stayed but, as with the Langham, the staff denied all knowledge of the man.

Catto went to the Salvation Army refuge in Vandon Street, the address Holroyd had given the clerk of the court at Bow Street, only to discover that Holroyd had never been there at all. If achieving nothing else, Catto was proving that Holroyd was a habitual liar.

But then he came up with an idea. He walked across the road to New Scotland Yard and sought out Detective Sergeant Walter Hardcastle, son of his DDI, and the man who had arrested Holroyd at Kempton Park.

'Is DS Hardcastle about?' he asked as he entered the Flying Squad office. He did not know the younger Hardcastle by sight.

'Yeah, that's me.' DS Hardcastle was a tall, stocky man with black hair, and had been a keen rugby player until the new head of the Flying Squad, the deceptively cherubic DCI Charles Cooper, had told him to choose between the Squad and rugby. 'What can I do for you?'

'I'm DS Henry Catto from A—'

Hardcastle interrupted Catto with a hoot of derisive laughter. 'Bad luck, mate. You must be working for my old man. Looking for an escape route, are you? There aren't any vacancies on the Squad at the moment.'

'Don't knock the guv'nor. He's all right.' Catto was not a particular admirer of the Flying Squad, whose members he regarded as glory-seeking mavericks, and he instinctively leapt to his DDI's defence.

'Only joking, mate,' said Hardcastle. 'My name's Wally, by the way. Have a pew, Henry, and tell me all your troubles, apart from complaining that my old pot and pan keeps your nose firmly to the grindstone.'

'D'you remember nicking a geezer called Rupert Holroyd, Wally?'

Walter Hardcastle hesitated for only a moment before replying. 'Yeah, got it. Kempton Park on the ninth. It'd been pissing with rain for two days and the racing was off. We only managed to nick half a dozen, including Holroyd. What's the problem, then?'

'We're pretty sure he's done a runner,' said Catto, and briefly explained the circumstances surrounding A Division's interest.

'And you think this topping's down to him, do you?'

'Yes, because I don't believe this cock-and-bull yarn Harold Barton, his brother-in-law butcher, spun us about finding two dead bodies and chopping 'em up, just in case we thought Holroyd was the bloke who'd topped 'em.'

Hardcastle laughed. 'I don't believe it either, and I don't suppose my old man does.'

'I'm not too sure about that,' said Catto, 'but I think we're bringing him round to our way of thinking.'

'That's the trouble with toffee-nosed ex-officers like Holroyd. They think that can get away with murder, literally.'

'I'd have agreed with you but for the fact that he's not toffee-nosed at all. His family's on its beam ends. Hardly got two ha'pennies to rub together. It's surprising he ever got a commission. According to army records, he was a clerk at the water board in Oakham before the war started.' Catto went on to tell Hardcastle about Holroyd defrauding Stoner by forging cheques.

'I know. That's what I nicked him for. You put him in the *Police Gazette*. Anyway, what d'you want me to do? Arrest him again?'

'In a word, yes. We're not prepared to wait until the

twenty-third of May on the off-chance that he'll turn up at
Bow Street for committal proceedings, because we're bloody
sure he won't. I thought that you blokes were best equipped
to find him, seeing as how you've got a roving commission.'

'I'll have a word with the guv'nor,' said Hardcastle, 'and
he'll brief the teams to keep an eye open. Any idea where he
usually hangs out?'

'No idea at all. We know he was in the habit of frequenting
West End nightclubs, but I dare say his money's run out by
now. On two occasions he claimed to have stayed at the Ritz
Hotel and the Langham Hotel, but he hasn't been at either of
them. He also told the clerk at Bow Street that he was living
at the Sally Ann in Vandon Street, but never went near the
place.'

'If he's been used to the high life, and he's already been
nicked for fraud, it wouldn't surprise me if he turns to crime.
Serious crime, I mean. He's bound to be short of the readies.
Leave it with me, Henry. Give me your telephone number and
I'll give you a call if anything crops up.'

It so happened that Catto's decision to speak to Wally
Hardcastle, done without the A Division DDI's knowledge,
proved to be a wise move. His plea for help from the Flying
Squad came to fruition a week later.

It was due in no small part to the network of informants that
the Flying Squad was so good at cultivating. Word was put out
that Detective Sergeant Hardcastle would be very interested to
know of any jobs that were likely to come up involving an
ex-officer called Holroyd. Generally speaking, the villainous
underworld of London is very resentful of what they see as
'toffs' muscling in on crime, thereby preventing the working-
class villain from earning an honest living. Wally Hardcastle
was confident that if Holroyd turned to crime, he would learn
about it very quickly.

In the spring of 1927, it was finally admitted that the Crossley
tenders used by the Flying Squad were too slow for pursuing
stolen motor cars. They were also too easily recognized by
the criminal fraternity because of the wireless aerial on the
roof of the vehicles that resembled a bedstead. Authority was

given for the acquisition of six Lea-Francis tourers boasting
a twelve-horsepower engine under their bonnets, and capable
of reaching speeds of seventy-five miles per hour.

Almost one of the first cases in which these high-powered
cars were used in a chase began at a bank in Brompton Road,
not far from Harrods' world-famous emporium.

There was only one female customer in the bank when the
man entered at eleven o'clock that Friday morning. Making
sure that he kept his back to the woman and the staff by
pretending to write a paying-in slip at a counter beneath the
window, he waited until the customer had left.

The man immediately pulled up a tightly knotted scarf to
cover the lower part of his face and drew a revolver. Meanwhile,
and ensuring that the engine was kept running, his accomplice
waited outside in the Lanchester saloon that the pair had stolen
earlier that day. The man inside the bank approached the senior
cashier and, brandishing the heavy firearm, demanded all of
the money the bank was holding. As it was a Friday, the
robbers had assumed that there would be more money in the
bank than usual, it being payday. What they had not realized
was that many of the customers of the Brompton Road branch
were salaried and paid by cheque once a month.

Even so, the robbers netted about a thousand pounds before
making good their escape. It was the bank's policy not to resist
any attempt at robbery, but to hand over cash rather than risk
the death of a member of staff. However, the senior cashier
discreetly pressed a silent alarm button positioned beneath the
counter. The alarm sounded in the distant control room at New
Scotland Yard to inform them that a bank robbery was in
progress at the Brompton Road bank.

Within minutes, Scotland Yard had circulated details of the
robbery to the crew of every one of the patrolling Flying Squad
cars. It was no stroke of luck that one of those cars had been
parked in Brompton Road about fifty yards east of the bank
– the result of a guarded telephone call to Wally Hardcastle
informing him that word was out about a couple of 'toffs'
who were planning a raid on the bank in question.

The message from the Yard went on to say that the stolen

vehicle was moving in a westerly direction towards Fulham. The Squad driver promptly started the engine of his Lea-Francis and accelerated past the bank until he sighted what the Squad described as 'the bandits'.

Although the Lanchester was a vehicle with a horsepower of nearly twice that of the Lea-Francis, its driver was not a match for the Flying Squad driver, whose expertise had been honed on the famous Brooklands racing track.

The pursuit was a short one. The bandits' Lanchester got as far as Earls Court Exhibition when it spotted the Lea-Francis on its tail. The driver saw the police sign that the detective inspector in the passenger seat had lowered at the same time as he heard the strident ringing of the police car's gong.

In his panic, the Lanchester driver attempted to take the sharp right-hand turn into North End Road much too fast and, with a loud rending of metal, finished up wedged against the wall of a chapel. The two occupants of the vehicle, apparently unhurt, fled.

'Bless you, my son, for being such a God-awful driver,' muttered the inspector, as he and the two officers with him quit their car and gave chase on foot.

The two bandits now made the mistake of running into Fane Street. Ignoring the lane on the right that would have taken them into Star Street and some chance of outrunning the police, they found themselves in a cul-de-sac. Turning to face the approaching detectives, they held up their hands in surrender. Although possessing firearms, they were only too aware of the hangman's noose, and to murder a police officer would have guaranteed their execution.

Two of the detectives ran their hands expertly over the two robbers and seized a Webley & Scott revolver from each of them. Many of these weapons were in circulation in the years following the war and had been retained by the officers to whom they had been issued.

'You're nicked, gentlemen,' said the detective inspector, 'for robbing a bank.'

The two prisoners made a miserable picture seated in the interview room at Walham Green police station in Heckfield

Place, Fulham. The speed with which they had been captured
shocked them but, not being habitual criminals, they were
unfamiliar with the practices of the Flying Squad. It was almost
as if they had read Ernest Hornung's creation *Raffles*, the
gentleman cracksman, and assumed that being ex-officers they
were clever enough to outwit the bumbling police.

'My name is Prosser, Detective Inspector Prosser of the
Flying Squad.' The tough-looking policeman sat down
opposite the two luckless criminals and lit a cigarette. 'And
this is Detective Sergeant Allenby. And in case you were
thinking of pulling strings, he's no relation to the famous
Field Marshal,' he added, with a sarcastic cackle. 'Turn out
your pockets.'

Each of the men placed a wallet, a handkerchief, a cigarette
case and some loose change on the table. The police had
already taken possession of the money that the pair had stolen.

'And now we'll have your names.' Prosser turned to DS
Allenby. 'Get your notebook out, Charlie.'

'Horace Beauchamp,' said the man who had been driving
the Lanchester. 'Major Horace Beauchamp.'

'And you?' Allenby pointed his pencil at the other man.

'Captain Rupert Hölroyd.'

'If I were in your shoes, gentlemen, I should keep quiet
about your past glory,' said Prosser mildly. 'The judge will
likely tack a few more years on to your sentence if he hears
that you held a commission during the war. He'll say you
should've known better.'

'Dates of birth?' asked Allenby, and the two robbers
promptly provided them.

'What d'you think we'll get?' Beauchamp posed the
question nervously, almost as if he feared the answer.

Prosser lit another cigarette from the butt of the first and
leaned back in his chair, contemplating the dingy ceiling of
the interview room. Eventually, he returned his gaze to
Beauchamp. 'From my recent experience at the Old Bailey,'
he began, 'the going rate for robbery with violence is about
ten years' hard labour.'

'But it's our first offence,' said Holroyd pitifully. 'And Horry
here only drove the car.'

Prosser laughed loudly. 'Don't make any difference,' he said. 'You're both principals in the first degree. Anyway, it was first offenders I was talking about,' he continued mercilessly. 'Of course, if you're unlucky enough to appear before Mr Justice Avory, you'll probably cop a round dozen. His Lordship doesn't care much for gentlemen robbers.'

'Anything else, guv'nor?' Allenby asked his DI.

'Not for the moment, Charlie. Time to take our friends along to the charge room and introduce them to the station officer so he can put 'em on the sheet. Come along, lads.'

The station sergeant entered the charge room clutching a large book and a few sheets of official paper. Placing himself behind the charge-room desk, he glared at the two prisoners.

'Stand over here,' he said, gesturing to the space in front of his desk.

The two men were ushered into place by Detective Sergeant Allenby. DI Prosser stepped up so that he was beside the station sergeant.

'Names?' The station sergeant dipped his pen in the inkwell. Having recorded the necessary details on the charge sheets, he turned to DI Prosser. 'What are the charges, sir?' When the arresting officer was a detective inspector, the station sergeant had to accept that officer's decision.

'Armed robbery and furious driving, Sergeant. That'll do for a start.'

The station sergeant put the charges to Beauchamp and Holroyd, cautioned them and recorded their replies. Then he told the gaoler to put them in separate cells. 'West London police court tomorrow morning, sir,' he said to Prosser.

Henry Catto grabbed the pedestal telephone and unhooked the earpiece. 'Catto.'

'Henry, it's Wally Hardcastle. My guv'nor, DI Prosser, nicked your man Holroyd this morning.'

'What for?'

'Armed robbery at a bank in Brompton Road, along with a bloke called Beauchamp, another ex-officer. I reckon you can say goodbye to him for at least a ten stretch.'

'Not if he gets topped for murder, Wally.'

DS Hardcastle laughed. 'That'd save the taxpayer a few bob in feeding him.'

'When's he up?'

'Ten o'clock tomorrow morning, West London court.'

'I reckon I'll see you there, then, along with your old man.'

'I won't be there, Henry. It's not my job.'

Catto finished his conversation, crossed the corridor from the detectives' office and knocked on the DDI's door.

'What is it, Catto?'

'Holroyd's been arrested for bank robbery, sir. Up before the stipe at West London tomorrow morning.'

'Who arrested him?'

'DI Prosser of the Flying Squad, sir.'

FOURTEEN

Detective Sergeant Marriott could see no great point in he and Hardcastle attending West London police court on the Saturday morning, but the DDI announced that he would be there and ordered his sergeant to accompany him.

After the night's haul of prostitutes and drunks had been dealt with by the magistrate, Holroyd and Beauchamp appeared in the dock. Brief evidence of their arrest and the reason for it was given by DI Prosser of the Flying Squad.

The stipendiary magistrate made very short work of dealing with them. His view of gentlemen robbers was not improved when he learned that, despite the advice of DI Prosser, the pair had insisted on their former army ranks being put on the charge sheets in the hope that this might afford them some leniency. But if they thought that the stresses and strains of battle would mitigate the inevitable outcome of their arrest, they were mistaken. In point of fact, it had the opposite effect. The magistrate, who wore the regimental tie of the Devonshire Regiment in which he had served as a lieutenant colonel, had been appointed to the Distinguished Service Order for his outstanding bravery while leading his battalion at the Somme. He struck out the military ranks on the charge sheets, an action prompted by the fact that the first battalion of Beauchamp's former regiment, the Connaught Rangers, had mutinied in India in 1920, and had subsequently been disbanded in 1922.

'Remanded in custody to appear at this court again on Monday the twenty-third of May. Take them down.'

'D'you propose to interview Holroyd now, sir, before they remove him to Brixton?' asked Marriott, as he and Hardcastle moved out to the lobby of the court.

'No, Marriott, we'll wait till Monday and then we'll have a chat with him when he's nice and settled in his flowery dell.'

Marriott wondered why Hardcastle had insisted on going to West London police court simply to witness Holroyd's remand in custody. It was not something he would have done in the past; he would have sent Marriott if, in fact, he had sent anyone. Nothing had been gained by his coming here this morning. The remand prison to which Holroyd had been sent could have been discovered simply by telephoning the court inspector. Not for the first time, he had cause to wonder whether Hardcastle was, indeed, becoming too old for the job.

His Majesty's Prison Brixton was in Jebb Avenue, a turning off Brixton Hill in south-west London.

'Hello, Mr Hardcastle. Haven't seen you here lately.' The gate warder, whose name was Jim Wise, shook hands. 'To be honest, guv'nor, I thought you'd retired.' Wise had the appearance of a man who should have retired himself. He was balding and had put on weight since his uniform was issued, so that it strained at the buttons. That, together with his ragged moustache and bushy eyebrows, gave the appearance of someone who was older than his sixty years. Marriott thought that he had been put on gate duty because he no longer possessed the physique to tackle a violent prisoner if that situation ever arose.

Hardcastle laughed. 'I'll bet you've got a few locked up in here who'd wish I had, Jim.'

'You ain't wrong about that, guv'nor,' said Wise with a laugh that made his not inconsiderable belly wobble up and down. 'Who d'you want to see this morning?' Returning to the reception office, he donned a pair of wire-framed spectacles and peered at a large book that rested on the counter in front of him.

'Rupert Holroyd, Jim, on remand.'

Wise ran his finger down the list of remand prisoners. 'Oh, the galloping major's mate,' he said, glancing back at Hardcastle. 'Well, I hope he's still in one piece, guv'nor. Hoity-toity ex-officers don't go down at all well in here. Too many old sweats who fought in the war have finished up in here.'

'I know, Jim. I put one or two of 'em in here myself,' said Hardcastle.

'What's more, guv'nor,' Wise continued, 'they gave that Beauchamp and Holroyd a bit of a reminder that they wasn't in the Kate no more, if you know what I mean.'

'Did you see much action yourself, Jim?' asked Marriott, recognizing Wise's three war medals. His brother-in-law, Frank Dobson, was a regular captain in the Middlesex Regiment, having survived four years of trench warfare, and had explained to Marriott how to 'read' medal ribbons, particularly the three known as Pip, Squeak and Wilfred.

'Not really. I was at Étaples.' Wise pronounced it 'eat apples'.

'What were you doing there, Jim?' Marriott appeared to express a passing interest, but his brother-in-law had told him a few tales about Étaples and what went on there.

'I was on the staff of the training camp.' Wise sounded reluctant to admit it; the 'canaries', as the staff were perversely known, had the unenviable reputation of being sadistic bullies. 'It's just Holroyd you want to see, then, is it, Mr Hardcastle?' he asked, quickly changing the subject back to the present.

'Yes, please, Jim. I'm not interested in the bank robbery; that's the Flying Squad's job. I want to talk to Holroyd about a couple of dead bodies.'

Wise chuckled again. 'Now that sounds a bit more like your style, guv'nor.' He glanced over his shoulder at the availability board. 'I'll get one of the lads to take him up to the usual interview room. You know your way, don't you?'

Rupert Holroyd had a black eye, probably the result of the 'reminder' that Wise had mentioned. Although, as a remand prisoner, he had been allowed to keep his own clothes, his suit was now looking a bit shabby. His appearance was not helped by the fact that the prison authorities had deprived him of his braces, and he had no laces in his shoes.

'I've got a complaint to make, Inspector,' said Holroyd arrogantly, the moment Hardcastle and Marriott entered the interview room.

'What about?'

'This.' Holroyd pointed at his bruised eye. 'I got beaten up by some of the prisoners.'

'It's no good complaining to me. Speak to the prison governor about it.' Hardcastle turned to the warder who had accompanied Holroyd to the interview room. 'I'm sure you can arrange for the governor to entertain Captain Holroyd to tea, so's he can tell him all about his complaint.'

'Of course, sir.' The warder emitted a sarcastic laugh. 'I'll arrange for the governor to stand by for when it's convenient for the gallant captain to make himself available, sir.'

'I want to talk to you again about two bodies we found at Ditton at the site of your failed garage, Holroyd,' said Hardcastle. 'One of which you identified as Guy Stoner.'

'That's right. So, what's the problem?'

'The problem, as you put it,' said Hardcastle, is that we've arrested your brother-in-law, Harold Barton, in connection with this matter.'

'You've arrested Harry? Whatever for?' Suddenly, Holroyd's arrogance left him.

'At the moment,' said Marriott, 'he's been charged with disposing of two corpses to prevent a coroner's inquest and is locked up somewhere in this prison. But I dare say my inspector will charge him with murder, along with you, Holroyd.'

'But that's outrageous!' Holroyd's voice rose in panic, his face had turned a deathly white and he was visibly shaking. 'Why on earth should you charge Harry with that? He had nothing to do with any bodies. Nor did I.' It was as much as he could do to get the words out.

'That's not what Barton said, Holroyd. He's given you up.' Marriott rested his pocketbook on the table. 'He said that you sent for him and he helped you to cut up the bodies before the pair of you buried them. What's more, I interviewed your sister, Ethel Barton, and your mother, Winifred Holroyd, and they both failed to confirm that you were in Oakham at all that weekend. Your brother-in-law suggested you were somewhere in Hampshire enjoying a bit of jig-a-jig.'

'My mother's gaga,' said Holroyd, 'and my bloody sister's not much better. She was always simple.'

'What's your version, then?' asked Hardcastle cynically. The more he spoke to Holroyd, the less he was inclined to believe anything he said.

'All right, Inspector, I wasn't in Oakham. I admit that. As Harold said, I was in Hampshire with a girl.'

'Name?' Marriott picked up his pocketbook and took out a pencil.

'Oh, I say, is that really necessary?'

'Don't mess me about, Holroyd,' said Marriott, who was getting rather annoyed with the man's pretence of being of a higher class than the two detectives. 'You were a clerk with the water board before the war. You're as working-class as the rest of them in here.'

'Her name is Vinny Quilter.'

'I suppose you mean Lady Lavinia Quilter, daughter of the Earl of Wilmslow?' said Marriott mildly.

Holroyd's mouth fell open. 'How on earth—?'

'Never make the mistake of underestimating the police, Holroyd,' said Hardcastle, lighting his pipe and leaning back in his chair. 'Not that you'll have much of an opportunity, because you'll be going from here via the Old Bailey to the condemned cell.'

'For God's sake!' Holroyd gripped the edges of the table until his knuckles showed white. 'I didn't murder anyone. Please, Inspector, ask Vinny Quilter,' he pleaded desperately. 'She'll tell you I was with her that whole weekend.'

'There's just one problem with that, Holroyd,' said Hardcastle, dropping a dead match into the tin lid that served as an ashtray. 'She's been reported missing. Did you murder her, too?'

'Missing? But she can't be. I saw her three weeks ago. Took her out to dinner actually.'

'When exactly?' asked Marriott.

'It was Monday the twenty-fifth of April.' Holroyd recalled the date without hesitation.

'How can you be so sure?'

'It was her birthday. I took her to Kettner's in Romilly Street for dinner.'

'How did you get in touch with her?' Hardcastle was doubtful.

'I telephoned her.'

'In that case, you can give Sergeant Marriott the telephone number.'

Holroyd hesitated. 'Look, Inspector, she doesn't want her father to know where she is. She told me that she had a falling out with him or, more to the point, with this woman he's married. She's called Dolly and she's twenty years younger than Vinny's father. Vinny said that her father fell for the woman after hearing her singing "I Wish I Could Shimmy Like My Sister Kate" at the Chiswick Empire where she was a chorus girl. Anyway, Vinny accused her of going after her father for his title and his money. The upshot was that Dolly and Vinny had a blazing row, and Vinny walked out.'

'That's all very fascinating, but will you now give the phone number to Sergeant Marriott?'

'Yes, but only if you promise not to tell her father where she is.'

'The only thing I can promise you, Holroyd, is charging you with murder if you don't come across with that information right now.'

Reluctantly, Holroyd provided a telephone number on the Mayfair exchange.

'We shall be seeing you again, Holroyd,' Hardcastle said ominously, as he and Marriott left the prisoner in the capable hands of the duty warder.

'Remind me, Marriott, who it was who interviewed Lord Wilmslow.'

'Catto, sir.'

'Very good. Fetch him in here.' Hardcastle paused. 'No, on second thoughts, you go.'

'Go where, sir?'

'To see Lady Lavinia. Not that I believe she'll be there. I think Holroyd is leading us up the garden path. If that's the case, I'll charge him and his brother-in-law with murder and be done with it. The lawyers can sort it out.'

'Very good, sir.' Marriott was not at all convinced that the Director of Public Prosecutions would be prepared to go to court on the evidence that had been accrued so far. At least, not for murder. But he forbore from saying so, at least until he had seen Lady Lavinia. If, in fact, she was to be found at the address to which the Mayfair telephone number was connected. And that was the next job.

It had not taken Marriott long to discover that the telephone, the number of which Holroyd had been loath to impart, was located in a flat in Tonkins Mews, one of the turnings off Park Street in the heart of Mayfair. He also discovered that the telephone account was in the name of Miss Sarah Carmichael.

The woman who answered the door appeared to be in her mid-twenties, perhaps even a year or two younger. She was wearing a pale-green frock that came to just below the knee and was so straight that it completely disguised her shape.

'Lady Lavinia Quilter?' Marriott raised his hat.

'No, I'm Sarah Carmichael. But Vinny's here. Do come in.' The woman ushered Marriott into the tiny hall. 'Vinny,' she shouted, 'there's a rather gorgeous-looking man here to see you.' Although fast approaching his forty-fifth birthday, Marriott still retained his chiselled good looks and actually appeared younger than his years would indicate. 'How long have you kept him a secret, eh, you crafty girl?'

'Hello. Who are you?' The woman who entered the hall from a room at the rear stared at Marriott. She was about the same age as Sarah Carmichael and dressed in similar fashion, save that her dress was yellow. 'Oh God, have we met? Was it that champagne party at Boodle's last Saturday? I'm afraid I got a bit squiffy that night.'

'I doubt it, Lady Lavinia. I'm Detective Sergeant Charles Marriott.'

'Daddy's sent you, hasn't he?' Her question was almost an accusation, and her mood changed in an instant.

'Your father has most certainly not sent me. As a matter of fact, I've not met him.' Marriott was being truthful; it was Catto who had interviewed the Earl of Wilmslow. Although the Winchester City Police had been informed that Lavinia was 'missing', they had apparently done little or nothing about it.

'Oh, sorry. Well, we can't stand here. Come into the drawing room.' Lavinia glanced at her wristwatch. 'I say, it's cocktail hour. Join us in a Manhattan, Sergeant, and tell me what you wanted to see me about.'

'Not for me, if you don't mind.'

'Oh, of course – mustn't drink on duty, eh?'

'It's not that, Lady Lavinia,' said Marriott. 'It's a trifle early for me.'

'Oh, do stop all that "Lady Lavinia" nonsense. For goodness' sake, call me Vinny.'

Marriott and Sarah Carmichael sat down while Lavinia busied herself at the cocktail cabinet. With a panache that betrayed her expertise, she poured rye whiskey and red vermouth into a cocktail shaker and added a dash of Angostura bitters.

'These glasses are supposed to be chilled,' she said, as she poured the concoction into them, 'but I can't be bothered. Now, Sergeant, what was it you wanted to see me about?' Lavinia sat down in the armchair opposite Marriott and took a sip of her cocktail.

'I'll get straight to the point. Did you spend the weekend of the eleventh to the fourteenth of March this year with Captain Rupert Holroyd at your father's country seat in Kings Worthy?'

Lavinia was quite unabashed at the implication of impropriety. 'No, I've never heard of him. I spent the weekend with Guy Stoner. He was a captain in the war. Anyway, who is this Holroyd chap?'

'Can you describe the Captain Guy Stoner you spent the weekend with?'

'Tall and well-built,' said Lavinia without hesitation. 'But he had a bushy moustache that tickled terribly when he kissed me. We were talking about getting married at one time, but it turned out that his uncle was a clergyman, and I'll bet he'd have wanted Guy to have a church wedding, although Guy didn't say as much. Well, Sergeant, that's not for me, I'm afraid. When I get married, it's got to be on the French Riviera with lots of sunshine and lots of champagne.'

'How long had you known this Guy Stoner?'

'About three months. We met at a nightclub called . . .' Lavinia turned to her friend. 'What was it called, Sarah?'

'The Twilight Cabaret Club. It's in Brewer Street.'

'Is it? I wouldn't know.' Lavinia gave a gay laugh. 'Thank God for cabbies. They know where everything is.'

'And you've never heard of Rupert Holroyd?'

'No, never.' Lavinia crossed the room and refilled her glass. She turned so that she was leaning against the cocktail cabinet. 'You haven't explained what this is all about.'

'The man you spent the weekend with was Rupert Holroyd, pretending to be Guy Stoner. Guy Stoner was murdered sometime before that, and from what you're saying about having known this man you were thinking of marrying, it would appear that Stoner had been dead for some time.'

Lavinia Quilter's face suddenly lost much of its colour, but she managed to maintain the sangfroid for which the aristocracy is renowned. 'I think you must be mistaken, Sergeant,' she said in rather superior tones, and drained her glass in one gulp before replacing it on the cabinet.

'Ironically, it was Rupert Holroyd who identified the remains of Guy Stoner after his body was found.'

Lavinia sat down in her armchair rather heavily. 'Oh my God!' she exclaimed and ran her hands through her bobbed hair.

Marriott produced the photograph of Stoner that the vicar had given Hardcastle. 'Guy Stoner's uncle said that his nephew claimed to have met you.'

'I don't know him at all,' said Lavinia, returning the photograph after a few seconds. 'One meets so many people. I suppose I might have danced with him, but most evenings out end in a blur.'

'If we asked you to attend an identification parade, would you be able to pick out the man you believed to be Guy Stoner?'

'Yes, I certainly would. Why did this Holroyd pretend to be Guy?' Suddenly, Lavinia grasped the implications of what Marriott had been saying. 'Oh my God!' she said again. 'You think this Holroyd murdered Guy and then pretended to be him.'

Marriott did not answer.

FIFTEEN

Before leaving the mews flat that Lady Lavinia Quilter shared with Sarah Carmichael, Marriott had telephoned Hardcastle and secured his agreement for an identification parade to be held the following day.

On the Tuesday morning, uniformed constables scoured the streets in and around Whitehall to find seven men of similar appearance to Rupert Holroyd. By eleven o'clock, these men had assembled in the parade room of Cannon Row police station and were joined by Holroyd who earlier that morning had been escorted from Brixton prison by two warders.

Promptly at eleven o'clock, Lady Lavinia Quilter arrived at the police station. She was the very picture of elegance in a beige cloth wrap with matching cloche hat and suede gloves. In one hand she held a leather handbag, and in the other an *en-tout-cas* umbrella.

The uniformed inspector who had been deputed to conduct the parade escorted her to the station yard and explained what she should do if she recognized the man she knew as Guy Stoner.

Handing her umbrella to the inspector, she moved speedily along the line of men and unhesitatingly, and without uttering a word, placed her hand firmly on Holroyd's chest.

Holroyd was stunned to be confronted by Lavinia Quilter and was rendered momentarily speechless. He had no idea why the identification parade had been held, but he was even more surprised when she picked him out. What really worried him was the possibility that he was about to be accused of another crime of which, thus far, he was unaware.

Once the parade had been dismissed, and Holroyd was on his way back to Brixton prison, Marriott showed Lady Lavinia up to Hardcastle's office and introduced her to the DDI. Divesting herself of her wrap, she handed it to Marriott, along with her umbrella and gloves, and waited until a chair had been brought in for her.

'D'you mind if I smoke, Inspector?' she asked, and took a small gold case from her handbag, having made the assumption that Hardcastle could not possibly refuse. Then she waited until he leaned across his desk and applied a flame to her cigarette.

'Are you quite certain, Lady Lavinia, that the man you picked out was the man who pretended to you that he was Captain Guy Stoner?'

'I most certainly am.'

'And did he spend the weekend of the eleventh to the fourteenth of March with you in Kings Worthy?' Hardcastle blew out the match and dropped it into the ashtray which he then moved closer to his visitor.

'Yes, I'm positive, Inspector. He left Durlston Park early on the Monday morning.' Lady Lavinia blew a smoke ring and shot a quick smile in Marriott's direction as if sharing her indiscretion with him. 'But has he been accused of some crime?'

'On the contrary, Lady Lavinia,' said Hardcastle. 'You have just prevented him from being charged with the murder of Guy Stoner and a woman named Celine Walker.'

'But why should you have thought that Rupert what's-his-name had committed murder?'

'I'm not in a position to tell you about that, ma'am. It is what we call *sub judice*,' said Hardcastle, even though he was uncertain whether he was correct in his assertion. 'No doubt the newspapers will report it all in due course, but that won't be until after the trial. Thank you for agreeing to attend the parade, and now Sergeant Marriott will show you out and call a cab for you.' But as the young woman reached the door, the DDI asked, 'As a matter of interest, Lady Lavinia, where did you meet the man you thought was Guy Stoner?'

'At the Twilight Cabaret Club.'

'In Brewer Street?'

Waving a hand vaguely in the air, Lady Lavinia gave a gay laugh. 'You may well be right, Inspector. I must admit that I rely very much on taxi drivers to get me to where I want to go.' Marriott helped her into her wrap and returned her umbrella. At the door, she gave Hardcastle a gay wave. 'Toodle-oo, Inspector.'

Marriott walked Lady Lavinia up Derby Gate to Parliament Street and called a cab for her.

With one foot on the step of the taxi, she paused and turned. 'Your inspector's a bit of an old stick-in-the-mud, isn't he, Charlie?' She laughed. 'You don't mind me calling you Charlie, do you?'

'Not at all, Vinny.'

'I suppose you're married, Charlie?'

'Yes, very happily.'

'Dammit! All the best ones are.' Lady Lavinia blew him a kiss and climbed into the cab.

Marriott slowly ascended the stairs to Hardcastle's office, still chuckling at the extent to which young women like Vinny Quilter behaved since the end of the war, but at once thought that it was that war that had caused the change. Or maybe the aristocracy always did behave like that.

'Well?' asked Hardcastle.

'That rules Holroyd out of the murders of Stoner and the girl, sir.'

'You think so, do you, Marriott?'

'If he spent that weekend with the earl's daughter, sir, I don't see how he could possibly have murdered Stoner and the French girl. Sir Bernard Spilsbury was adamant that the murders had taken place that weekend.'

'I'm not so sure, Marriott. She might just be saying that to protect him. Did she honestly think he was Stoner?'

'I don't know what she thought, sir,' said Marriott, becoming a little irritated by Hardcastle's doubts. It was as though the DDI was looking for a loophole, and with it a reason to clear up two murders, even if it meant seeing the wrong man hanged. 'We mustn't overlook the fact that the Earl of Wilmslow was at Kings Worthy that weekend and also met Holroyd. Do you want *him* to come up to London to attend an identification parade as well?'

Hardcastle glared at his sergeant. 'I'll thank you to keep a civil tongue in your head, Marriott.'

'I'm sorry, sir, but I really do think that the evidence is strongly in favour of Holroyd being innocent.'

'He's a bank robber, Marriott.' It was Hardcastle's belief that once a man ventured into the world of serious criminality, he would thereafter commit any felony, including murder.

'That doesn't necessarily make him a murderer, sir,' said Marriott, as if reading Hardcastle's thoughts. He had been trying to dissuade the DDI from that blinkered view ever since he had started working with him.

'I think you need to concentrate on this here Twilight Cabaret Club, Marriott.' As Hardcastle so often did when he could find no justification for one of his wild theories, he changed direction. 'It seems to me that it crops up too often. First there's Walker bribing a waiter so as he could meet Celine and eventually marry her, and now the Lady Lavinia says that's where she met Holroyd masquerading as Stoner. I still think that Holroyd might have had something to do with them toppings down at Ditton. Who was it who made enquiries at this here club?'

'Catto and Ritchie, sir.'

'Send 'em up there again. And this time tell 'em to dig deeper.'

Despite Hardcastle switching his interest to the Twilight Cabaret Club, Marriott was sure that the DDI still had doubts about Holroyd. Being a younger man, and aware that changes were taking place in law enforcement, Marriott relied on evidence to a far greater extent than Hardcastle and was more than satisfied that Rupert Holroyd was not responsible for the Ditton murders. He knew that these days defending counsel were unlikely to accept evidence simply because it was given by a senior detective officer, as had been the case in former days, and would challenge it rigorously.

As he had tried to explain to Hardcastle, the Earl of Wilmslow had also met Holroyd and believed him to be Stoner. Not that he had met either him or the real Stoner before, and therefore had no reason to be suspicious of the identity to which Holroyd had laid claim. But the fact remained that Lord Wilmslow actually saw Holroyd in the flesh that weekend and could testify to the fact that he was nowhere near Ditton some sixty or so miles away.

Marriott's job now was to overcome the DDI's intransigence and persuade him not to waste any more time in speculating about how he could find Holroyd culpable. Marriott's own view of the man was that he was an ex-officer who had enjoyed the life of what the army scathingly termed a *temporary* gentleman, with a servant and mess life, and all that went with it. It was unsurprising that he wanted to continue with that mode of life, but he was soon to discover that robbing a bank was not the solution. The reality, of course, was that Holroyd had seen very little of the real life of an army officer, having spent most of the war knee-deep in mud tending his guns. Colonel Patmore, the Assistant Provost Marshal, had said that after the war Holroyd had applied for a permanent commission but had been rejected. He had gone on to say that Holroyd was not exactly 'top drawer', implying that the army had no room for a former water company clerk in the peacetime officer corps.

'Henry!'

'Yes, Sergeant?' Henry Catto rose from his place at the detectives' table and crossed the office until he was in front of Marriott's desk.

'Pull up a chair, Henry.' When Catto was settled, Marriott continued. 'The DDI wants you and Ritchie to go back to the Twilight Cabaret Club and find out as much as you can about this business of waiters being bribed to put clients in touch with the showgirls. Don't hesitate to make a few threats, but we've got to get to the bottom of this damned murder. If you get any trouble from the owner of the place, let me know.'

Catto laughed. 'I don't foresee having any trouble with him, Skip.'

Marriott laughed too. 'No, I think you're right, Henry.'

The immaculately attired man who greeted the two detectives when they arrived at the club at seven o'clock was the same man who had been on duty the last time they called. The owner had described him as the admissions manager, rather than the doorman.

'Good evening, gentlemen,' he said, with his customary suavity. 'Unless I'm much mistaken, you are the gentlemen from the police. Doubtless you'll be wanting a word with the major.'

'Thank you,' said Catto.

'I'll just advise him that you're here.'

A minute or so later, Major Leo Craddock limped into the foyer. Hooking his walking cane over his left arm, he shook hands with the two CID officers. 'No trouble, I hope, gentlemen.'

'I hope not,' said Catto, as he and Ritchie followed Craddock in his slow progress upstairs to his office.

'Scotch, gentlemen?' Without waiting for a reply, Craddock poured three stiff measures of Laphroaig. 'Now, what can I do for you?' he asked, as the detectives sat down. 'It's Detective Sergeant Catto and Detective Constable Ritchie, if memory serves me correctly.'

'Yes, it is.' Catto succinctly described the reason for his visit and emphasized that there seemed to be a link between the Twilight Cabaret Club and the murders of Guy Stoner and Celine Walker. 'I'm not suggesting that your establishment was involved in any way, Major, but it just happens to be the venue where the principals met.' He went on to repeat the story that Gerald Walker had told about bribing a waiter to pass a note to Celine Fontenau, as she had been then, and how Walker had subsequently married her.

'This is all very disturbing, Sergeant Catto,' said Craddock. 'I think I said, the last time you were here, that I try to dissuade the girls from fraternizing with the guests. Marjorie Hibberd does her best and the waiters are scared stiff of her, but human nature being what it is, a man and a woman will always find a way of meeting if there's a mutual attraction.' From downstairs there came a sudden burst of lively music, interrupting what Craddock was saying. 'Dixieland jazz,' he commented with a shrug. 'Our younger guests are very keen on it.' Returning to the matter in hand, he asked, 'Would it be helpful if I found the waiter who passed that note, Sergeant Catto?'

'It would certainly be a start,' said Catto. 'D'you think you *can* find him? Presumably he'll be facing the sack.'

'Oh, he'll get the sack all right.'

'In that case, he's bound to deny any misconduct. So how are you going to identify him?' asked Ritchie.

Craddock laughed. 'My head waiter is an Irishman and is very good at winkling out the truth.' He paused. 'At one time, he was my squadron sergeant major and a few years after the war he called here quite by chance looking for work. He was obviously down on his luck and I gave him a job. He turned out to be just as good a head waiter as he had been an SSM.'

'Would it be asking a lot if I requested you not to sack this waiter, whoever he is, Major?' said Ritchie. 'We might need to speak to him again on other matters connected with these murders.'

'Surely to God you don't think that one of my waiters is mixed up in a murder, Mr Ritchie?' Craddock sounded appalled at the very thought of it.

'Not at all, Major,' Catto answered hurriedly. He was annoyed that Ritchie had gone in with his customary bluntness and intended to remind him of Baden-Powell's oft-quoted maxim: 'Softly Softly Catchee Monkey.'

'I think it's time that I sent for Patrick Lynch. As I said earlier, if anyone can find this chap, he can.' Craddock leaned across to his desk and made a telephone call.

Two minutes later, the door opened and a man appeared on the threshold. 'You wanted to see me, sir?' Ramrod straight, his thumbs aligned with the seams of his trousers, he was immaculate in a tailcoat upon which was a row of miniature medals, worn at Craddock's insistence.

'These two gentlemen are from the police, Sarn't Major.'

'Are they indeed, sir?' Lynch nodded briefly in the detectives' direction. 'Not from Vine Street, I hope.'

'No, Mr Lynch, I'm Detective Sergeant Catto and this is Detective Constable Ritchie, and we're from the Whitehall Division, investigating two murders.' Catto assumed that Lynch had made the acquaintance of Station Sergeant Goddard and had probably taken an instant dislike to the man.

'That's all right, then.' Lynch spoke as though murder was an everyday event. But for a man who had daily witnessed death on the Western Front, that came as no surprise.

Craddock explained to Lynch what the two police officers hoped to discover.

'Ah, I see, sir.' Lynch glanced at Catto. 'Can you tell me this gentleman's name and the date he sent this note to Celine Fontenau, Sergeant?'

Although Catto knew the date, he checked by referring to his pocketbook. 'It was a Mr Gerald Walker and the incident took place on the ninth of October 1926.'

'I know who that would be, sir,' said Lynch to Craddock. 'I've had my eye on him for some time now. A bit of a crafty spalpeen is that one. Are you going to give him his cards, sir?'

'Very likely, Sarn't Major,' said Craddock, 'but I'll see what he has to say for himself. As you are well aware, I'll not stand for that sort of conduct. I'll ring down for him.'

'I could go and fetch him, sir.'

'No, I'll not have my senior staff running about after waiters, Mr Lynch. What's the man's name?'

'Albert Higgs, sir.'

'Why don't you take a seat, Sarn't Major?' said Craddock, as he lifted the telephone from his desk.

'Rather stand, sir, if it's all the same to you.'

'You wanted to see me, sir?' Albert Higgs did not so much enter the office as appear to insinuate himself around the edge of the door. He was a weasely little man with a pencil moustache, pomaded hair and the rounded shoulders of one of life's perpetual servants. He glanced apprehensively at Major Craddock, and with a sweeping gaze took in the head waiter and the two men he knew instinctively to be police officers.

'On the ninth of October last year, Higgs,' began Lynch, 'you accepted a substantial sum of money from a Mr Walker to pass a note of assignation to Celine Fontenau, one of the dancers.'

'You must've got me mixed up with someone else, Mr Lynch.' Higgs's nervous and unconvincing reply was almost a whine.

Lynch took a step closer to Higgs. 'I don't think you know how much trouble you could be in by lying to me, Higgs.' He spoke in low menacing tones. 'We're not talking about taking bribes – that's bugger all – but these two officers are investigating a murder.' He paused for effect. 'The murder, in fact, of Celine Fontenau. If I was in your shoes, Higgs, I'd be falling over myself to tell these gentlemen everything I knew.'

'Well, it's not something I usually do, Mr Lynch.' Already Higgs was beginning to formulate his defence.

'How many times did you pass notes to Celine Fontenau?' Lynch had now moved so close to Higgs that their faces were almost touching.

'About four times, Mr Lynch.'

'And who were these gentlemen who were so keen to meet the young lady, apart from Mr Walker, eh? The truth now.'

Higgs hesitated, as though about to claim that he did not know the identities, but seeing the expression on Lynch's face, he yielded.

'There was a Captain Stoner, a Major Beauchamp and a Mr Talbot.' The names came out in a rush, as though revealing them would somehow purge Higgs of guilt.

Catto had not interrupted Lynch's interrogation of Higgs but sat silently absorbing all that the waiter had reluctantly divulged. If the Beauchamp that Higgs had mentioned was Major Horace Beauchamp, then he was almost certainly the man now standing accused of bank robbery with Rupert Holroyd. Interestingly, the other name mentioned was probably Holroyd. He had used the name of Oliver Talbot for letters arriving at the Paddington newsagent when he was trying to sell the Ditton garage.

'And how much did these fine gentlemen give you for passing a note, Higgs?' asked Lynch. When the waiter paused, he added, 'I'm getting a little impatient, man.'

'They each give me a pound, Mr Lynch.'

'*A pound!*' Lynch was amazed. 'God give me strength.'

'Wait outside, Higgs, until I send for you,' said Major Craddock. He was clearly furious about the man's conduct. Patrick Lynch was beside himself and probably regretting that Field Punishment Number One, which involved tying a defaulter to the wheel of a limber for two hours a day, was no longer within the major's power.

'I really cannot keep this man in my employment, Sergeant Catto,' said Craddock. 'He sets a very bad example. Receiving tips is one thing and is an accepted part of a waiter's income, but to endanger the welfare of the young women we employ is quite unacceptable.'

'I agree, sir,' said Catto. 'As far as I'm concerned, Higgs is unlikely to be of any further assistance to the police.'

'Good. Fetch him in, Sarn't Major.'

When the miserable Higgs returned, his expression indicated that he knew what was about to happen next.

'Your conduct is quite unacceptable, Higgs,' said Craddock. 'You are dismissed with immediate effect.' He turned to the head waiter. 'I'll thank you to see Higgs off the premises, Sarn't Major.'

'It'll be a pleasure, sir.'

SIXTEEN

I t was now just over two months since the fire at the Ditton garage, and more than a month since the discovery of the two bodies, both of which had been identified. Hardcastle was becoming increasingly irascible about the lack of progress, but the irony of the situation was that he was involving himself less and less in the day-to-day enquiries. Although this rather pleased his junior officers, particularly Marriott and Catto, it at once laid them more open to blame when results did not satisfy the DDI's demanding and often unreasonable expectations.

On the morning following their visit to the Twilight Cabaret Club, Catto and Ritchie reported to Hardcastle.

'You'd better go and see this Beauchamp, then, Catto, and find out what he knows about it all. Where is he?'

'Wormwood Scrubs, sir.'

'Best place for him,' muttered Hardcastle. 'Report back when you've seen him.'

Leaving the police station, Catto and Ritchie crossed the narrow roadway to Commissioner's Office and made for the Flying Squad office.

'Is DI Prosser here?' asked Catto, looking around.

'That's me,' said a thickset man who had the appearance of being useful in the event that he was involved in a rough-house. 'Who are you?'

'DS Catto, A Division, sir. DDI Hardcastle has directed me to interview Horace Beauchamp up at the Scrubs. I thought I should let you know as a matter of courtesy.'

'What's that about, then?'

'My DDI fancies him for a couple of murders, guv.'

'Oh, yes. Wally Hardcastle told me about that,' said Prosser. 'But don't ask Beauchamp any questions about the bank robbery in Brompton Road. I don't want you buggering up my job, because Beauchamp's a sly bastard. Anyway, you know the form. Incidentally, Skip, I had a word with the military about him. It seems he was court-martialled and cashiered. Something to do with nicking mess funds. Bloody amateurs,' he added scornfully.

The forbidding façade of His Majesty's Prison Wormwood Scrubs was not a welcoming sight, even for visiting police officers.

'I'm Detective Sergeant Catto, Metropolitan Police,' said Catto, displaying his warrant card to the gate warder, 'and this is Detective Constable Ritchie,' he added, indicating his colleague.

'And what can I do for you two upstanding officers of the law?'

'We'd like a word with one of your remand prisoners, a Horace Beauchamp.'

'Hold on.' Coughing affectedly, the gate warder ran a finger down the large ledger on the shelf that did duty as a desk. 'Ah, we've only got a geezer called 'Orace Bowchamp. Is that the fellow, Sarge?'

'That's him.' Catto was not sure whether the warder was making an attempt at humour or whether he really did not know how to pronounce Beauchamp's name.

'I'll get one of my colleagues to escort you up to the interview room, Sarge.'

Horace Beauchamp was typical of many regular army officers. About forty years of age, he had the bearing of someone who had spent all his adult life in the army, rather than being a hostilities-only officer. He had a red face – possibly due to an excess of gin – and a moustache, and bushy eyebrows from beneath which piercing blue eyes studied the two policemen.

'I'm Detective Sergeant Catto and this is Detective Constable Ritchie. We're from the Whitehall Division investigating crimes that you might know something about.'

'I know you.' Beauchamp ignored Catto's allegation and instead pointed a finger at Ritchie. 'I'm sure I bumped into you in Wipers in 1915. You're Captain Stuart Ritchie, Grenadier Guards.' He paused. 'Ah, got it. In the mess at Poperinghe when we were in rest.'

'The bloody war's over and I'm not in the army any more,' said Ritchie tersely. He was a firm believer in leaving the past where it belonged: behind him.

'A copper, eh?' Beauchamp gave a humourless laugh that was almost a sneer. 'Bit of a comedown after the Household Brigade, eh, old boy?'

'Not as much of a comedown as awaiting trial for robbing a bank,' said Ritchie drily, before adding a final condemnation. 'Weren't you gazetted to the Connaught Rangers, the regiment that mutinied in India in 1920?'

'You gave a waiter at the Twilight Cabaret Club a pound to pass a note to Celine Fontenau, Beauchamp,' said Catto, cutting swiftly through military reminiscences that were showing signs of developing into an unseemly slanging match.

'It's *Major* Beauchamp.'

'Not any more,' put in Ritchie. 'According to the military, you were court-martialled and cashiered for stealing from the mess funds.'

'That was all a mistake,' protested Beauchamp. 'I only borrowed the money.'

'You should fit in nicely with everyone else in here, then,' said Ritchie. 'They're all innocent, too.'

'Getting back to what we were talking about,' said Catto, 'did you in fact meet Celine Fontenau later on?'

'Have you seriously come all the way out to Wormwood Scrubs to ask me that?' Beauchamp gave another of his sneering smiles. 'Not that it's got anything to do with you, but yes, I took the filly out a few times. But why are so interested in my love life?'

'Because I'm trying to discover who murdered her,' said Catto mildly. 'And as you were intimately acquainted with her, you seem to be a good individual to start with.'

'Christ, man! Murdered her?' Beauchamp's jaw dropped and he stared at Catto. 'What the hell are you talking about?'

'Oh, very good, Beauchamp!' said Ritchie sarcastically. 'That was a really convincing performance.'

'I hope you're not accusing me of having killed her.' Beauchamp did not make any comment about the omission of his rank this time. 'I only took her out the once—'

'Just now you said you'd taken her out a few times,' said Ritchie, after glancing down at his pocketbook. 'Which is it?'

'All right, it was just the once, and that was what you might call a business arrangement. I took her to a hotel and had it up with her.' Beauchamp glossed over the fact that he had been caught out in a lie, or perhaps it was arrogant boasting. 'When we'd finished, I sent her on her way five pounds the richer. Lively little filly was Celine, and I had hoped to bed her a few more times, but she was fully booked, so she said.'

'Are you suggesting that Celine Fontenau was a prostitute?' Catto had no problem keeping the surprise from his voice. This was something he had come to expect during the course of his enquiries. 'How could you afford to give her five quid?' he asked unwisely.

'He robs banks,' said Ritchie quietly.

'Some of us have private incomes,' commented Beauchamp with another of his irritating, sneering laughs. He was, of course, boasting again, and there was little doubt in Catto's mind that he had acquired the money illegally.

'Who else went out with Celine?' asked Catto.

'There must have been dozens. As I said, she told me she was fully booked for the foreseeable future.'

'Did Guy Stoner go out with her?' Catto thought that even a prostitute would object to having sexual intercourse with an overweight, bombastic individual like Beauchamp whose breath probably smelt permanently of tobacco and alcohol.

'Oh, yes. He was very keen on her.'

'How did you come to know Stoner?'

'He was a friend of Holroyd's, and he introduced me to Stoner at the club. There were quite a few of us who got together there. But why all these questions? Don't you know who murdered the girl?'

'Not yet,' admitted Catto reluctantly, 'but we'll find out.'

'If I were you, I'd ask Stoner. He was the chap who went with her most often. I think the damned fool was even talking about marrying the girl, but God knows what they'd have lived on, because I don't think he had any money. Anyway, one doesn't marry one's tart. It's not the done thing.' Beauchamp sneered again.

Catto was unsure whether Beauchamp was professing ignorance just to annoy the police or whether he really was unaware that Stoner also had been murdered. It was unlikely Holroyd had told Beauchamp that Stoner was dead, because he would have to explain how he knew, and most certainly he would not have mentioned that he had emptied Stoner's bank account.

'Does the name Gerald Walker mean anything to you?' asked Catto.

'No. Who's he and what's he got to do with this fairy tale of yours?'

'Only that he was married to Celine Fontenau.'

'You find me a prostitute who doesn't claim to be married.' Beauchamp laughed. '"Husband" is usually a euphemism for her pimp.'

'The Twilight Cabaret Club was where you made your first contact with Celine Fontenau, was it?' asked Ritchie. 'You hadn't previously met her somewhere else.'

'That's where I first set eyes on her.'

'And you slipped Albert Higgs a pound to pass her a note, did you?'

'Who the devil's Albert Higgs?'

'The waiter you bribed.'

'How the hell did you know that?' For some inexplicable reason, Beauchamp seemed disconcerted that the police had discovered how Celine's clients arranged to meet her. Perhaps it was the apparent depth of their enquiries that worried him, and he wondered what else they might have discovered.

'We always find out these things when someone has been murdered,' said Ritchie quietly. 'It helps us to track down the killer.'

'Well, don't look at me. I had nothing to do with it. When did it happen, anyway?'

Ritchie did not answer that question, but Catto posed one of his own. 'Where were you during the weekend of the eleventh to the fourteenth of March this year?'

'Good God, man! I don't know.'

'Well, you'd better start thinking because I've got you on my list of suspects for the murder of Celine Fontenau, cully.'

'Now, look here. Just because you're a copper, you can't

make a wild accusation like that or you'll be hearing from my lawyers, whom I shall instruct to issue a writ for slander.'

'Have you forgotten where you are, Beauchamp?' asked Catto mildly. 'In case you have, I'll remind you. You're in Wormwood Scrubs on remand for armed robbery. You haven't got two ha'pennies to bless yourself with, so don't start talking about lawyers and actions for slander, because you haven't the faintest idea what you're talking about. If I decide to charge you with the girl's murder, your armed robbery will pale into insignificance.' He stood up and banged on the interview room door. 'You can take Beauchamp back to his flowery dell, mate,' he said, when the escorting warder appeared.

'Right, guv'nor. Move yourself, Bowchamp.'

Henry Catto was not in a good mood when he and Ritchie set off on their walk down Du Cane Road towards East Acton Underground station.

'In future, Ritchie, when you're with me, you don't go in for verbal fencing like you were doing with Beauchamp just now. I don't give a damn which regiment you were in, or which one he was in, or the circumstances under which he left it. It has no relevance to whether he murdered Stoner and the girl. Don't rise to his sarcasm; just ignore it. You'll find that it'll annoy men like Beauchamp even more. He's the sort who hates to be ignored. Got it?'

'Yes, Sergeant,' said Ritchie. 'It's just that men like him infuriate me. I met a few in the army, and—'

Catto stopped and turned to face Ritchie. 'There you go again, Ritchie. Just forget you were in the bloody army, will you? You're in the Metropolitan Police now and you'll do as you're told. If you don't like it, perhaps you ought to consider a change of career.'

Neither officer spoke again during the remainder of the journey back to Cannon Row.

Catto knocked on Hardcastle's door the moment he got back to the police station.

'According to Beauchamp, sir, Celine Walker was well

known to the punters at the Twilight Cabaret Club as a
prostitute.'

Hardcastle remained silent as he considered the implications
of the report Catto had just made. He went slowly through
the procedure of filling his pipe as though it had some cathartic
effect on his thought process. Finally, he lit it and expelled a
plume of smoke towards the ceiling.

'I wonder if Craddock knew what his chorus girls were
up to.'

'He professed ignorance, sir,' said Catto. 'He claimed that
Marjorie Hibberd, his choreographer, kept an eye on the girls
to make sure they stayed on the straight and narrow. She
certainly seemed to be genuine enough, and while I was there,
Craddock sacked the waiter who'd admitted passing notes to
Celine from clients wanting to make an assignation.'

Hardcastle laughed. 'An assignation, Catto? You mean from
men who were after a bit of jig-a-jig. Anyway, waiters are
expendable. There are hundreds on the dole, so sacking one
of 'em wouldn't hurt Craddock's business one little bit, and
it'll have made him look as though he was an upright club
owner who wasn't prepared to stand for any hanky-panky.'

'What d'you suggest we do next, sir?' Catto knew what he
would do, but the case was the DDI's.

'You and I will visit this here Twilight set-up, Catto, and
have a few words with Master Craddock. I think he needs to
be put right on a few things.'

It was a quarter to eight that same evening when Hardcastle
and Catto arrived at the Twilight Cabaret Club.

'I'm Divisional Detective Inspector Hardcastle and I want
to see Craddock, and I want to see him now.'

The man whom Craddock called the admissions manager
took an instant dislike to Hardcastle's brash approach, his view
being that courtesy costs nothing, even if you are a policeman.
'I'll see if the major is free.' Raising his head slightly as if
he had suddenly detected an offensive smell beneath his nose,
he turned to the telephone and made a brief call. 'There is a
person called Hardcastle wishing to speak to you, sir,' he said
when Craddock answered. 'He says he's a detective inspector.'

Replacing the receiver on its hook, he turned back to Hardcastle. 'The major will be down shortly.'

'Leo Craddock at your service, Inspector.' The club's dinner-jacketed owner limped into the foyer a minute or two later. 'And Sergeant Catto, too, I see. Good to see you again, Sergeant. Perhaps you'd care to follow me, gentlemen.'

As Craddock and the two detectives skirted the dance floor, Hardcastle stopped in amazement. He stared at the dancers who appeared to be performing a number of physical jerks to the accompaniment of ragtime music.

'What on earth are they doing?' asked Hardcastle.

'It's called the Charleston,' said Craddock. 'Another import from the United States. In fact, it's named after Charleston in South Carolina, but I've no idea why. Doubtless it'll be replaced by another craze before long.'

Once the two detectives were seated in Craddock's office, he offered them a drink. Hardcastle refused, leaving Catto no option but to refuse as well.

'How may I help you, Inspector?' Craddock poured himself a stiff measure of Laphroaig and sat down.

'It's come to my notice that Celine Fontenau was a prosti-tute, Major.' Hardcastle made the accusation bluntly and without any preamble. 'Furthermore, I have been told that she was well known as such by quite a few of the patrons of this establishment. What have you to say to that?'

'I can hardly believe it, Inspector.' The look on Craddock's face clearly indicated that this news came as a complete shock and that he was unaware of the woman's activities. 'May I ask where this information came from?'

'You know better than to ask me that, Major.'

'Yes, I'm sorry, but could I at least ask if it came from one of my employees?'

'No, it didn't. It came from one of your clients, but that's all I'm telling you.' Hardcastle, like all detectives, jealously guarded his informants, even though he did not place Beauchamp in that category. To reveal that the allegation had come from a cashiered army officer currently awaiting trial for robbery would undoubtedly cast doubt upon the veracity of the information. But Hardcastle was not above using any ploy available to him to get reliable information. He called it using a sprat to catch a mackerel.

Craddock finished his whisky and immediately poured himself another. 'Was there a suggestion that any of my other girls were engaging in prostitution, Inspector? Because if that is the case, I'll sack the lot and start again. The employment market is awash with dancers – far more than there are vacancies for.'

'My information only concerns Celine Fontenau. It's up to you to find out whether there are more. I'm sure I don't have to tell you that it's an offence to harbour prostitutes.' As usual, Hardcastle was stretching the law a point or two.

'I can assure you, Inspector, that I had no knowledge of this.'

'How long has Marjorie Hibberd been with you, Major?' asked Catto.

Craddock pursed his lips as he considered his answer. 'Three or so years, I suppose, Sergeant. I took her on just after I opened here.'

'Are you married, Major?' asked Hardcastle suddenly.

'No, the right girl never seemed to come along, Inspector.' Craddock smiled, a little diffidently.

'Very well,' said Hardcastle, rising to his feet. 'I may have to see you again, Major Craddock, but bear in mind what I said about employing prostitutes who masquerade as dancers. It's not unheard of in my line of business.'

'Come into the office, Catto,' said Hardcastle, once the two detectives were back at the police station, 'and tell me what you think of the galloping major. What you *really* think, I mean.'

'As I said before, sir, he seems genuine enough to me. I reckon he was really shocked when you told him that Celine was on the game.'

Hardcastle patted his jacket pockets until he found his pipe, and then put it in his mouth without lighting it. 'Maybe,' he said eventually. 'But he ain't married, Catto, and it's just possible that he was enjoying the fruits of his labours, so to speak. That's why I asked him if he was wed.'

'I don't know about that, sir. I'm more interested in Marjorie

Hibberd, the choreographer who's supposed to keep an eye on these girls.' Catto paused before tentatively adding, 'It's just possible that she's actually acting as a madam to organize it all. Either with the major's knowledge or without it.'

For a few seconds, Hardcastle stared at his subordinate in stunned silence. When Catto had previously served on A Division, it was the sort of look from the DDI that would have scared the living daylights out of him, but not any more.

'I think you're clutching at straws,' Hardcastle said eventually. 'But there might just be something in what you say. Have a look into her if you like, but don't waste too much time on it.' As Catto stood up to leave, he added, 'You can take the rest of the day off and start tomorrow.' He made it sound as though he was being extremely generous. Indeed, being an old-school detective, he firmly believed that he *was* being extremely generous.

'Thank you, sir.' Catto glanced at the clock over the door of Hardcastle's office. It was twenty minutes past nine. Catto's arrangement to meet his latest girlfriend had been stillborn, and she was probably now his ex-girlfriend.

SEVENTEEN

C atto's first stop in his search for background information on the Twilight Cabaret Club's choreographer
was at Somerset House in the Strand, where records
of births, deaths and marriages in England and Wales were
kept. Major Craddock had suggested that Marjorie Hibberd
was about fifty years of age and had referred to her as *Mrs*
Hibberd. Not that that meant anything. One of the things that
Catto had learned early in his career was that the cooks in big
houses were always called 'Mrs' whether or not they were
married. He had certainly come across several women who
claimed to be married, but were not, and had never been able
to fathom why they did so. Perhaps the same custom applied
to choreographers.

Catto started his search with the marriage records in 1895,
working on the basis that Mrs Hibberd might have been married
when she was about eighteen, but he was lucky enough not to
have to search too far. In the first quarter of 1897, he found an
entry recording the marriage of a George Hibberd, aged twenty-
five, a stage manager, to a Marjorie Bowen, aged twenty. The
ceremony had taken place at St Bartholomew's Church in Ann
Street, Brighton, which caused Catto to wonder if George
Hibberd could have been the stage manager at a Brighton
theatre. It was also possible that Marjorie was a dancer there
at some time and that was how they had met.

Knowing how old the Hibberds were at the time of their
marriage, it was a comparatively easy task to discover their
dates of birth. Armed with that information, Catto would now
be able to make a thorough and accurate search of Metropolitan
Police records.

It was a search of the Criminal Records Office, did Catto
but know it at the time, that became the first step in solving
the murders of Guy Stoner and Celine Walker, née Fontenau.

In 1922, the Brighton magistrates had convicted Marjorie

Hibberd of keeping a bawdy house at Albert Road, Brighton, and had sentenced her to three months' imprisonment. There were only a few details of the conviction and Catto determined that he would go to Brighton to find out more. Although he could have obtained those details by making a telephone call to the seaside town's police, he had a feeling that it would profit him even more were he to make some other enquiries while in the area.

Brighton police station was housed in the same building as the headquarters of the Brighton Borough Police in a road called Bartholomews, very close to the seafront. Catto and Ritchie arrived in the popular seaside resort at about ten o'clock on the morning of Thursday the nineteenth of May, just over six weeks since the discovery of the dismembered bodies of Guy Stoner and Celine Walker in Ditton.

The elderly sergeant manning the front office of the police station surveyed the two smartly dressed men. 'And how can I help you gentlemen on this fine sunny day?'

'I'm Detective Sergeant Catto of the Metropolitan Police and this is Detective Constable Ritchie, Sergeant.'

'Ah!' The sergeant brushed his moustache with the back of his hand. 'Are you gents on holiday and seeking lodgings or on duty and seeking information?' he asked.

'Oh, we're not on holiday,' said Catto, 'but information is what we're after.' He went on to explain his interest in Marjorie Hibberd, and that she might be able to assist in some way with enquiries into a double murder.

'Murder, eh? Well, now, let's see what we can do to assist you.' The sergeant's brow wrinkled in thought for a moment or two, and he brushed his moustache yet again. 'Your best bet is to have a word with the sergeant in charge of records on the first floor, Sergeant Catto. I'll get a PC to show you the way.' He shouted for someone called Broderick and told him where to take the visiting officers from the 'Mets' as provincial officers were wont to call the London force.

'I'm DS Charlie Caldicott,' said the sergeant in charge of the records section, once Catto had introduced himself and Ritchie, and explained what he was looking for. Caldicott began by looking in a large book, followed this by searching through a card index system and finally took a manila folder from a filing cabinet. 'Marjorie Hibberd, née Bowen, born second of February 1877. Married George Hibberd on the twentieth of March 1897 and he died twentieth of November 1918.'

'What did he die of, Charlie?'

'Caught the flu during the pandemic that year, Henry.'

'What was his occupation at the time of his death?'

Caldicott glanced down at his docket. 'Stage manager at the Brighton Hippodrome. It's in Middle Street, only a short stride from here if you're thinking of going there. According to this,' he continued, tapping the docket, 'Marjorie Bowen, as she was at the time of her marriage, was a dancer in the chorus at the theatre. I suppose that's how they met.'

'How did this bawdy house conviction come about, Sergeant?' asked Ritchie.

'It was five years ago. She was running a brothel in Albert Road. Information came from several of the neighbours . . .' Caldicott paused. 'It's quite a well-to-do neighbourhood and they complained, not because they thought it was a brothel, but because they thought it had been turned into a boarding house. They're a snooty lot round there, and when they found out what had really been going on, they were probably overcome with the vapours.' He chuckled at the thought. 'Being suspicious coppers, we took an interest and, lo and behold, found she was running a very classy sort of knocking shop. There were about six girls working there and business was booming, especially in the holiday season. Marjorie got three months and never returned to Brighton after her release from Holloway nick.'

'She's in London now, as a choreographer at the Twilight Cabaret Club in Brewer Street.'

'She's probably good at it, too. From what I heard, she was a top-rate dancer. I'll make a note of where she's gone, just in case she decides to come back.' Caldicott scribbled a few lines in the docket.

'Just one other thing . . .' Catto took out his pocketbook, flicked over a few pages and, using his pencil as a pointer, indicated one of the many names that he had recorded during the investigation. 'Does that name mean anything to you, Charlie?'

Caldicott opened his manila folder again and spent a moment or two glancing through it. 'Of course,' he said eventually, looking up. 'I thought it rang a bell. Two or three of the tarts who worked there mentioned he was inside, but when the house was raided, there was no sign of him. Nobody knew where he'd gone – or if they did, they weren't saying.'

'Is there a warrant out for him, Charlie?'

'No, there wasn't enough evidence to tie him into either the actual running of the place or living on the immoral earnings. One informant suggested that he owned the house, but there was nothing lodged with the borough council to indicate that he did. Marjorie Hibberd settled the rates bill every year and she remained tight-lipped. The rest of 'em didn't know anything anyway. The only whisper our people picked up was that he was ex-army, but so were millions of others.'

'Thanks for all that, Charlie. Ritchie and I'll take a stroll up to the Hippodrome and see if they can tell us something that'll put flesh on the bones, so to speak.'

'We're police officers,' said Catto.

'Fred Harris at your service, gents,' said the ageing door-keeper as he emerged from his cubicle near the stage door. He had wispy greying hair, a pair of spectacles held together with a piece of sticking plaster and a worn-out waistcoat with a watch chain suspended between the two lower pockets. He showed no sign of surprise at the arrival of the police. 'Can't say as how I've seen you before, but never mind. Couple of tickets for tonight's performance, is it?'

'No, thanks, Mr Harris,' said Catto. 'We're from the Metropolitan Police and we're investigating a murder.'

'Pity. It's a good show we've got on this week. The local bobbies usually pop in of a morning to pick up their free tickets, see. They comes in of a morning on account of 'em being early turn, so's they've got the evening off, meaning as how they can see the show. It's the manager's idea. He likes to have a few bobbies in the audience in case there's any trouble.'

'Fascinating,' murmured Catto. 'I was wondering what you can tell me about George Hibberd.'

'Ah, dear old George, God rest his soul, yes. Here, I'll tell you what: come and have a seat in the auditorium. Be a bit more comfortable.' Harris led the way along a dank corridor, through a fire door and into the area immediately in front of the orchestra pit. 'Thems is the fauteuils,' he said, pronouncing it 'four tails', and indicated the front row of seats. 'Cost you half a crown to plonk your backside in one of them. Mind you, it was well worth it in the old days. We had 'em all here, you know, guv'nor. Oh, yes. There was Sarah Bernhardt, bless 'er, Lillie Langtry . . .' He paused, a dreamy expression on his face. 'She was the Prince of Wales's bit of fluff, you know. Lovely girl was the Jersey Lily. Then there was Buster Keaton—'

'Can we talk about George Hibberd, Fred? Much as I like hearing about the theatre, we do have to get back to London.'

'Ah, yes, o'course. Now then . . . George. One of the best stage managers we ever had. I was stage-door keeper already when he arrived here in 1912, but the flu did for him a week after the end of the war. Mind you, a lot of good souls went the same way.'

Catto realized that Harris would need prompting. 'I believe he married a dancer from here – a girl called Marjorie Bowen.'

'Yes, you're right, guv'nor. Blimey, you've got a good memory. She was a good-time girl, was our Marge. Started out as a trapeze artist. Got into a bit of trouble with the law later on, so I heard. Mind you, that'd come as no surprise to them of us what knew 'er. Always up for a bit of a tumble was our Marge – professional like, if you take my meaning – and if she weren't available, she'd always fix the customer up with another of the chorus girls what was ready to turn a trick.'

'Did the management know about this, Fred?' asked Ritchie.

'Gawd blimey, no, guv'nor.' Harris was horrified at the thought. 'There'd have been hell to pay if they'd found out. No, it was all kept very quiet and only a few of the girls was involved. Some of the usherettes would take a bob to pass a note to our Marge, and she'd do the rest. Much better for the stage-door johnnies than hanging around in the cold in the hope of taking a doxy out to dinner in exchange for a favour, as you might say.' He afforded the two police officers an exaggerated wink.

'And did George know what was going on?'

'No, he couldn't have.' Harris scratched at his stubbled chin. 'Marge's bit of trouble was in 1922, and I'm pretty sure she never started on the game till after old George was pushing up daisies. She never had no income apart from dancing, see, and dancing don't pay that much.' It sounded as though Harris was attempting to excuse her behaviour.

'I would have thought she was a bit too old to go on the game at that age,' said Catto. 'She'd have been about forty-five.'

'Never! She can't have been.' Harris's face expressed surprise. 'Are you sure, guv'nor?'

'I've seen her birth certificate,' said Catto.

'Well, you could knock me down with a feather, and that's no error,' said Harris. 'That girl had the figure of a twenty-year-old, and the stamina to go with it. Er, so I've been told,' he added hurriedly.

'Were you one of her customers, then, Fred?' asked Ritchie, more out of devilment than a need to know for evidential purposes.

'Chance would have been a fine thing,' said Harris, his face adopting a look of lost opportunities. 'But I couldn't have afforded her. Anyway, my heart condition couldn't have coped with her, not from what I heard of her athletics. Like I said, she'd been a trapeze artist.'

Catto and Ritchie were back in London by three o'clock that afternoon, and immediately reported to the DDI.

'What did you learn?' Hardcastle filled his pipe and patted his pockets in an attempt to locate his box of Swan Vestas.

Catto explained, as succinctly as possible, what he and Ritchie had learned from the Brighton police and their conversation with Fred Harris, the stage-door keeper. The DDI was particularly interested in the man that DS Caldicott told them had vanished from the Albert Road brothel just before the police raided it.

'Tipped off by some local copper, I suppose,' said Hardcastle, ever the cynic. 'I want you to take an interest in this man, Catto. Find out all about him, because I don't think he's been straight with us, despite what we've learned of him so far.'

'D'you want him arrested, sir?'

'I'll leave that to your judgement, Catto. You know the rules. If arresting him is justified, well, then, arrest him.' At last Hardcastle found his matches and lit his pipe.

Secretly, Catto was pleased to have been entrusted with further enquiries in connection with the murders of Guy Stoner and Celine Walker, but it was apparent that Hardcastle was losing interest in it. It was not very long ago that Hardcastle would have been at the forefront of every aspect of a murder enquiry. But now, like Marriott, Catto considered the possibility that Hardcastle was past it and was contemplating retirement.

On Friday morning, Catto and Ritchie made their way to Vauxhall Bridge Road where the firm of Hudson and Peartree, makers of bakers' ovens, had its offices.

A Corps of Commissionaires man stood at the main entrance. 'Can I help you, gentlemen?'

'We're police officers, and we'd like to speak to Mr Gerald Walker.'

'I'm only here for the day, sir, the usual man having been taken ill. Consequently, I don't know any of the people who work here. If you step inside, sir, there's a lady receptionist who I'm sure will be able to assist you.'

There was a discreet sign on the receptionist's desk informing the world that her name was Miss M. Marsh.

Catto explained who he was and told Miss Marsh who he wished to speak to. It was then that Catto received a surprise.

'Gerald Walker? A clerk, you say?' The receptionist, a grey-haired lady of about fifty, with glasses and a severe expression, glanced down at her staff list. After a moment or two of study, she looked up again. 'I'm afraid there's no one of that name listed. Do you know how long he's worked here? If he's a recent arrival – say, in the last week – he might not have been included in the list yet.'

'Mr Walker informed us that he had worked here for twenty years. If it helps, he told us that his job was taking orders and that he had a separate telephone line that went direct to his desk for that purpose.' Catto took out his pocketbook and pointed to the number that Walker had given the A Division detectives when they had interviewed him.

'I'm afraid you've been misinformed, Sergeant. We only have one telephone number here, and all calls go through the switchboard. The telephone number that you have there is nothing to do with Hudson and Peartree, I can assure you.' Miss Marsh dismissed the idea with a wave of the hand.

'Mr Walker also told us that he had an apartment in Chapter Street, a turning just off—'

'I know where Chapter Street is,' said Miss Marsh, who disliked being patronized.

'And he said that it was paid for by his employers.'

The receptionist scoffed. 'I've never heard of such a thing,' she said. 'I've worked here for thirty-five years and I can say, without fear of contradiction, that there are very few people who know more about the workings of Hudson and Peartree than I do. The very idea of a clerk being provided with accommodation by the company is, well, preposterous.'

Catto put his pocketbook away. 'I think you're right, madam. I've clearly been misinformed.'

'Is it possible that Mr Walker did work here at some time in the past but has since resigned?' asked Ritchie.

'No,' said Miss Marsh firmly.

'Where are we going now, Skipper?' asked Ritchie as he and Catto walked down Vauxhall Bridge Road.

Catto glanced at his watch. 'The Grosvenor Hotel, Stuart. They've got a decent bar and I need a pint after that fiasco.'

Once the two detectives were ensconced at a quiet end of the bar in the saloon of the old railway hotel, Ritchie asked, 'What d'you make of this story that Walker told us, then?'

'We've been conned,' said Catto.

'Yeah, I appreciate that, but so has the guv'nor.'

Catto laughed. 'Maybe, but I can't see the DDI admitting it. He'll put it on someone else, you mark my words. However,

I'll speak to the GPO and get details of the subscriber to the telephone number that Walker gave us. Provided Walker is his real name,' he added gloomily.

'It's looking more like he was the bloke who owned the bawdy house at Brighton, isn't it?'

'Maybe, but what I've got to do now is get as much information about Walker, and anything else that we can find out about Marjorie Hibberd, before we speak to the DDI. He'll still go bloody mad when we tell him about the fast one that Walker's pulled, but if we've got something to give him, it'll at least soften the blow.'

Ritchie bought another round of beer. 'I've got a suggestion to make, Skip,' he said tentatively, 'but it rather depends how quickly we can get the address of that telephone number Walker gave us.' He went on to outline what he had in mind.

'That's a good idea,' said Catto, when Ritchie had finished. He drained his beer. 'Gerald Road nick is only a short walk from here. We'll get round there and use their telephone to speak to the GPO.'

After the usual chaffing when the station officer told Catto that B Division was always willing to assist officers of the Royal A Division, Catto got in touch with the GPO. Within minutes, he had the address. And it was not an apartment in Chapter Street.

'That number belongs to a house in Charlwood Place, which runs parallel with Belgrave Road.'

'Do we go there, Skip?'

'Now is as good a time as any, Stuart. We don't know what he does for a living, but sure as hell he's not a clerk at Hudson and Peartree.'

EIGHTEEN

The Georgian town house in Charlwood Place was clearly an expensive dwelling, certainly for someone who had professed to be a clerk, although that was now in serious doubt. Catto hammered on the heavy brass knocker and after about five minutes the door was opened by Gerald Walker attired in a long Paisley-patterned silk robe. The first thing Catto noticed was that his hair was dishevelled, as though he had just got out of bed, even though it was now two o'clock in the afternoon.

'Oh, Sergeant Catto!' Walker was unable to disguise his shock at seeing the detective on his doorstep and sensed that it boded ill. 'What brings you here?'

'You told us that the company you work for – Hudson and Peartree – had provided you with an apartment in Chapter Street, not Charlwood Place.'

'Quite right, but since our last meeting they offered me this house and I could hardly refuse, could I?'

'It seems rather grand accommodation for a clerk,' said Ritchie who, like Catto, was playing along with Walker's fiction.

'May we come in?' asked Catto. 'There are one or two things we'd like to discuss with you.'

'Er, yes, but I hope it won't take long because I am rather busy.' There was no denying that Walker was reluctant to admit the two detectives and he ushered them hurriedly into the temple-tiled hall. He was about to open the door of a side room when a barefooted woman came down the stairs.

'Who is it, Gerald?' Marjorie Hibberd was also wearing a robe, but it was much shorter than Walker's, and she had taken time to arrange her hair. 'Oh, Sergeant Catto. What are you doing here?' Her surprise was as apparent as Walker's had been.

'I might ask you the same question, Mrs Hibberd.'

'Mr Walker and I live together, and I think I'm right in

saying that our living arrangements, although perhaps not regarded as socially acceptable, are not illegal and have nothing to do with the police.' Marjorie Hibberd immediately went on the offensive. It was not her first hostile meeting with the police and, doubtless, she had learned a few tricks from the other inmates at Holloway, the north London women's prison where she had served her sentence.

Following Marjorie Hibberd's lead, Walker now became more assertive. Suddenly, the downtrodden character who had been interviewed by Hardcastle vanished and was replaced by what Catto took to be the man's true persona. 'What d'you want?' he demanded truculently.

Catto had had enough. 'You told us that you were a clerk with Hudson and Peartree.'

'And so I am,' said Walker, beginning to sound a little less confident.

Catto laughed. 'Are you seriously suggesting that a company as big as Hudson and Peartree would allocate expensive accommodation like this to a clerk? And the telephone number you gave us has nothing to do with the company or taking orders, and before you start arguing the toss about what I'm saying, I've checked it with the GPO. In fact, that's how I found out where you lived. Furthermore, Detective Constable Ritchie and I visited the head office of the company this morning and a Miss Marsh informed us that nobody by the name of Gerald Walker worked there and never had. In short, they'd never heard of you.'

'She was wrong,' said Walker lamely. 'Whoever Miss Marsh is.'

'I think you'd better leave, Sergeant,' said Marjorie Hibberd. 'Mr Walker lost his wife not long ago, as you well know, and is still grieving.'

'By living with an old Brighton friend, I see,' commented Ritchie quietly.

'What d'you mean by that?' demanded Marjorie, the pitch of her voice rising slightly.

Ritchie laughed. 'You can come down off your high horse, Mrs Hibberd. We know all about the brothel you were running in Albert Road, Brighton, and we also know that you were sentenced to three months' imprisonment as a result.' He then took a chance. 'And the house in Albert Road was owned by you, Mr Walker, wasn't it?'

Both Catto and Ritchie were expecting a denial from Walker, but none was forthcoming.

'So what? I owned a house in Brighton. Is that against the law?' Walker's reply was heavy with sarcasm.

'And presumably you rented it out to Mrs Hibberd.'

'What's wrong with that?' Walker was beginning to get a little edgy. He was uncertain what Catto was driving at, but he had a feeling that it would not be to his advantage.

'How much did she pay you in rent?'

But before Walker had a chance to answer, Marjorie Hibberd intervened.

'Don't answer that, Gerald,' she snapped. 'And if I were you, I'd refuse to answer any more questions without a solicitor being present.'

Catto made a decision. 'Gerald Walker, I am arresting you for living on the immoral earnings of prostitution in Brighton on divers dates in 1922.' To which awesome announcement he added the usual Judges' Rules caution.

'I'll go out and call a cab, Sergeant,' said Ritchie.

'This is outrageous,' protested Marjorie Hibberd. 'I'll get a lawyer for you, Gerald, darling.' Judging by the expression on her face, it was obvious that she regretted her initial intervention. Too late, it occurred to her that Catto was bound to infer, from that slip of the tongue, that Walker *had* been involved with her in the running of the Brighton brothel. Furthermore, despite his brief show of bravado, Walker was a weak character and there was no telling what he might say to the police when she was not there to guide him. And that worried her.

Catto escorted Walker to his bedroom and waited while he dressed. He had known prisoners to escape from a first-floor window before, and he had no intention of being held responsible for allowing Walker to do so.

Ritchie returned, and he and Catto conducted Walker out of the house to the waiting cab.

'Where to, guv?' asked the cab driver as he yanked down the flag of the taximeter.

'Scotland Yard,' said Catto, mindful of Hardcastle's maxim that if you tell a cabbie to take you to Cannon Row, you are just as likely to finish up at Cannon Street in the City of London.

The moment that Walker had been lodged in a cell, Catto made his way to the DDI's office.

'You've done *what*?' demanded Hardcastle, once Catto had explained about the arrest of Gerald Walker.

'I've got a feeling that he knows something about the murders of Celine Fontenau and Guy Stoner, sir.' Catto refused to be browbeaten by Hardcastle's bullying outburst.

The DDI ignored that comment. 'Have you informed Brighton police that you've got him in custody for one of their jobs?'

'No, sir. I thought you might think there was not enough evidence to justify nicking him, so I held off telling them.'

Hardcastle grunted. 'I'll see what he's got to say for himself about the murders before I decide whether to give him to Brighton. Get him up to the interview room, and then you can start writing a report about your visit to Charlwood Place. Tell Sergeant Marriott to join me downstairs.'

Walker continued to lounge in his chair when Hardcastle and Marriott entered the room. It was a churlish attempt to convey that he had nothing to worry about. 'Why have I been arrested?' he demanded truculently. There was no repetition of the servility he had displayed on the occasion of his last interview with Hardcastle.

'Detective Sergeant Catto told you the reason,' snapped the DDI, 'but I want to talk about something else.'

'Oh, really?' Walker tried to hide his fear with that overweening comment, but this man frightened him. Suddenly, he suspected that Hardcastle was aware of his involvement in the murders.

'We have fingerprint evidence in connection with the murder of Captain Guy Stoner and your wife, Mr Walker,' said Marriott mildly.

'Well, they're not mine,' Walker blurted out. 'I had nothing to do with it.'

'You know who Captain Stoner is, then.' Marriott spoke softly. His approach often produced more positive results than did the DDI's hectoring.

'I, er, no, but you mentioned him when I came to see you following the report in the newspaper.'

'No, we didn't, Mr Walker.' Marriott thumbed through the statement he had made following the DDI's first interview with Walker, and the later one following his identification of Celine Fontenau who, Walker had claimed, was his lawfully wedded wife. 'Where did you get married to Celine Fontenau, Mr Walker?'

'Er, Marylebone register office.' Walker named the first office that came to mind, but he was not the first man to underestimate the thoroughness of police enquiries.

'I don't think so,' said Marriott. While Catto had been doing a lot of the legwork, Marriott had been delving into Walker's background. He had searched the marriage records at Somerset House from the date of Celine Fontenau's arrival in the United Kingdom and found no trace of a marriage between her and Walker. Now, he glanced down at the report from the Assistant Provost Marshal's office that he had received only that morning in response to his request for any details of Walker having been a soldier. There had been no time to inform Hardcastle, but whatever the DDI might say later, there was no doubt in Marriott's mind that this was the moment to put it to Walker. 'It seems that your army career was not very distinguished.'

'I wasn't in the army. I told you, I was in a reserved occupation for a firm making field kitchens.'

'Marriott, what the hell are you playing at?' Hardcastle demanded, turning on his sergeant with an expression of annoyance on his face. 'What's this all about?'

'Let me finish, sir, and I'll explain in a moment.' Marriott faced Walker again. 'You were certainly associated with kitchens. You were a cook attached to the Army Ordnance Corps at the base depot in Boulogne for the entire war.'

'How did you know that?' Walker was aghast that the police knew so much about him.

Marriott briefly nodded in Hardcastle's direction, the accepted signal that it was time for the DDI to take over the questioning.

'We know you murdered Guy Stoner and Celine Fontenau, Walker. Your fingerprints were found on a crowbar that was used, and I'll see you dancing on the hangman's trapdoor before the year is out.' For a change, the DDI had spoken almost as mildly as Marriott. In fact, Hardcastle was in error. No discernible fingerprints had been found on the crowbar, only on the car-jack handle.

Walker went white in the face and for a moment it seemed that he might faint again, as he had done when identifying Celine's remains at St Mary's Hospital.

'It wasn't me. It was Marjorie.' Walker blurted out his accusation almost as a reflex action.

'I'm sorry, Walker, I didn't quite hear that.' Hardcastle made a little pantomime out of leaning forward and cupping a hand around his ear.

'It was Marjorie Hibberd who did for them.'

'How d'you know?'

'I was there.' Walker made it sound as though a great weight had been lifted from him, without realizing that he had just implicated himself in the crime. 'And I want to turn King's evidence.'

'Oh, you were there, were you?' Hardcastle ignored Walker's desperate plea for immunity in exchange for testifying against his lover. 'That makes you an accomplice, if not a principal in the second degree. But before we go into that, you can tell me exactly what happened.'

Marriott, already concerned about the admissibility of evidence, scribbled a note and passed it across to the DDI. It bore the two words: 'Judges' Rules.'

Hardcastle glanced at the note and irritably brushed it aside. 'Tell me about Marjorie Hibberd, Walker.'

'It's true what you said about me owning the house at Brighton, and I was involved in recruiting the girls who worked there. After the Brighton business collapsed, and when Marjorie came out of prison, we set up at Charlwood Place.'

'Are you admitting that you're running a brothel at that house?'

'Yes. And one of the girls we recruited was Celine Fontenau. In fact, we have six girls working there at the moment.'

'Haven't there been any complaints from the neighbours? They must have seen men coming and going,' suggested Marriott.

'Marjorie wasn't greedy. She made sure that men only came by appointment, and the appointments were spaced out – only on some days of the week – so as not to arouse suspicion.'

'Let's go back to the night of your fortieth birthday party at the Twilight Cabaret Club, Walker,' said Marriott.

'What about it?'

'The head waiter at the club is a man who's well aware of what's going on, and he doesn't remember anything about a party where you and your friends all got drunk on champagne. The night you sent a note to Celine.'

'There wasn't a party,' admitted Walker miserably. 'It was Marjorie's idea to recruit the girl. She made me do it. I sent a note up to Celine and invited her out to dinner. Afterwards, I took her back to Charlwood Place and Marjorie set her up as one of the girls.'

'So, how did she meet Guy Stoner?'

'He was a client, but he made the mistake of falling in love with her.'

'Why was that a mistake?' asked Hardcastle.

'It often happens, Inspector. A customer thinks he's in love with a tom and wants to take her away from her sordid way of life.'

Marriott smiled at the reasons Walker had put forward. It was well known among prostitutes in the West End that some of their tricks often fell head over heels in love with one of them and expressed the desire 'to take you away from all this'.

'But these girls sometimes gave up the game and got married, anyway,' said Hardcastle. 'What was different this time?'

'Marjorie was furious about losing one of her best performers. I've never seen her so mad. She told Stoner that she'd put it about that he picked up tarts. But Stoner was a nasty bastard,

Mr Hardcastle. He told Marjorie that he was going to shop
the whole set-up to the police and that she'd finish up in
prison.'

'You were privy to this conversation, I take it.'

'No, but Marjorie told me afterwards what Stoner had threatened her with. She'd been inside before and she told me that
she'd had a terrible time. The other prisoners beat her up
because she spoke nicely – hoity-toity, they called her – and
they'd go into her cell and steal all her clothes and leave her
naked and shivering. She'd have done anything to avoid going
back to Holloway, particularly as she knew it would be a
lengthy sentence next time. She's a tough bird is Marjorie,
but that lot in Holloway were tougher, and she didn't fancy
going back inside again.'

'She won't,' said Hardcastle. 'At least only long enough for
them to measure her for the drop. Go on.'

'If she'd peached on me, I'd have gone inside as well, and
I didn't fancy that. But I swear I didn't know what she was
going to do, and that's the God's honest truth.'

Hardcastle didn't believe for one moment that Walker
was unaware of what Marjorie Hibberd had in mind, but
he made no comment about it. 'So, what was your part in
all this?'

'I had to get Stoner to some place that was quiet. I'd found
out that he and his mate Holroyd had got this sort of garage
place down at Ditton, and that sounded good. It was well away
from Soho, and I knew that Stoner was actually living there,
so I put the arm on Celine to tell me when he was next going
down there.'

'And when you found out, you told Marjorie and took her
down there because she didn't know where it was.'

'Yeah. But I didn't know she was going to murder him, Mr
Hardcastle. I thought she just wanted to talk to him.' Even as
the words came out of his mouth, Walker must have realized
how implausible they sounded. 'You see, I didn't know Celine
was going to be there. Stoner was in the workshop when we
arrived, and straight away Marjorie grabbed this car-jack
handle and hit him with it.'

'Did she say anything?' asked Marriott.

'Not a word. She was a powerful woman, you see. She'd been a trapeze artiste when she was younger, before she took up dancing. I reckon she must've killed him with that one blow. But then Celine appeared from nowhere. I suppose she must've been in the office. There were a couple of camp beds in there, and I suppose—'

'Yes, all right. I can guess the rest. What did Celine do?' asked Marriott.

'Well, she'd seen everything, and she started screaming in French that Marjorie was a murderess.'

'If she was speaking in French, how did you know that's what she was saying?' asked Hardcastle, becoming highly suspicious about Walker's account.

'I learned quite a lot of French when I was stationed in Boulogne, Inspector. Anyway, Celine obviously sensed that she was in danger, and turned to run away, but Marjorie went after her and hit her with the car-jack handle. Celine went down and lay still.'

'And you're saying that you took no part in these murders, that you were just an innocent spectator.'

'All I did was throw the car-jack handle back into the workshop while Marjorie dragged Celine's body in there, too. Then she turned on me. She blamed me for not knowing that Celine was there, because she'd had to kill her, too; otherwise she'd have peached on us.'

'Where did you first meet Marjorie Hibberd?' Marriott made it sound as though he had only posed the question out of interest.

Walker was momentarily disconcerted by the sudden switch in questioning, and wondered what to say, but then he decided there would be no point in lying, and that this quiet detective probably knew the answer anyway. 'At the Brighton Hippodrome. Why?'

'What were you doing there? In the audience, were you? A stage-door johnnie?'

Walker laughed. 'No, I was an actor. Started as soon as I came out of the army. I'd taken part in one or two concert parties for the lads in Boulogne, and rather took a fancy to it. Trouble was that the pay of an actor wasn't up to much, not unless you made it to the West End stage, and not always then. To tell you the truth, running our team of girls paid much better.'

'So, it was your acting skills that enabled you to play the part of the stricken, grieving husband so convincingly the first time you showed up here,' said Marriott. He felt like leaning over the table and hitting the smug little pimp sitting opposite.

'That's all very interesting, Walker. But, in fact, that's all pie in the sky. Marjorie got you to murder them.' Hardcastle lit his pipe and sat back in his chair to await Walker's reaction to an accusation that implied he had not believed a word of what Walker had just been saying.

'Oh my God, no! I never killed them. Honestly. You've got to believe me, Inspector.' Having been open and honest with the two detectives – at least, his version of openness and honesty – Walker realized that his play-acting had been in vain.

'Make no mistake, Walker,' said Hardcastle, 'you're for the drop.'

'She made me tell her when Stoner was going to be at Ditton,' Walker pleaded desperately. 'She threatened to grass on me to the police about it if I didn't help her out.'

'About what?'

'About procuring the girls for her in Brighton and here, and she said I'd get a long stretch in the nick because judges have taken against people who run brothels. Then she told me what the other cons did to ponces inside. She frightens the life out of me, Inspector. Always has.'

'Why didn't you tell me that you'd received information from the army about Walker, Marriott? I never want to go into an interview without being fully prepared. You should know that by now.' Hardcastle was very annoyed at what he perceived to be disloyalty on the part of his sergeant.

'I only received it a minute or so before you sent for me to interview Walker, sir.'

Hardcastle grunted. 'Yes, well, don't let it happen again.'

'Very good, sir.' Marriott had learned over the years

that there was no profit in arguing with the DDI. 'Are you going to charge Walker, sir?'

'There's no doubt in my mind that he was a principal in the second degree, Marriott, but what's more important right now is to arrest Marjorie Hibberd. It's a pity that Catto didn't bring her in at the same time as Walker.'

'I doubt that he had grounds for arresting her at that time, sir.'

'Maybe not.' Hardcastle rarely admitted to being wrong. 'But you can send him and Ritchie up to that club right now. She might be so confident that she thinks her cat's paw Walker wouldn't have told us what he did. She might just have gone to work as usual. If not, it'll take months if not years to locate her, because if she's got any sense, she'll have upped sticks and run. Possibly even abroad,' he added gloomily.

Marriott tended to agree with the last part of Hardcastle's comment. He did not think that after Walker's arrest that afternoon she would have waited for the police to come back and arrest her. Nevertheless, he returned to the detectives' office and called Catto and Ritchie over to his desk.

'You're to go to that club where Marjorie Hibberd works and arrest her, Henry. Walker has just accused her of murdering Guy Stoner and Celine Fontenau and running a prostitution ring from among the team of dancers that she claimed to be protecting.'

'If she was running a team of prostitutes, Skipper,' said Catto, 'surely Major Craddock must've known about it. D'you want him arrested as well?'

'Not yet,' said Marriott. 'Living on immoral earnings or running a bawdy house is nothing compared with two counts of murder. Anyway, C Division can always go after him if they want to.'

NINETEEN

'**G**ood evening, gentlemen,' said the admissions manager, as effusive as ever. 'I presume you wish to see the major. You're becoming regular visitors.'

'Yes, please,' said Catto. 'By the way, is Mrs Hibberd here?'

'Our dear Marjorie? Yes, she's here somewhere. Did you want to see her, too?'

'Not particularly,' said Catto in an offhand way.

'I'll just call the major, then.' The doorkeeper – because in reality that is what he was – made a brief telephone call, and a few minutes later, Leo Craddock limped into the foyer.

'Good evening, Sergeant Catto. Ah, and Constable Ritchie, I see. Would you care to come up to my office, gentlemen?'

'Thank you, Major,' said Catto, and he and Ritchie followed Craddock's slow progress up to the first floor.

'Well, now, gentlemen, to what do I owe the pleasure of your visit this evening?' Craddock's hand hovered over a bottle of Laphroaig, an unspoken invitation to join him in a drink.

But Catto shook his head. 'You recall the first occasion we called here, Major Craddock, I mentioned that we were investigating two murders.'

'Yes, I do,' said Craddock, pouring himself a whisky. 'Have you arrested anyone yet?'

'We have made one arrest, but there are other people involved. To that end, I'd like to speak to Marjorie Hibberd if she's here this evening,' said Catto, although he had already ascertained from the doorman that she was here.

'You think she might be able to help, eh?' Craddock reached for his telephone and made a call.

'We're convinced that she'll be able to,' said Ritchie. He knew why Catto had refrained from mentioning the real reason for their visit. Loyalty to one's ostensibly trusted employee might even extend to warning her of the intentions of the police, although he doubted that Craddock would be silly enough to protect a murderess.

Marjorie Hibberd appeared in Craddock's office within minutes of his telephone call. Following the prevailing fashion of shapeless and sleeveless dresses, she wore a velvet creation in mauve with a gold silk edging to the hem.

'You wanted me, Major?' she glanced at the two police officers, convinced that their visit to Charlwood Place that morning and the arrest of Gerald Walker was somehow connected to their arrival here.

'Actually, these officers would like to speak to you, Marjorie.'

'Have you come to tell me that you made a mistake in arresting poor Gerald this morning?'

'No, Mrs Hibberd,' said Catto. 'We've come to tell you that he is to be charged as a principal in the second degree to the commission of two murders, namely those of Guy Stoner and Celine Fontenau.'

'What on earth makes you think that he'd have murdered his own wife?' Marjorie Hibberd almost spat the words. 'It's absolutely ludicrous.'

'Celine Fontenau was not Walker's wife, as you well know,' said Catto as he and Ritchie stood up. 'Marjorie Hibberd, I'm arresting you for the wilful murders of Guy Stoner and Celine Fontenau. You do not have to say anything, but anything you do say will be taken down in writing and may be given in evidence.'

'Whatever are you talking about?' demanded Craddock, his face registering shock. 'You're making a terrible mistake. I've known Marjorie for a number of years and—'

'I suggest that you don't interfere, Major Craddock,' said Ritchie. 'Such intervention may be misconstrued or even regarded as obstructing police in the execution of their duty.'

For a moment or two, Craddock stared at Ritchie, amazed at the policeman's command of English, but he took Ritchie's advice and remained silent.

'My lawyers will sue you for every penny you possess,' said Marjorie, her voice rising a little.

'You will now be taken to Cannon Row police station,

Mrs Hibberd, where you will be charged with two counts of murder,' said Catto, ignoring the woman's empty threat.

It was approaching eight o'clock that evening by the time Catto and Ritchie returned to Cannon Row police station. Once Hardcastle had been told of the arrest of Marjorie Hibberd, he went straight down to the charge room, arriving at the same time as the station officer entered with the charge book and a sheaf of papers.

'All correct, sir,' said the station officer.

Hardcastle nodded in response to what he regarded as a pointless report, made whether things were all correct or not. But, perversely, he was annoyed if the report was not made.

'You needn't think you'll get anywhere by questioning me,' said Marjorie, 'because I'm not saying anything about this ridiculous allegation that I murdered those two people.'

'I have no questions to ask you,' said Hardcastle mildly. 'I have all the evidence I need.' He turned to the station officer. 'The charge is the wilful murders of Guy Stoner and Celine Fontenau, Sergeant.'

'Very good, sir.' The divisional detective inspector's decision made the sergeant's task much easier. He had no option but to put the charges without questioning the arresting officers. Once the formalities were complete, the sergeant asked, 'To be kept in custody, sir?'

'Of course she'll be kept in custody, Sergeant. I hope you're not suggesting that someone charged with two counts of murder should be released on bail.'

'No, sir,' said the sergeant, wondering why DDIs had to be so bloody awkward, given that they knew the rules, 'but I'm obliged to ask.'

As was to be expected on a Saturday morning, Bow Street police court was bustling with activity. Black vans with darkened windows were delivering detainees who had been collected from various London prisons and police stations. Inside the marble-floored entrance hall, names of witnesses or people surrendering to bail were called at intervals. Policemen rushed hither and thither, and a layman could be forgiven for wondering how any semblance of order could come from such chaos, but somehow it worked tolerably well.

Most of Friday night's prostitutes had been gathered up in London's West End and would appear at Marlborough Street police court, but there were still a few who had been arrested within Bow Street's catchment area. It was these 'ladies of the night' who firmly believed that they were entitled to appear before the magistrate first, taking precedence over drunks and the assorted rag, tag and bobtail who regularly appeared there. They were, therefore, a little put out that a man and a woman who had been charged with murder should appear first in the dock of Number One Court.

'You are Marjorie Hibberd and you live at Charlwood Place in the City of Westminster?' asked the clerk of the court.

'Yes,' said Marjorie. 'And I am innocent of this ludicrous charge—'

The clerk raised his hand. 'You will be given the opportunity to enter a plea at a later date, Mrs Hibberd. This is merely a preliminary hearing.' He turned to the other prisoner in the dock. 'You are Gerald Walker and you live at the same address as your co-defendant?'

'Yes, sir,' said Walker.

The clerk stood up, turned and handed a sheet of paper to the magistrate.

'Mr Hardcastle?' The Chief Magistrate glanced at the DDI as he ascended the witness box.

'The charge is murder, Your Worship, and there will be two counts on the indictment if Your Worship agrees that there is a case to answer.'

'Very well. I'll not take a plea this morning.' The Chief Magistrate looked down at the ledger. 'Remanded in custody to appear again at this court on Monday the thirtieth of May. Perhaps you will then be in a position to inform the court when committal proceedings are likely to commence.'

'I'm obliged, Your Worship,' said Hardcastle as the two prisoners were escorted down the steps from the dock to the cells below. As he was leaving, he heard the clerk say, 'Ethel Davis, you are charged with soliciting prostitution in Drury Lane . . .'

*   *   *

Sir Patrick Sloane KC had his chambers at Grant Court in the Temple, a rabbit warren of barristers' accommodation that lay between Fleet Street and Victoria Embankment. In common with many others in his profession, he worked in a room that was too small to afford any degree of comfort to the number of people who, from time to time, arrived for a conference. Nevertheless, he had somehow contrived to find chairs for Hardcastle, Marriott and Catto who were now squeezed together around the barrister's desk.

'Since our last conference, Mr Hardcastle, I have consulted the Director of Public Prosecutions, Sir Archibald Bodkin.' Seeing the frown on Catto's face, Sir Patrick said, 'We have to have his fiat to go ahead in cases of murder, Sergeant Catto. His decision was that Hibberd be charged with murder and that Walker should also face a similar charge. Walker's request to turn King's evidence was rejected by the DPP, mainly because, Mr Hardcastle, in your statement you say that Walker is an inveterate liar.'

'And so he is, sir,' said Hardcastle. 'He invented a background that was totally false, and I'm not convinced by the statement he made claiming that Hibberd was solely responsible for the murders.'

'I gather from your report that you believe him to have been an active participant.'

'I do, sir.'

'As for the man Holroyd and his brother-in-law . . .' Sloane began to sort through the untidy heaps of papers on his desk while muttering incomprehensively.

'His brother-in-law's name is Harold Barton, sir, if that's what you were looking for. He was the butcher who has admitted dismembering the bodies at Ditton.'

'Exactly so. I'm much obliged, Mr Hardcastle. Holroyd and Barton will be charged with disposing of the corpses with intent to prevent a coroner's inquest. It's a common law offence and could carry life imprisonment, although it never does. On the other hand, they're more likely to get off with a slap on the wrist unless their actions impeded your enquiries. Rather depends which judge we get on the day. There again, of course, I might suggest that they are dealt with summarily. We shall see.'

'Holroyd is in custody and facing a charge of armed robbery, sir,' said Hardcastle. 'Unconnected with this murder case.'

'Is he, by Jove? Sounds a bit of a bad hat. In that case, I'll not object to it being dealt with summarily. The stipe will probably give him three months to be going on with until he appears at the Old Bailey.' Sloane chuckled at the thought. 'So, there we have it, Mr Hardcastle. I'll let you know when we have a date.' He stood up and shook hands with the three detectives. 'See you down at the Bailey.'

The trial of Marjorie Hibberd and Gerald Walker opened at the Central Criminal Court, Old Bailey, in the City of London, on Thursday the fifteenth of September 1927 before Mr Justice Squires. That morning's papers were, however, more interested in the news that Isadora Duncan, the American dancer, had met a bizarre death in Nice when her scarf had become entangled with the rear wheel of the car in which she was travelling. She was thrown on to the road where she died of a broken neck.

'Oyez! Oyez! Oyez! All persons having business before this court of oyer and terminer and general gaol delivery pray draw near.' After the court crier had had his moment of glory with that age-old proclamation, the judge took his seat after exchanging bows with counsel. 'Sir Patrick?'

'I appear for the Crown, my lord,' said Sloane, 'prosecuting both defendants, and my learned friend John Digby is for the defence of both accused.' He then named their respective juniors.

'Thank you, Sir Patrick. Bailiff, swear the jury.'

Although women had been allowed to sit as jurors since 1919, it had been decided by some faceless court official, who had seriously underestimated the strength of character of women, that it would be better not to expose their tender sensibilities to the gruesome evidence that was likely to be given. He had completely overlooked the fact that many women had nursed in base hospitals during the war and been witness to the most horrific injuries. The outcome of the official's unwarranted assumption was that there were no challenges, peremptory or for cause, to the empanelment of an all-male jury.

Both defendants pleaded not guilty.

Over the next few days, the trial followed the customary course of such proceedings.

Hardcastle gave evidence of arrest and testified to Walker's allegation that Marjorie Hibberd had committed both murders. Defence counsel gave a bravura performance in attempting to turn the DDI's testimony against him by pointing out that his statement mentioned Walker's unreliability. John Digby was slightly disconcerted to discover that Hardcastle agreed with him when the point was raised. But he had crossed swords with the wily DDI before and should have guessed that Hardcastle's ready admission did not influence the outcome.

Sir Bernard Spilsbury, in the eloquent testimony that had come to be expected of him, described the cause of death in each case and gave a chilling description of the manner of the victims' dismemberment. Prompted by Sir Patrick Sloane, he expressed the opinion that it was done with such skill as to lead him to believe it was the work of either a surgeon or a butcher.

It was, however, the arrival in the witness box of Detective Superintendent William Bell, head of the Yard's Fingerprint Bureau, that put the outcome beyond doubt.

'I have examined the car-jack handle handed me by Divisional Detective Inspector Hardcastle and I have made a comparison with the fingerprint impressions found on that car-jack handle with the impressions of the accused persons that were taken at the time of their arrest and taken again by or on behalf of the governors of Holloway Prison in respect of Hibberd, and Wandsworth Prison in respect of Walker. I can say without doubt that the car-jack handle bears the fingerprints of both Marjorie Hibberd and Gerald Walker.' Bell then explained in great detail how he had come to that conclusion. He supported it by distributing photographs to members of the jury, after which he described the sixteen points of similarity between the prints of each of the accused and the marks found on the car-jack handle.

Digby, the defence counsel, rose to cross-examine. 'Am I to understand, Superintendent,' he asked, 'that you are suggesting the two accused jointly committed the murders?' But his attempt to muddy the waters was immediately dashed.

'I cannot express an opinion about that which is rightly the preserve of the jury, sir.' Detective Superintendent Bell had given evidence on many occasions and was unlikely to be caught out that easily.

'Are you certain that these are the finger impressions of the accused, and not someone else's?' asked Digby, desperately trying to find a flaw in the fingerprint evidence.

'The chances of two different people having identical finger-prints has been estimated at sixty-four million to one, sir,' said Bell.

When it was Digby's turn to present the defence case, the unfortunate position of representing both Hibberd and Walker caused him to decide not to put either of them in the witness box. He believed that it would merely result in accusations being made by each against the other, and the prosecution would thus be helped to build the case against them. Marjorie Hibberd expressed a willingness to enter the witness box to accuse Walker, but Digby realized the danger of that, even if she did not appreciate it.

The jury took two whole days to consider their verdict, but at four o'clock in the afternoon of the second day they returned to the courtroom.

'Gentlemen of the jury, are you agreed upon your verdict?' asked the clerk of the court.

'We are,' said the foreman, and delivered their decision that each defendant was guilty of the murders of Guy Stoner and Celine Fontenau.

The judge asked each defendant if they wished to say anything before sentence of death was passed upon them, but they remained silent, stunned by the verdict and that which was to follow. He donned the black cap.

'Marjorie Hibberd,' he began, 'you stand convicted of murder. The sentence of the law upon you is that you be taken to a lawful prison and thence to a place of execution. That you be there hanged by the neck until you are dead and that your body be buried within the precincts of the prison in which you shall have last been confined before your execution, and may the Lord have mercy on your soul.'

After which, the judge's chaplain intoned the single word 'Amen'.

Marjorie Hibberd stared stoically ahead and said nothing, but it was a different reaction when the judge repeated the sentence to Gerald Walker.

Half fainting, so that he had to be supported by the two prison warders, he shouted and screamed his innocence.

'Take them down,' said the judge.

It was two weeks after the Court of Criminal Appeal had dismissed the appeals of both Marjorie Hibberd and Gerald Walker that the Home Secretary opened the docket requiring him to confirm the sentence of death passed on Gerald Walker. It was the third time that he had perused the document. Although not opposed to the death penalty, he was a scrupulously just man and the thought that he might be responsible for sending an innocent man to the gallows appalled his sense of fair play. The reason for his concern was not so much the evidence of DDI Hardcastle, the senior investigating officer, that Walker was an unreliable witness, as much as the letter that the Home Secretary had received from Marjorie Hibberd. Written from the condemned cell at Holloway Prison, it stated that although Gerald Walker had certainly alerted her to where she could find Guy Stoner, he had taken no part in the actual murders.

She did not understand, of course, that it made no difference to the penalty because he was an accessory to the murders and was treated in law in exactly the same way as the principal.

What prompted this sudden statement was unclear, but it was likely that she actually loved Walker and that they had lived together ever since she was released from prison following her conviction for running a brothel at Albert Road, Brighton. It was even possible that an intimate liaison had started before that.

As a consequence, and after long and careful consideration, the Home Secretary commuted Walker's sentence to one of life imprisonment. He then drew the docket concerning Marjorie Hibberd across his desk and, after one last reading, took out his fountain pen and wrote on the cover, *Let the law take its course.*

As Sir Patrick Sloane had predicted, Rupert Holroyd and his brother-in-law, Harold Barton, each received a sentence of three months' imprisonment for dismembering and secreting the bodies of Guy Stoner and Celine Fontenau. In Holroyd's case, his sentence was but a precursor to the main act. Two weeks after the end of the Hibberd and Walker trial, Holroyd and Horace Beauchamp appeared at the Old Bailey and were each sentenced to ten years' penal servitude for a bank robbery that, in the event, had netted them nothing.

It was raining on the Monday morning when, undeterred by the weather, the usual crowd of ghoulish sightseers gathered in Parkhurst Road, North London. At seven minutes past eight, a warder appeared and posted a notice on the gate. It said that Marjorie Hibberd had been executed in accordance with the law. Some members of the crowd nodded their approval. Others, opposed to the death penalty, murmured their dissent. The crowd dispersed and went about their business.

'The one thing I don't understand, sir,' said Marriott, 'is why Gerald Walker came to us to report his wife missing when he knew exactly what had happened to her. Not that she was his wife, of course.'

It was the day after Marjorie Hibberd's execution and the two detectives were mulling over the case in the DDI's office.

'That,' said Hardcastle, 'is what I call criminal bravado. You see,' he continued, lighting his pipe as he warmed to his subject, 'people of Walker's type love to think they're clever enough to outwit the police. But, deep down, they want to know what we're doing about it. In a way, they think we can't work out what they're up to. But they're trying to discover whether we're getting nearer the truth and nearer to them, so they can arrange their next move. They're a bit like an arsonist, Marriott, who will often be in the crowd watching the brigade putting out the fire that he started.'

'I suppose we should have worked that out, sir. If we'd discovered earlier that he wasn't the clerk he pretended to be, we might've got him and the Hibberd woman to trial quicker.'

Hardcastle walked across to his window and for a moment or two watched an Underground train pulling out of Westminster station below. Then he turned. 'I suppose these clever psychologists would know the answer to that, Marriott.'

TWENTY

One morning in November, Hardcastle was seated in his office, checking the latest report that he had prepared for the Director of Public Prosecutions. It was also the morning that he heard that Gerald Walker had died in Dartmoor Prison. The official verdict was that he had died as the result of a heart attack, but Marjorie Hibberd's warning about what happened to pimps in prison made Hardcastle wonder.

'Excuse me, sir.'

'What is it, Marriott?'

'A telephone call from Mr Wensley's clerk, sir. Would you see Mr Wensley as soon as possible?'

Hardcastle sighed, stood up and took his bowler hat and umbrella from the stand.

The PC at the main entrance of New Scotland Yard opened the door and saluted.

Tapping on the chief constable's door, Hardcastle entered without waiting for a summons.

'Good morning, Ernie. Take a seat.'

'Thank you, sir.' Hardcastle was convinced he was about to be given another out-of-town murder to deal with, but Wensley's next statement was one that he had not expected.

'I'm afraid I have to tell you that Arthur Fitnam died this morning, Ernie.'

'I'm sorry to hear that, sir. Arthur was a good detective.'

'I'm offering you his post as DDI V Division. It's time you had a rest from the hurly-burly of the Royal A Division.' There was a twinkle in Wensley's eye as he said that. 'On the other hand, given that you've got . . .' He paused and glanced down at the open docket that contained Hardcastle's record of service. 'Given that you've been in the Job for thirty-six years, you might even be considering retirement.' He closed the docket and placed it in his out-tray. 'You deserve a rest, Ernie. But I don't want an answer now. Mull it over and discuss it with Mrs Hardcastle if you like. After all, we'll still have a Hardcastle in the Job. Your boy Walter is doing very well, and if he goes on the way he's going, I can see him rising up the ranks very quickly.'

Hardcastle alighted from the tram at the top of Kennington Road and walked the few yards to Boxall's the newsagents.

'Good evening, Mr Hardcastle.' Kathleen Boxall had taken over the shop when her father, Horace, had died at the end of the war. Now forty years of age, she was unmarried. Like so many unfortunate women of her generation, she had been betrothed to a soldier. In her case, her fiancé had been a sergeant in the Machine Gun Corps who was killed at Cambrai when his tank was hit by shellfire. She had never wanted to risk getting too close to anyone ever again.

'Ah, I can see you know me well, Kate,' said Hardcastle, as, unasked, Kathleen placed an ounce of St Bruno tobacco, a box of Swan Vestas and a copy of the *Evening News* on the counter as he entered the shop.

'I was trained well by my dad,' said Kathleen. 'He told me that you were our oldest customer, Mr Hardcastle.'

'I doubt that I'm that old.' It was the second time in one day that Hardcastle had been reminded of his age.

'Oh, I didn't mean it like that, Mr Hardcastle,' said Kathleen hurriedly. 'I meant that you had been a customer longer than anyone else around here.'

'Oh, I see. Yes, Alice and I have lived here now for thirty-four years.'

'Have you really? Good gracious. I suppose you must be thinking about retiring soon, then. Will you move away? Some nice little bungalow by the seaside, perhaps?'

'We'll have to see, Kate.' The thought of a bungalow by the sea horrified Hardcastle. He placed a half-crown on the counter and pocketed his change.

'Give my regards to Mrs Hardcastle,' said Kathleen, as Hardcastle left the shop.

* * *

Hardcastle let himself into his house and put his umbrella in the stand and his bowler hat on a hook, as he always did. He took out his hunter and compared its time with that of the longcase clock, as he always did. Satisfied that the hall clock was accurate, he put his watch away and pushed open the door to the sitting room.

'You're early tonight, Ernie.'

'A glass of sherry, love?' Hardcastle kissed his wife.

'Please, Ernie.'

Hardcastle poured his wife a glass of Amontillado and himself a whisky. As he always did.

GLOSSARY

APM: assistant provost marshal (a lieutenant colonel attached to the military police).

BAILIWICK: area of responsibility.

BEAK: a magistrate.

BIT OF FLUFF: sexually attractive woman.

BLADDER O'LARD: Scotland Yard (rhyming slang).

BLOW THE GAFF, To: to reveal a secret or to turn informant.

BOB: a shilling (now 5p).

BOGEY: derogatory term for a police officer.

BRADBURY: a pound note. From Sir John Bradbury, Secretary to the Treasury, who introduced pound notes in 1914 to replace gold sovereigns.

BRADSHAW: a timetable giving routes and times of British railway services.

BRIEF, a: a warrant *or* a police warrant card *or* a lawyer *or* a barrister's case papers.

CAT'S PAW: a dupe.

CULLY: alternative to calling a man 'mate'.

DICKEY BIRD: a word (rhyming slang).

DOXY: a woman of loose character.

DROP, the: a hanging.

FIVER: five pounds sterling.

FLOWERY DELL: cell, as in prison cell (rhyming slang).

FLUFF, a bit of: a girl; a sexually attractive woman.

GANDER, to cop a: to take a look.

GILD THE LILY, to: to exaggerate.

HA'PENNY: a half penny (pre-decimal coinage).

HALF A CROWN or **(colloquially) HALF A DOLLAR:** two shillings and sixpence (12½p).

HAVE IT UP, to: to engage in sexual intercourse.

HOLLOWAY: women's prison in North London.

JIG-A-JIG: sexual intercourse.
JILDI: quickly (*ex* Hindi).

KC: King's Counsel: a senior barrister.
KNOCKING SHOP: a brothel.

MANOR: a police area.
NICK: a police station *or* prison *or* to arrest *or* to steal.
NICKED: arrested *or* stolen

ON THE GAME: leading a life of prostitution.

PICCADILLY WINDOW: a monocle.
PIG'S EAR, to make a: to make a mess of things.
PIP, SQUEAK & WILFRED: WW1 medals, namely the 1914-15 Star, the British War Medal 1914-18 and the Victory Medal 1914-19, so named after newspaper cartoon characters of the period.
POT AND PAN, OLD: father (rhyming slang: old man).
PUSHING UP DAISIES: dead and buried.

RAG, TAG AND BOBTAIL: term describing a low-class or disreputable persons.
SALLY ANN: affectionate term for the Salvation Army.
SOMERSET HOUSE: formerly the records office of births, deaths and marriages for England & Wales.
STIPE: a stipendiary magistrate (a qualified barrister presiding alone in a petty sessional court).
STRETCH, a: one year's imprisonment.
STRIPE, to: to maliciously wound, usually with a razor.
TOUCH OF THE VAPOURS, a: to be overcome with faintness.
TUMBLE, a: sexual intercourse.
TURN UP ONE'S TOES, to: to die or be killed.
TWO-AND-EIGHT, in a: in a state (rhyming slang).

WHITE-FEATHER JOHNNY: man avoiding military service.